**Bronwyn Scott** is a communications instructor at Pierce College and the proud mother of three wonderful children—one boy and two girls. When she's not teaching or writing she enjoys playing the piano, travelling—especially to Florence, Italy—and studying history and foreign languages. Find her on Bluesky, @bronwynscott.bsky.social. She loves to hear from readers.

## Also by Bronwyn Scott

*The Viscount's Christmas Bride*
*Cinderella at the Duke's Ball*

### Wed Within a Year miniseries

*How to Court a Rake*
*How to Tempt an Earl*
*How to Seduce a Viscount*

### Enterprising Widows miniseries

*Liaison with the Champagne Count*
*Alliance with the Notorious Lord*
*A Deal with the Rebellious Marquess*

### Daring Rogues miniseries

*Miss Claiborne's Illicit Attraction*
*His Inherited Duchess*

Discover more at millsandboon.co.uk.

# BECOMING HIS DOLLAR DUCHESS

Bronwyn Scott

MILLS & BOON

All rights reserved including the right of reproduction in whole or in part in any form. This edition is published by arrangement with Harlequin Enterprises ULC.

This is a work of fiction. Names, characters, places, locations and incidents are purely fictional and bear no relationship to any real life individuals, living or dead, or to any actual places, business establishments, locations, events or incidents. Any resemblance is entirely coincidental.

Without limiting the exclusive rights of any author, contributor or the publisher of this publication, any unauthorised use of this publication to train generative artificial intelligence (AI) technologies is expressly prohibited. HarperCollins also exercise their rights under Article 4(3) of the Digital Single Market Directive 2019/790 and expressly reserve this publication from the text and data mining exception.

® and TM are trademarks owned and used by the trademark owner and/or its licensee. Trademarks marked with ® are registered with the United Kingdom Patent Office and/or the Office for Harmonisation in the Internal Market and in other countries.

First published in Great Britain 2026
by Mills & Boon, an imprint of HarperCollins*Publishers* Ltd,
1 London Bridge Street, London, SE1 9GF

www.harpercollins.co.uk

HarperCollins*Publishers*, Macken House, 39/40 Mayor Street Upper, Dublin 1, D01 C9W8, Ireland

Becoming His Dollar Duchess © 2026 Nikki Poppen

ISBN: 978-0-263-41872-9

03/26

Printed and Bound in the UK using 100% Renewable Electricity at CPI Group (UK) Ltd, Croydon, CR0 4YY

For Catie and Sam
because dreams are always worth chasing.

# Chapter One

*San Francisco, late February 1890*

*Pas de pain, pas de vie.* No bread, no life. Bread sustained both those who ate it and those who baked it. Zephyrine Duval, third-generation French San Franciscan knew this perhaps better than anyone. Bread, sourdough bread particularly, was her life. She'd been immersed in it as soon as she could stand on a chair next to the kneaders, punching her own small loaf with tiny hands, maybe even before then. She had earlier memories, too, of bouncing on *grand-père*'s shoulders as he walked the bakery, overseeing each step of the elaborate, careful process—a process she could recite along with her ABCs by the time she was four.

Zephyrine patted her coat pockets, searching for a key, the coat's warmth a welcome comfort against the foggy marine layer that crept in off the bay. No, it wasn't in that pocket. That one held a small square package newly arrived from her friend, Lulu, who lived in New York. It must be the other pocket. Yes, there it was.

She looked up at the bold, black-lettered sign hanging above the door at 820 Broadway: *Duval French Bakery est. 1851.* Her eyes lingered on the motto written above it in smaller script. *Pain est vie.* Bread is life. Bread had certainly been life for the financially distressed Duvals of Picardy, France. The unrest and uncertain economy of the motherland had compelled her *grand-père* and her father, who'd been a young man at the time, to take advantage of the 1849 Gold Rush and try their luck in San Francisco. Her *grand-père* had believed life in California could hardly be worse than what was on offer in France, and he'd been right.

For the Duvals, life in California had turned out, in fact, to be a whole lot better. This was a story Zephy knew by heart—the family legend. By 1855, her father and *grand-père* had gone from baking bread out of their tiny apartment on Broadway to owning the building and warehouses associated with number 820. Forty years later, the Duvals had a fleet of delivery wagons, a mansion on Gough Street, a château in Napa Valley and money to send back to the cousins who'd stayed behind in Picardy, struggling. It was a proud legacy. *Her* legacy. She was part of this story. She contributed to the business her family had built, and her contributions kept it running. These days, she helped her father keep the books, she oversaw the bakery when business kept him away, she met with the master baker who nourished the all-important mother dough, and she was the one who innovated new ways to promote the Duval brand against the constant competition from the Boudins. It was exhilarating, but it was also consuming. It left no time for other dreams or pursuits like travel or a life that was truly her own beyond the bakery. It certainly made for a complicated relationship with the family business—something that she both loved and at times resented.

Mostly, though, she loved it. Zephyrine fit her key to the lock on the bakery's front door and stepped inside. She took her first, deep breath of the morning, inhaling the warm, tangy, comfort of sourdough baking in the great ovens. For her, this was the golden hour, the time when she had the bakery mostly to herself. The busy place was quiet, humming only with the subtle sounds of the early bakers shoveling loaves in and out of the ovens preparing the orders that would go out on the delivery wagons this morning. Later, her desk would be piled with correspondence and contracts. Later, the bakery would be filled with the bark of instructions, the chatter of conversation, as workers kneaded and shaped tomorrow's loaves. The rounders, the shapers, the moulders, the women who worked the front counter would all arrive in an hour to take up their positions. For now, there was only bread and peace.

'Bonjour, Mademoiselle Zephy.' Pierre, their lead baker, looked up a moment from scoring the unbaked loaves with the family's signature fleur-de-lis. A strand of grey hair peeped from beneath his flat-topped baker's toque in testament to the twenty years he'd spent with them.

'*Bonjour.* How is the bread today?' Zephy asked. Anyone who worked with sourdough knew that it was a living, breathing creature and sometimes just as temperamental. One should never take it for granted.

'*Le pain est très bon.* The dough has behaved itself. The loaves are golden and the crusts are as they should be.' He laughed as she passed.

She greeted the other bakers, all of them by name. To work for the Duval bakery meant to be part of the Duval family, part of the legacy. Her father insisted on only hiring French. 'After all,' he would say, 'there are over thirty thousand French in the city. San Francisco isn't called the Paris of the West for nothing. *Liberté, Égalité, Fraternité*, even here.' The city had given the Duvals a new start, and her family was proud to repay the favour by giving others the same.

Zephyrine pushed open the door to the office, using her shoulder for extra force. The door had a habit of sticking during the winter. The cold outside and the heat inside caught the wood in a constant limbo of contracting and expanding. Not unlike the dough she worked with, and not unlike herself. She laughed a little as she took off her coat and hung it on a peg, retrieving the package from her pocket before going to her desk. She spent her days being big for her father, for the business, being everywhere all at once, being all things, and yet she had to do so in ways that were small, that did not call undo attention to her gender, ways that didn't undermine her father's credibility with other businessmen in the city, nor undermine her own femininity as her mother was quick to point out when she felt her daughter had stepped over the line. Zephyrine knew she had more latitude in San Francisco than she would have anywhere else, and yet the limits still chafed. What would it take to be truly free?

She took a seat behind the desk and turned the brown paper wrapped package in her hands, tracing its shape. It *felt* like a little book, like a pocket-sized *Baedeker* one might carry for sightseeing. Had Lulu—Louise Cameron—sent a guidebook from her latest travels? Zephyrine gave a wistful sigh. Lulu had gone to Europe last spring for the Season and stayed on afterwards for quite a while, sending letters full of details, but she'd not heard from Lulu since before Christmas. She ought to be home now. Perhaps this was a souvenir?

Zephy gave a second wistful sigh and untied the string. Lulu had the best adventures while she was stuck on the other side of the world in San Francisco. Oh, to be sure, San Francisco was an adventure in itself, full of people from all over the globe. She could walk down the streets and hear Chinese, French, German and Italian all spoken. She could shop at specialty food stores featuring delicacies from Europe and purchase the latest in Parisian fashions. But it wasn't the same. It was *better*, she scolded herself, immediately feeling disloyal to her city, to her family. And yet, the desire to visit the castles and cathedrals, to walk the narrow streets, to see the museums, and the art of people who'd lived centuries earlier, to discover how other people lived in the present rumbled within her. Lately it was more of a grumble than a rumble as spring approached and with the new season no travel plans once again. Time was slipping away. She would be twenty-two in September. The more responsibility she took on at the bakery the harder it would be for her to get away, even briefly. She didn't want to be gone forever, just for a while, just long enough to see a piece of the world, long enough to find herself, to come to terms with life.

She unwrapped the package, carefully setting aside the paper for later use and smiled. It was not just one book but two. The first was as she'd thought—a pocket guide. To London. Lulu knew her well. London was the city of her dreams, home of kings and queens, the city where fairy tales came to life during the Season; riding in Hyde Park, balls every night, an endless parade of gowns, teas and dashing gentlemen. She reached for the second book, a little gasp of surprise escaping her as she realised what it was. *Titled Americans: A List of American Ladies Who Married Foreigners of Rank.* A guide of its own sort, then—a guide to those dashing gentlemen and where to find them perhaps? She laughed. How like Lulu to send such a thing.

Zephy opened the book and thumbed the pages, perusing name after name of American women who'd gone to Europe and now bore titles. French titles, Italian titles, German titles and, the most coveted of all, English titles. The list was quite cosmopolitan in its make-up. Oh, and their addresses, too! How intrepid of the authors, but perhaps that audacity crossed a certain line. She wondered how Miss Ridgeway, formerly of Philadelphia, now the Countess De Ganey, or Mrs Moreton Frewen, of 18 Alford Street in Mayfair, felt about their residences being published for all and sundry.

She did stop to read a biography or two. Girls from ordinary places: Indiana, Philadelphia, Georgia, were now turned into ambassadors' wives, baronesses, countesses and duchesses. From the look of the list, there were happy endings to spare—*if* that was what a girl was looking for. Zephyrine wasn't sure *she* was looking for *that* kind of happy ending. She needed to find herself before she found a husband. But up until that part, the fairy tale did sound delightful.

Her fingers stilled on the pages as the content changed. *This* was different: The list of women's names had given way to men's names under the heading 'A Carefully Compiled List of Peers Who Are Supposed to Be Eager to Lay Their Coronets…at the Feet of the All-Conquering American Girl.' Her eyes widened. Titles, addresses *and* incomes were listed for these gentlemen and in some cases very frank gossip about who really controlled the family purse strings.

If Lulu were here, they'd have had a good laugh over a book full of names of desperate gentlemen. Lulu was in no more hurry to marry than she was. But Lulu was three thousand miles away in New York. Zephyrine would have to settle for her friend's letter instead, tucked at the back of the book.

Zephy slid a fingernail beneath the seal and began to read, prepared to be regaled with Lulu's London exploits. Wait. What? Zephy re-read the opening paragraph of the letter again, the news setting her thoughts to racing. Louise was *still* in London. She'd not gone home to New York. Instead, she'd become engaged to an earl. *I am to be the Countess of Southford. The wedding is set for the second week in June. Please come and be my bridesmaid.* Was that a plea or excitement she read in her friend's tone? Like herself, Lulu had been ambivalent towards marriage, but apparently that had changed since last they were together. Now Lulu's life was moving full speed ahead while her own remained woefully status quo.

Zephy pressed the letter to her chest. Lulu was getting married! London beckoned. The answer to her friend's request was already whispering in her mind. *Yes.* She would go to London and help Lulu see this through. Her mind began to whir with ideas. Perhaps London was just the beginning? After the wedding, she might venture to France to see family she'd never met, perhaps go as far even as Italy. Her thoughts were a flurry of excitement. London was merely the gateway if she could just get there. Her decision was made. All that remained now was to persuade her parents, a large obstacle to be sure, but not an insurmountable one. With them, timing would be everything.

She waited until dessert that evening. Her parents were in high spirits, oohing and aahing over the latest dessert crafted by their chef. A French household of distinction did not have a mere cook, it had a *chef*, and the Duval household took such distinction a step further. They were also blessed with a *pâtissier*—the best in town. Tonight, their *pâtissier* had duplicated a new recipe sent by a friend from France, *tarte tatin*: caramelised apples baked in pastry dough. Most recently it had been served at the Hotel Tatin where it had become an instant sensation. Zephy took a bite and thought the accolades were justly deserved.

'Etienne has outdone himself,' her mother praised with a satisfied smile. 'A beautiful meal from start to finish.' It was the highest compliment Celine Duval could give. She prized herself on her palette and so did San Franciscan Society. Her mother, who'd begun life as the émigré daughter of a chocolatier was the centre of gustatory San Francisco. No fine meal was complete without her attendance or her sanction. Her mother took an elegant sip of the chilled sauterne accompanying the tarte. 'How was your day, *ma chère*?'

'Nearly as good as the tarte.' Zephy smiled. This was her moment. Her mother's palette was pleased, and all of Celine Duval's attention was turned her way. She would not get a better opening. 'Louise has written. She has news.'

Her mother's eyes brightened at the prospect of gossip. Her mother liked Louise, who had spent a summer with them a few years back, and her mother also liked being able to claim connections to New York Society. The Camerons were part of Mrs Astor's 'Four Hundred', and their wealth approached Croesus-like proportions.

'How did she like London? We must have her back for another visit soon. Her parents, too.'

'I think a visit is out of the question for a while.' She gave her mother a sly look. 'She liked London well enough to stay.' At least, Zephy hoped that was the case. She hoped her friend had fallen madly in love, been swept off her feet, given the fairy tale she deserved, and that she wasn't being forced into anything. Zephy let a smile break across her face. If her parents could see she was excited, perhaps they would be excited, too. 'Lulu is getting married to the Earl of Southford.' She let that piece of information register, watched her mother's face light up.

'She's to be a countess? How splendid. Her parents must be so pleased,' her mother gushed. Zephy glanced to her father's end of the table where he merely frowned.

'I wonder how much Cameron paid the earl for the privilege of a title?' He harrumphed, setting aside his napkin. 'That's more American money going across the Atlantic. What was the point of the revolution if Americans are just going to go bowing back to England after barely a hundred years? Frenchmen died for American freedom.'

Oh dear, she did not want to get her father started on politics or there'd be no talk of going to London. Zephy swiftly redirected the conversation back to Lulu. 'The wedding is in June. Lulu wants me to be a bridesmaid, and I want to go. It would be an honour to be her attendant.' She flashed a smile at her mother, hoping her mother was imagining the gowns, the parties, the photographs and publicity—

her daughter alongside the daughter of one of Wall Street's most successful investors. Perhaps her mother was already thinking what that would do for advertising the bakery—Duval's bread: fit for a countess.

'You'd go all the way to London?' her father groused. 'You'd be gone for months. London is halfway around the world from here. San Francisco is not like New York where a ship leaves for England nigh on everyday—*et voilà*—in five days you're there.' He gave a Gallic snap of his fingers. He groused when he was worried and he complained when he was worried, and tonight he'd done both within moments of each other. 'There's the train to consider as well.'

Zephy neatly turned the argument. 'It's a week on the train and then five days by ship, give or take a few days in New York depending on sailing schedules. Within two weeks from departure, I can be in London. We live in a marvellous age, Papa. Of course, I'd want to leave right away. Lulu is still in London with her fiancé's family, but the Camerons are home in New York briefly to announce the wedding. They've invited me to travel with them, and they hope to be back in London by the end of March. There are so many things to do in regard to wedding preparations.'

'You could be home by the end of June, then,' her father mused, counting the weeks behind his dark eyes. Dark eyes that seemed tired. He was often tired these days, and that concerned her. Perhaps there was more behind his reluctance to let her go than he was letting on.

'Well,' she began tentatively, trying to read her father in order to make the right argument. One wrong word, and he could prove intractable. 'I had hoped to stay a while and do some travelling. Perhaps see France. I've never been, and since we have relatives there, I could connect with them.' Her father had a soft spot for family. She hoped that would be a winning argument.

Her father's eyes shuttered. What had she said? 'France is out of the question. That's too long. We need you here. Who will take care of the accounts? Who will open the bakery every day?'

'Pierre can open the bakery. He's there early as it is, or one of the counter girls. And I thought you could do the books. You used to do a fair amount of the accounting even when *grand-père* was alive. I've only taken over because you were ill this past autumn.' She paused, a finger of fear trailing down her spine. Was her father sick again? Or perhaps he'd not fully recovered after all? Was his illness something more than a cough? That cough had been bad enough. It had stolen his breath, made it hard for him to manage the stairs at home let alone a journey to the bakery. 'The doctor said you were recovered.' That had been back in December, right before Christmas. She split her gaze between her mother and father. What was going on? There was definitely an undertone here, something she was not part of.

'I am recovered,' he assured her, although she didn't quite believe him. 'But this past autumn was a reminder that I am not a young man anymore. It is time to start thinking about the future of the bakery, the future of our family legacy. Your *grand-père* is gone. What will happen when I pass? Who will carry on? Or will we simply be bought out by the Boudins?' He made a gesture of despair. 'I hear they're looking at taking the property at 815 Broadway across from us now.'

She pushed the last remark aside. She'd deal with the Boudins' potential encroachment later. 'I will, of course. You know I love the bakery.' She more than loved it, even when it held her back. She *knew* it from the process of feeding the mother dough to final loaf, and more besides. She couldn't just bake bread, she could sell it, too.

There was another look between her parents and a long silence. She broke it with her next argument, hoping she wasn't launching it too soon. 'Louise Boudin runs the bakery now herself.' Isidore Boudin had passed away two years ago, right before *grand-père*. She'd always thought her grandfather had been hanging on out of sheer stubbornness to outlast his old countryman and rival.

'*You* are not a widow like Louise Boudin,' her

mother interjected, her gaze stern. '*You* are a rich, educated, well-bred young woman. *You* are the Sourdough Heiress of San Francisco.' That was a moniker the newspapers had labelled her with when she'd made her official début into San Francisco Society four years ago. She'd not liked it then any more than she liked it now, but the name had stuck. Mostly because it was true. She did the books: She'd seen the accounts, and she knew exactly how much she was worth—enough to impress the Mrs Astors of New York. In other words, there were certainly heiresses worth less.

'You need a husband to lend you consequence. Lulu has the right idea.' Her mother's eyes remained locked on hers a moment longer before turning to her father. 'Perhaps you *should* send her to London. Maybe she could find a husband, too, like Lulu Cameron. The Boudins could never compete with a viscount or a duke. Think of the advertising. I can see it now, the Duke of Broadway or the Duval Duke. Americans love a good duke. Democracy can go hang when there's a duke in the room.'

Zephy quickly grasped what had just happened. Her mother had become her ally but at a price. She could get as far as London under the guise of husband-hunting, although she wasn't sure her mother saw it as a guise so much as the real thing. Zephy wasn't sure how she felt about that. Hadn't she just dismissed such a notion for herself earlier today?

Her father exploded from the end of the table, making it exceedingly clear how he felt about the idea. 'An *Englishman*? For *my* daughter when there are perfectly good young Frenchmen here in the city?'

After decades of living with a hot-headed Frenchman, her mother was unbothered by her father's outbursts. She merely dismissed his protest with an elegant wave of her hand. 'Alexandre, she's not interested in the boys here.'

'An Englishman with a title doesn't understand business. He doesn't even understand how to manage his own money, or he wouldn't come looking for ours. The French families here are like *us*. They understand business, they understand bread. What more could we ask for? Besides, I thought we'd agreed.' Another look passed between them, and Zephy felt a moment's panic. They'd agreed? On what or, perhaps, on who? She ran a quick catalogue in her mind. Who was her father thinking of? He, perhaps her mother, too, obviously had someone in mind, and that made her very nervous. Theoretical husbands were easily overlooked, even tolerated. Husbands in the flesh were much harder to disregard.

Her father fixed her with a dark stare. 'We feel Claudel Aubert's son, Mathieu, shows great promise.

He's twenty-eight and ready to marry. Plus, he knows the business well.'

The panic was real now. Zephy clenched the napkin in her lap. No, not him. Anyone but him, really. The Auberts owned a small bakery in the French quarter, one of the fifty-three bakeries in town.

'I strongly disagree.' Zephy met her father's gaze steadily, refusing to dilute her opinion. 'He is *not* ready to marry. He keeps a mistress off Dumont Street, and he's always down at the wharfside saloons.'

Her mother's gaze fixed on her father. 'You did not tell me this, Alexandre.' Then Zephy felt her gaze shift to her. 'And you, *mon Dieu*, how do *you* know such sordid things?' She waved her hand. 'Never mind how you know. I can guess. This is what comes of having a woman in business. An unmarried girl should not know such unsavoury things. It is all fine for such discussion between men, but this is not acceptable for you, *ma chère*. What man will want a woman who lacks a sense of delicacy?' She turned. 'Alexandre, this is why she must go to London. Your daughter is an *heiress*. She needs a gentleman, not an émigré's son with no polish on him.'

Her parents' eyes held, a silent battle being waged between them. Some of the life seemed to visibly go out of her father. He held up his palms in surrender.

'Very well, I can't battle you both. But I have my terms.'

Zephy held her breath, waiting for the verdict, for the price. 'Zephyrine may go to London, for a little while, to hunt a husband like other American heiresses.' Zephy felt excitement flicker. She was going to get to go! If she had to pretend to be looking for a husband, she could do it. Hunters didn't always come home successful, after all. She could say she tried and failed.

Her father's next words dashed those hopes. 'I suppose we can tolerate an Englishman in the family if he's got a title. Your mother's right. We can use it for marketing if nothing else. But...' that one word lingered over the supper table '...should you fail, you will marry Mathieu Aubert. It's a good alliance for us. We cannot risk the future with uncertainty. If you mean to run the business, you must have a husband. I will not allow it any other way, and I *will* stand firm on this, Zephyrine. You may make your arrangements and pack your trunks, but that is the price of my permission.' He rose from the table and stalked from the room.

Zephy turned towards her mother. 'Talk to him, make him see reason. I'm not ready to wed anyone yet.' But the woman who'd been her ally moments ago shook her head.

'Your father's right, and his offer is fair. He's not

getting any younger, and the *family* needs you to be settled. If you care at all about our legacy, you will do this for all of us.' Her mother smiled. 'Come, it's not so bad. We will shop and send you off like the heiress you are. You will have London at your feet in no time.'

She hoped her mother was right. If she didn't conquer London, she'd have to face a lifetime with Mathieu Aubert. But she *would* conquer London. She thought of Lulu's little book of names—names of Englishmen desperate to wed, to trade their titles for money. Perhaps that book could be her lifeline. She had time, time to come up with a plan, time to find a way out or, if not a way out, a way around. She was a good thinker; surely she would find one. What she was *not* going to do, though, was think about defeat. She was not going to let her father's ultimatum ruin what should be a joyous moment for her.

She would focus on the positive. She was going to London! She had nearly five months of freedom stretching out before her, and there was so much to do; telegrams to send, arrangements to be made, shopping and packing, a journey to take. At the end of that journey, Lulu and adventure awaited. She wasn't going to waste a minute of it. Her time had come at last.

## Chapter Two

*London, April, six weeks later*

At last, she was going to her first London ball! Zephy could hardly contain herself, although she tried, she really did try. If she gripped the delicate ivory fan in her lap any harder it would surely snap from her excitement. She wasn't the only one excited, though. Lulu sat beside her in the Cameron town coach, anticipation rolling off her in waves. Tonight, Zephy was making her social début, but Lulu was making her official appearance for the first time in Society since the December engagement as the fiancée of the Earl of Southford, the woman who would be the future countess. Zephy exchanged a covert glance with her friend. They both wanted this evening to go well.

Zephy played with the silken folds of her pale blue gown, one of gowns she'd had made before she'd left. The modiste had called the delicate shade *water and mist*. To Zephy, it was the colour of home, the colour of San Francisco Bay with the fog rising like an opera curtain, revealing the city inch by inch. She needed a touch of home this evening. There'd been so much change in a very short time, all of it exhilarating, exciting and new, everything that she'd hoped for when she dreamed of London, but her hands were aching for a chance to sink into the sourdough starter she'd brought with her and diligently fed each day in the Camerons' kitchen. To sink her hands into the dough would be to sink into the familiar, to grab onto an anchor before she was entirely swept away.

Tonight was the culmination of a six-week whirlwind since she'd received Lulu's invitation. There'd been the rush of packing, the thrill of the overland adventure on the train, America speeding past the train window, followed by some time in New York with Lulu's family. There'd been small parties and dinners, a chance to quietly socialise with Mrs Astor's Four Hundred. Her mother would have loved that, especially Delmonico's privately catered oyster supper the night before they'd sailed. There'd been the ocean voyage on the Inman Line's ship, the SS *City of New York*, the reunion with Lulu at the Camerons' townhouse off Grosvenor Square, rented for the Season from a viscount with financial difficulties who was taking rooms in Piccadilly instead. From there it had been a breathless pace of dress fittings, teas and socials while the Season began to move towards its zenith.

Now that Easter had passed, the balls would pick up in pace, Lulu assured her, as if their schedule hadn't been hectic enough already. Hectic and wondrous. Zephy hadn't minded a minute of it. This was what she'd come for, to step into the fairy tale unfolding before her, to be part of it for a short while. There were even moments when she could forget about her father's ultimatum, forget that she either needed a husband or a plan in order to avoid Mathieu Aubert and keep her place at the bakery. Tonight, she could make strides towards acquiring the former, but in terms of designing a plan to avoid both Mathieu and an unwanted husband, she was still at a loss.

The coach inched forward in line one last time. They were here! Mrs Cameron gave them each a final looking-over, beaming with pride. 'You're both beautiful. My darling girl, you will make all the jealous old biddies regret their words about Southford marrying an American. And, Zephyrine, your gown brings out your eyes so delightfully. The gentlemen won't be able to pry their gaze away. Remember who is here tonight,' she rushed on. 'The Duke of Sunderland and several other eligible men who have not yet shown their faces at events this spring.'

Mr Cameron looked away from the window. 'Don't go getting Zephyrine's hopes up, Eliza. Everyone knows Sunderland is only here to keep his younger brother in check. He's not looking for an American heiress. He's just about the only aristocrat who isn't. He's a stickler for tradition, and his finances are solid.' Mr Cameron winked at Zephy. 'Never worry, my dear. There are plenty of broke barons inside those doors. We'll find you one if your heart's set on it.'

Zephy laughed. 'It's a good thing my heart isn't set on a duke, then.' At least not that one. The duke sounded like a prude, the very antithesis of a good time, the one thing she would make sure she had while she was in London, in spite of her obligations.

Lady Featherfield's ball was *not* Hale Eberley's idea of a good time. It managed to combine two odious tasks into a single evening of displeasure: fending off débutantes with or without their mothers, and making sure his brother, who was twenty-eight and ought to know better, stayed out of trouble. Financial trouble, matrimonial trouble—in short, all forms of trouble were fair game when Leo was involved. Put Leo in a ballroom full of women to charm and there were bound to be misled daughters and angry papas come morning. It would suddenly become his problem to sort out while Leo played least-in-sight.

Hale fought the urge to lean against one of the Doric columns gracing the Featherfield ballroom as he surveyed the floor. Gentlemen did *not* lean. But neither should a gentleman be dragged against his will to spend an evening in purgatory for sins he didn't commit. It was not his fault Leo had run through his quarterly allowance in record fashion at the gaming tables and then tried to earn it back with a reckless carriage race on Richmond Road that had nearly ended poorly not just for himself but for others. Hale could not tolerate the latter. A true gentleman looked out for others, a tenet drilled into him early and often by his late father, a respectable man if not a loving one. He'd paid more attention to his estates than he had his sons. Hale had loved him anyway.

Over-loud laughter reached him above the general din of conversation and music. Ah, so it began. Hale slowly swivelled his gaze towards the sound, knowing what he'd find before his eyes reached the spot. Leo stood amid a group of dashing young men and expensively dressed young women. American women.

Hale could pick them out in any setting. Pretty, fresh, confident. There wasn't a demure bone in their American bodies. They said what they thought, they did what they wanted. There wasn't an ounce of dissembling or discretion in their breeding. Then again, they hadn't been bred with any intention in mind. They simply were, and there were more and more of them every year. That was Manchester's fault, Marlborough's fault. When dukes married Americans it gave everyone ideas. Wrong ideas. If dukes could do it, why not viscounts and barons? If two American heiresses from nondescript stock could do it, why couldn't anyone else? And so they had. Everyone had thrown themselves into the game. For twenty years, Americans had flocked to British ballrooms, and British nobles had welcomed them.

'Are you looking over the new crop?' William De-Vole, Viscount Bilborough, sidled up with punch glass in hand. 'It's good to see you out.' Bilborough clapped him on the shoulder.

'I'm keeping an eye on Leo. After last week's fiasco, I need to ensure he toes the line for a while.'

'Ah, the fiacre fiasco.' Bilborough chuckled knowingly.

Hale groaned. 'Is that what they're calling it now?' Leo had run a public fiacre full of passengers off the road during his madcap race, nearly causing it to turn over. 'Mother will have a fit.' He protected Leo from himself, and he protected their mother from the realities of Leo. It was far better for her to believe Leo was simply an exuberant young man.

'So any prospects this year for the vaunted position of the Duchess of Sunderland?' William gestured towards Leo's group with his punch cup.

'I don't need to survey the new crop of débutantes. I am about to be betrothed to Lady Julia. Even if that weren't so, *I* certainly don't need an American duchess,' Hale clarified with a small sense of pride.

'Maybe it's not about need but want. Just look at them, so pretty and bright. You have to admit they light up a room. The blonde is Louise Cameron, Southford's fiancée. The other blonde is May Cornell. Her father is in railroads. The brunette is Cecily Milford, a tobacco heiress. The one in green is Alice Woods, estimated to be worth twenty thousand per annum.' Good Lord, everything *was* bigger in America. Even their fortunes were big, flashy and obvious.

'And the dark-haired one, the one standing next to Leo? He's danced once with her already,' Hale interrupted impatiently. He was not interested in their dowries. His only interest came from his brother being in their milieu.

William leaned closer for discretion. 'That, my dear friend, is the Sourdough Heiress of San Francisco. Miss Zephyrine Duval.'

'Good God, what a name.' A *bread* heiress, for heaven's sake. A *baker*'s daughter. Her father wasn't even a merchant but an artisan.

'The family is French,' Bilborough said off-handedly as if that explained everything. 'Rumour has it she's worth three fortunes.'

'As I've mentioned, I do not need an infusion of American dollars.'

'Said no English aristocrat ever.' Bilborough chuckled. 'Since when did anyone have too much money? I despair of you some days, Sunderland. The charming Miss Duval is a friend of Louise Cameron's. She's here for the wedding. Isn't she spectacular?'

'Spectacularly wrong,' Hale replied without hesitation. It was *her* laugh he'd heard. She'd been too loud in a crowded ballroom where it was impossible to hear anyone say anything, and yet she'd managed to rise above the din. Hale let his eyes rove over her. He could hardly *not* notice her. She was too much of everything. Her gown was too fashionable, too expensive with its yards of cool blue silk and falls of creamy lace sewn into the gores of the skirt, and her hair too luxurious and sleek like the dark pelt of a mink, silk itself. It seemed to showcase every earthy shade. When she moved her head, the light caught Titian highlights hidden within walnut depths. In profile, her jaw seemed too sharp, too defined, her chin too pointed.

Bilborough looked at him. 'It might be time for spectacles, old chap. She's beautiful. There isn't a man in this room who isn't taken with her. Except for you, of course,' he added with a laugh.

'All these men and she's chosen my brother? She's hardly a good judge of character, then, is she?' Hale groused.

'Did you consider it might be the other way around? That your brother chose her?' Bilborough mused over the rim of his cup. He took a swallow and grimaced. 'This tastes awful. Why do I keep drinking this swill?' He deposited the cup on the tray of a passing footman.

'Because you're an optimist.' Hale laughed. 'You hope this time it will be different.'

'You might be right. Still, if bad punch is the price for optimism I'll take it. I'd rather be a thirty-four-year-old optimist than a thirty-four-year-old cynic such as yourself.'

'*Realist*,' Hale corrected. 'I am a realist. A good duke has to be, otherwise he'll disappoint and be disappointed in turn. Too many people count on me for me to live on hope alone.' This was an old discussion, one that he and Bilborough had had many times over the years, usually sober, but on occasion in their cups.

'Are you going to rescue her, then?' Bilborough nodded towards Leo's group where people were partnering for the next set. 'Aren't you worried about *that*?'

'A gentleman knows better than to dance twice with a young woman unless he wants to signal his intentions. Even Leo knows that much. He also knows he is in no position to support a married household.'

'Precisely.' Bilborough gave him a pointed look. 'You might not need her money, but Leo does. Heiresses have been known to marry second sons, especially when that second son is the heir presumptive. Can you imagine a fortune of that size in Leo's hands?'

Hale could imagine it, too well. It would make the fiacre fiasco look like child's play. 'She ought to know better than to accept.' The Sourdough Heiress of San Francisco could defend herself with all that vaunted American ingenuity. Bilborough exchanged a look with him, one that said *But she's American. They don't think the rules apply to them.* Dammit if Bilborough wasn't right. To save her from Leo, and to save Leo from himself, he was going to have to dance with her. 'If you'll excuse me, Bilborough, duty calls.'

Hale made it just in time to insert himself next to Leo. 'I must beg an introduction,' he said to Leo. 'You have all the loveliest girls to yourself, brother.'

Leo flashed him a cool smile, resentment simmering in his green eyes. Hale returned the stare. This was a look he was used to. In the years since he'd assumed the title, the relationship with his brother had become strained. They both knew Leo would like to refuse but couldn't without looking churlish. 'Miss Duval, allow me to present my brother, the Duke of Sunderland.'

She offered a gloved hand and made a small curtsy. 'Your Grace, the pleasure is mine. I am told you are not often out in Society. It is my lucky night. My very first London ball and I get to meet the elusive duke.' She gave him a wide smile and an open stare, making no secret that she was taking him in, cataloguing him like a rare specimen, no doubt for a long letter home.

Music for the new set was beginning, and Leo was edgy, wanting him to be gone. Perhaps Bilborough had the right of it after all. If so, the situation was worrisome indeed. 'Might an elusive duke have this dance, Miss Duval?' If he didn't ask now, Leo would whisk her out onto the dance floor for all to see and comment on. There would be comments anyway: He could feel the eyes of Society upon their little threesome, but better the comments be about him than Leo. Better for him and better for her, even if she didn't know it yet.

'A dance would be lovely. I dare not refuse for fear I may not get another chance.' She laughed, the same open laugh he'd heard earlier and took his arm.

'Don't believe a thing he says about me,' Leo managed a parting shot in joking tones, wrapping the warning in one of his too-charming smiles.

'He assumes, of course, that we will talk about him at all,' Hale offered wryly as they took up their position on the crowded floor. He put his hand to her waist and cursed his continued bad fortune that this dance would be a waltz. His purgatory had no limits, it seemed, despite his good deed.

'We won't?' she parried, laying a hand on his shoulder with a touch that was firm, competent, lacking in all missishness. 'I assumed you asked me to dance either in order to warn me off or to steal me for yourself.' Sharp, periwinkle eyes the shade of her gown met his, a knowing smile teasing her bee-stung mouth. She was beautiful *and* bold.

'I am not in the habit of stealing women from my brother.' Hale moved them into the dance, slowly at first to get a sense of her, how she moved, how to match his steps to hers. She was not short but neither was she tall, and he was a big man. He was used to accommodating partners.

'Ah, so it *was* meant to be a rescue.' There was laughter in her eyes. 'Tell me, Your Grace, do I look like someone who needs to be rescued?' She gave a toss of her head, the chandelier lights picking out the Titian depths in her walnut-dark hair once more.

He swung them through the turn at the top of the ballroom. 'You look like someone who runs through Society heedless of the complexities until it's too late. You should not dance with any gentleman twice in a single night unless there's an arrangement between you.' They were picking up speed now. She was a competent dancer, and their bodies had found their rhythm.

'You think I am a simpleton.' Her blue eyes flashed.

'I think you're an American and there are certain nuances that escape you.'

'Do those nuances escape your brother as well? Even if I were unaware, surely he knows better for both of us. He would not have set me up to fail, as it were.' Dear heavens, she was brash, arguing with him amid a waltz, contradicting his well-intended advice. A strand of her enigmatic dark hair had come loose and dangled in a soft curl, framing her face, bringing a sense of delicacy to her boldness. Sometime during the dance, during the argument, they'd moved closer together, the standard distance having disappeared, much to his displeasure. He'd not intended for that to happen.

'I cannot possibly respond to your question without impugning my brother or myself. To admit he had nefarious intentions in asking for a second dance is to malign his honour. While to admit that you did not need rescuing suggests I misread the situation.'

'The latter suggests that you were *wrong*,' she corrected with a victorious smile. The minx knew exactly what she'd manoeuvred him into. She gave a cock of her head, her silvery-blue gaze bordering on unnerving as she studied him. Most men would not dare to scrutinise a duke so, and certainly not a woman. 'Your Grace, *are* you familiar with the concept of being wrong, or shall I explain it to you?'

Oh, the cheek of her knew no limits. He met her enquiring gaze steadily, coolly. 'I have, on rare occasion, been wrong, Miss Duval.' But not on this occasion, which was what made the situation so galling. He had played the hero, rescued her from social censure and the potentially less-than-honourable intentions of his brother and this was how he was repaid? 'So yes, I am aware of the concept.'

This was why he eschewed Americans. They were far too audacious for his tastes. Who wanted a duchess who argued with him? A wife who told him he was wrong? Who would be an obstruction at every turn? Not him. There were too many examples of unhappy transatlantic marriages to suggest it could be otherwise. Mandeville, now the eighth duke of Manchester and the Marlboroughs may have had their fortunes restored, but they'd paid the cost with their reputations. Those husbands were the unhappiest of men.

The music wound down, and Hale made his bow before leading her from the floor. 'Thank you for the dance, Miss Duval.'

'Thank *you*, Your Grace. It was most…insightful.' She gave a sly, teasing smile as he returned her to her friends. He noted with relief that Leo was absent, out dancing with someone else. Perhaps the dance had been worth it after all, if it had diverted Leo's attentions.

'I'd say I'll look forward to another dance this evening, but that seems to be a most scandalous wish, based on our discussion.' She gave another head tilt. 'It's a shame really when you're such a fine dancer. I should have liked another waltz. Another time, perhaps?'

'Perhaps.' Hale nodded and took his leave. Perhaps never. Perhaps when hell froze over. Perhaps if they were the only two left on the planet. Dammit all if those blue eyes weren't laughing at him, as if they saw right through his cool one-word lie to the hot truth beneath. His brother owed him one—well, actually, more than one. Leo owed him quite a lot. He'd saved Leo from more trouble than he knew. His brother was no match for the American with the laughing blue eyes and a bee-stung mouth. Who did she think she was to dare argue with a duke?

## Chapter Three

'Who does he think he is to lecture me about proper dance protocol? He doesn't even know me. I'd done nothing wrong. If anyone should have been lectured, it was his own brother who made the situation, in his opinion, intolerable.'

Zephy plopped with no small amount of force onto the chaise in Lulu's room and tugged off a dancing slipper. The clock in the hall was just striking three. Dear heavens, they really had danced the night away! She held up her slipper with a satisfied smile. 'Look, Lulu, there's a little hole right here. I've had partners aplenty despite the duke's disapproval.' Take that, you supercilious prude, she thought. There was a plethora of perfectly nice gentlemen who liked her American airs. The duke's own brother included. That last must gall him. Perhaps that's why he'd done it—making a show of intervening, of dancing with her only to lecture her—not that anyone had overheard what he'd said to her—to save his brother from a dubious fate.

Lulu looked over her shoulder from her dressing table, unscrewing her ear-bobs. 'The duke didn't disapprove of you. He was merely managing a situation. One might say he was looking out for you as much as he was his brother. In answer to who does *he* think he is, Zeph, he's the Duke of Sunderland. He possesses a title eleven generations old. He has two hundred and seventy-five years of tradition behind him. There isn't a more eligible gentleman on the marriage mart.'

'Even though he went about it like a complete cad?' Zephy huffed. He'd been a perfect boor, and the perfection hadn't stopped there. It had extended to his shirt, which had been blindingly white, his dark coat superbly fitted across broad shoulders. Everything about him had been correct—his fashion neither too retiring nor too avant-garde as his brother's had been. Where the duke had worn the classic evening coat with tails, his brother had worn the new, less fitted tuxedo jacket that had only recently been viewed as acceptable for evening wear. The duke's cologne had been the ideal mix of spiced bergamot and citrus, sophisticated yet with the sharp, fresh undertones of spring. And one could not forget that perfect swoop of hair so black as to be ebony... Oh, how she'd wanted to mess it up, to mess *him* up in retaliation for scolding her. But he had danced divinely, and she had meant it when she'd said it was a pity they couldn't dance again. No partner the rest of the night—and there had been many—had matched him.

Lulu met her gaze in the mirror. 'Yes, Zephy, even if he's a cad. Titles matter here, more so than a man's personality. Sunderland is the embodiment of nearly three centuries of tradition.'

That again. Good heavens, it was hard to think of three centuries of anything. Her entire country wasn't even half that old. The sourdough starter that sustained the family bakery was forty years old. And to think she'd felt pride just six weeks ago standing beneath the Duval bakery sign proclaiming forty years of business. In fact, she still felt pride in those forty years, centuries-old ducal titles notwithstanding.

'Southford has a title, and he isn't stuffy,' Zephy countered. Lulu's fiancé was blond and blue-eyed with an easy smile and polite manners. She could see why her friend had fallen for him.

'Southford's title is only four generations old.'

Zephy laughed. 'Well, it's good you got to him now, then, while there's still some life left in him and he's not a dried old stick like the duke.' She sobered. 'He *does* have some life in him, doesn't he, Lulu?' Southford would be forty in the autumn, and that seemed incredibly old to Zephy.

'Yes, of course.' Lulu smiled, too brightly perhaps in her attempt to allay any concern. 'We rub along well, and we have several shared interests. We will build a good life together, of that I am sure.' But what of passion, Zephy wondered? Or was it only the French who thought of such things?

'At any rate, you needn't trouble yourself with the duke again,' Lulu went on. 'He might be officially eligible, but rumour has it he means to offer this Season for Lady Julia Parkhurst. Her father is the second Marquess of Barrow, but her maternal grandmother was the daughter of an earl whose title went quite a ways back, and the marquess's wife's family has a Scottish title.'

Zephy smiled. 'Listen to you, Lulu, you've become quite the English lady over the last year, reciting Debrett's to me like you were born to it.' Lulu had taken to English life like the proverbial fish to water. 'You make it look easy.'

'It hasn't been, though.' Lulu sighed, and it seemed to Zephy that her whole face, which had radiated happiness all evening, collapsed. 'This is a whole different world, with different rules and expectations. It looks like a fairy tale from the outside, but it's not. Southford's mother does not like me no matter how many tables of precedence I commit to memory. She tolerates my money but not me. Southford is my only ally, and I fear after the honeymoon I'll be on my own to manage as best I can while he returns to his obligations. He assures me all will be well, but I know he doesn't really understand the position I'm in.' Tears threatened in Lulu's hazel eyes.

'Oh, Lulu.' Zephy rushed to her friend's side and wrapped her arms about her. 'You've been so brave. A new husband, a new house, a new life, all half of a world away from New York. Perhaps your mother can stay for a while?'

Lulu gave a faint smile and shook her head. 'No, I have to do this on my own. Even so, my mother can't stay forever.' She brightened. 'Enough of such maudlin talk. We should be celebrating. Our first large, formal outing of the Season has been a success. Southford was pleased with me, and all the young gentlemen were pleased with you. Unless I'm wrong, the next two days will be busy.'

'Why is that?' Zephy rose as Lulu's maid entered the room. Her own maid would be waiting for her in her own chamber, and Zephy disliked the idea of keeping her waiting so late at night, or was that *morning*?

'There's the garden party at Rivercross in Richmond tomorrow, and the day after is Mother's at-home. Your gentlemen will be sending flowers and vying for your attentions. It's quite a spectacle to see them all crowded into the drawing room. That was me last year.' She gave a wistful smile. 'Enjoy it while it lasts.'

'I intend to,' Zephy replied solemnly. She was

acutely aware her time in England would go by too fast, and there were decisions to make that would affect her future. She desperately wanted to confide in Lulu, but after her friend's disclosures tonight, Zephy wasn't about to burden her with her own troubles. Lulu had enough to worry about without her adding to the pile.

'Goodnight, Lulu.' Zephy stifled a yawn behind her hand. 'The garden party sounds nice. It will be good to be out in the fresh air and the country.'

And it would have been if not for two small details Lulu forgot to mention: that Rivercross was one of the many homes owned by the second Marquess of Barrow, Lady Julia Parkhurst's father, and that the Parkhursts, eager to see their daughter make an advantageous match, had invited the not-so-charming Duke of Sunderland to grace their party.

'Well, at least his brother will be here, too, and he's quite charming,' Lulu said by way of apology.

'You should have told me sooner,' Zephy scolded. Lulu had waited to drop those vital pieces of information until they were sailing down the Thames on Southford's yacht enjoying the soft spring breeze off the water. There was literally nowhere for Zephy to go, short of jumping into the river.

'You wouldn't have come,' Lulu responded defiantly. 'I know you, and you would have found a reason to stay behind.' She slid Zephy a sharp look.

'Although, maybe not. I've never known you to play the coward.'

'Life is too short to spend it with annoying people,' Zephy countered. One annoying person in particular. But this time, she was prepared. She knew what to expect.

The Georgian villa with its columns and neo-Palladian architecture came into view. Women in white gowns and men in linen suits dotted the sloping green yard that ran down to the waterside where boats were tied up. Other guests had shared Southford's idea and had come in their own yachts.

Before she even alit, Zephy's eyes were looking for *him* among the partygoers. It shouldn't be that hard to pick out one annoying man from the crowd. He'd be the tall dark-haired grumpy one making sure all was proper and that no one was having too much fun.

She was here. The American Sourdough Heiress. It wasn't hard to pick her out of the crowd. Although, upon reflection, perhaps it should have been. She was dressed in a white linen afternoon gown like the other young women, her dark hair smoothed and gathered into a neat chignon at the nape of her neck, even though his eyes were already straining to catch another glimpse of those peekaboo Titian highlights.

There were subtle differences, of course. Her hair did not sport the ropes of braids other girls wore, and the sash at her waist was done in the same lovely shade of blue as her ball gown while other girls wore pink or green. These were minor differences, and yet Hale knew his eyes would never have overlooked her, never classified her as merely another member of the group. If only he could put his finger on the reason. He couldn't blame his notice of her this time on her laugh. His gaze had sought her without provocation.

'Hale, there you are.' The dulcet tones of Lady Julia Parkhurst diverted his attention, as had the use of his first name and the way she so effortlessly slipped her hand through his arm. When had they moved to this stage of informality more appropriate for an affianced couple? And why did he balk at it today? Wasn't an engagement to this charming, lovely, well-positioned young woman in his immediate future anyway? Nothing had been spoken, but the knowledge was in the air. All interested parties *knew* it was only a matter of time, and yet today that knowledge felt more like a chain than an accomplishment.

'Lady Julia.' He favoured her with a smile. 'You look as lovely as ever.' And she did. She'd inherited the Parkhurst eyes, deep brown pools meant for drowning in, and her mother's blond hair: a fetching picture all around.

'I must steal you away at once. We have tennis set up on the side lawn, and I need you to partner me. Your brother is boasting he and Miss Elliott can best us.'

Hale shot a last look in Zephyrine Duval's direction and gave a nod. His afternoon would be much better spent teaching his brother a lesson and getting used to the company of Miss Parkhurst than following a baker's daughter about the party.

On those grounds, the party was a success. The guest list and the gardens of Rivercross were extensive. There were plenty of spaces and activities so that one might go the entire party without meeting all the guests. As it was, he did not encounter the unsettling American again until later in the afternoon, and even then, the encounter was unexpected. If he'd not stepped aside from the party for a moment's peace in Lady Barrow's rose garden, he might have avoided seeing her altogether. Or hearing her. He was forever hearing her.

'Jumping jiminy! *Zut alors!* Ouch, dammit all!' The heated epithets were followed by a rather aggressive rustling farther down the path. Hale exhaled, letting out a long-suffering sigh. Someone was in distress, and it took little guessing to know who that someone was. Who else at this party would swear with such *versatility*? Certainly, no English ladies he knew would use such language, even if they thought they were alone. He could not imagine such words slipping past Lady Julia's delicate lips, yet his first name had.

Still, the gentleman in him would never allow a cry for help to go unheeded. Hale turned and went reluctantly down the path. Perhaps he deserved this. This was his penance for deserting his almost-betrothed on the pretext of needing to speak with someone on a *matter of business*.

He found Miss Duval not far into the garden, attached to a rosebush. Hale surmised instantly most of the problem was *her*... Why didn't that surprise him? The more she twisted, the more tangled she became. 'It seems you've found yourself in another sticky situation.' He stopped a few feet from her.

She seared him with a look, frustration evident. 'My skirts are stuck, and I can't seem to free myself without tearing the fabric.'

He came forward unwilling to tease her more. 'Stand still for a moment before you rip something, Miss Duval, and I'll have you extricated.' He knelt on one knee and began the careful work of detaching her skirts from the thorns. 'All of your thrashing has made it worse.'

'I was not *thrashing*,' she objected. 'I hardly had a choice. Was I simply to stand here and do nothing but hope for someone to come along?' Argument and objection were her defence mechanisms, a cover for her embarrassment, Hale thought. She'd not liked being caught, least of all by him. Perhaps she'd have preferred a different rescuer? His brother maybe?

'There, last one.' He stood up and dusted the knee of his trousers. 'May I ask what you were doing out here, alone?'

'Not if it means you are going to lecture me.' She reached a hand down to shake her skirt into place, and he caught it just in time—the red dot on her fingertip. He grabbed her hand. 'I beg your pardon, Your Grace,' she said balking at the gesture.

'There's blood on your finger. You will get it on your skirt.' He held her hand up for her to see and reached for a handkerchief from his jacket pocket. 'Here, wrap you finger in this.'

'It's hardly a wound.' But she did take the handkerchief and do as instructed.

'Now that's settled, perhaps you might answer my question?' They'd begun to stroll, turning deeper into the garden as she wrapped her finger in the cloth.

She slid him a mischievous look that was a warning and a breath of fresh air all at once. 'I suppose there's no harm in telling you because you're not in it, but you have to promise to keep it a secret.'

'All right, I promise. What am I not in?' How bold of her to think she knew him well enough after the acquaintance of a waltz to trust him with a confidence. And perhaps how naive to think that he'd keep his word. Of course, he would keep it. But not all gentlemen were imbued with his sense of honour, especially if they had something to gain by exposing her secret. Or using it against her perhaps as leverage.

With her other hand she reached into the pocket of her skirt and pulled out a book. 'Have you ever seen this before? It's a list of titled gentlemen who are looking for wives—rich wives.' She passed the book to him, and he flipped through the pages in horror as he recognised some of the names *and* addresses.

He handed the book back to her and made his displeasure known. 'That book is a scandal, an invasion of privacy. My God, it has turned those men into prey to be hunted.' It was one thing to implicitly know that some men had and were willing to trade titles for American dollars. It was another to see that exchange addressed explicitly, blatantly, in print. He'd heard such information existed. However, he'd believed it to be only informally compiled in ladies' letters to each other. But this official codification and distribution was a whole other level.

She laughed at his stern disapproval and tucked the book back into her pocket. 'They're hardly prey. The men are overtly willing to be chased. They *want* to be found. *Need* to be found in some cases. How better to be located than to draw a map?'

Her candour was astounding. 'Do you argue with everyone, Miss Duval, or just me?'

'I do not argue,' she protested with honest heat. 'But

I will not stand by and allow someone to state incorrect assumptions when the truth is obvious.'

He could see that she meant it, but so did he. Hale stopped beside a rosebush burgeoning with flowers. 'I would say these roses are red. Would you agree?' There wasn't any room for argument. The roses were as red as possible.

She furrowed the arch of her slim dark brows, and he nearly laughed at the absurdity of it all even as he braced for her answer. The minx *was* going to disagree with him. He could see it in her face. 'To be honest, I do think they tend more towards cherry than red. Some of them I would even say are not red but carmine, with just a touch of purple to them, so deep is their colouring.' She moved to the bush beside it. 'These are certainly roseate—a combination of red *and* pink,' she explained.

'I know what *roseate* is,' he assured her. 'But I think I've made my point. *You* are contrary.'

'*I* am contrary because *you* are misinformed? I am contrary *because* I disagree with you? I was unaware dukes had cornered the market on determining the truth. Makes it all rather subjective, doesn't it? Which is counterintuitive to what the truth is supposed to be.'

Sometimes retreat was the best option. This was definitely one of those times. There'd be no winning with her. They were arguing apples and oranges. He returned to the original point of the conversation, and they began walking again, leaving behind the *red* rosebushes. 'Why did you come out here with the book? Were you looking someone up? Wanting to affirm their eligibility?' He shouldn't be surprised. It was what the Americans did; it was why they were here, year after year. But deep down, some long-forgotten part of him wanted her to deny it.

She slid him that sharp, scrutinising look he was coming to expect from her. 'You assume I am hunting a desperate husband. Perhaps it is the other way around. I came out here to hide from one.' She was always so cool, so certain she had the upper hand, that it took a moment for her words to register with him.

'Why would you hide? Aren't you here to find a husband like your friend, Miss Cameron, has?' Like several American heiresses before her had. Many of them came and rode the coattails of their successful friends just as she was. Success begat success, and with Miss Duval's looks she would have no trouble picking up a beleaguered baron and attaching *Lady* to the front of her name. Although, what she thought that would do for her escaped him.

'I am here for Lulu's wedding, to support her, and to give myself a journey. This is my chance to see a bit of the world before I have to make certain decisions.' Her answer surprised him, intrigued him, because for a moment, Miss Duval's bold bravado had slipped. Instead of bravado, there was a wistfulness to her tone, even what he suspected was a rare hint of uncertainty. And of course, the words themselves: *before I have to make certain decisions.* What might those decisions be? How weighty they must be if they had the power to get beneath her cool exterior, to leave her exposed. There was vulnerability in her honesty, in the soft smile she offered perhaps by way of apology for unburdening herself, and Hale found he couldn't let the issue go.

Against his better judgement, that smile, that vulnerability drew him in, tapping into his need to protect. What could this bold American need protection from? He shouldn't ask, but the temptation was too great. The words *What decisions?* were on the tip of his tongue when he became aware of the crunch of gravel and the sound of voices on the path, aware too that the spring sun had begun to descend.

'Ah, there you are, my dear,' Lulu burst around the corner, followed by Southford and Lord Blankenship. Beside him, Hale felt Miss Duval stiffen, the bold bravado back in place like a knight's visor. Intuition flared: She'd come in here to escape Blankenship, and now the man she'd sought to avoid had entered her sanctuary.

Miss Cameron slipped an arm through Miss Duval's. 'Southford is ready to sail home. We are just waiting on you. Lord Blankenship will join us.' She beamed with a meaningful smile to her friend. But

Miss Duval did not return it. That was all the confirmation Hale needed to take action, appealing to Southford's sense of rank and duty.

'I do apologise if I've upset any plans, but I offered to sail Miss Duval home on my yacht. My brother and my mother will be in attendance, so there's no question of impropriety. I had hoped to show her a few sights on the river given that she's new to London.' He felt Miss Duval relax in the wake of his fabrication.

Southford nodded. What else could he do but give way to a duke's dictates? 'Of course, Your Grace. It is very generous of you to take an interest in my fiancée's friend. We are expected at the Rutledges' for cards this evening, so please do keep that in mind. Ladies need time to change and all that.'

'Absolutely. We are expected at the Rutledges' as well.' That was also not entirely true until just now. His mother and brother were indeed pledged for the evening, but his own attendance was in reserve. He'd not yet decided. For a man who prided himself on the truth, he'd invented several pretexts since he'd met Miss Duval. He offered his arm. 'Miss Duval, shall we go collect my mother? Good day, Southford, Blankenship, Miss Cameron.'

'Thank you. That's three times you've come between me and a difficult situation,' Miss Duval said in low tones as they made their way out of the rose garden. 'Be careful, Your Grace, or it might become a habit.'

'Don't worry,' he assured her with a laugh. 'It takes more than a few days to form a habit.'

She laughed up at him, blue eyes dancing. 'Well, I'm here until July, so beware, there's still plenty of time.'

'I'll take note and be on my guard.' Perhaps it was the easy way she bantered without intending to flirt, although other men might mistake it for thus, that appealed to him. He recognised she was not so much outspoken as she was plain-spoken. Despite her confidence, she'd needed him today, and she had been honest enough to admit it. That was a kind of bravery all its own.

He could respect that. But it didn't mean he was going to change his mind about the courting of Americans by his peers. Still, he could admit to a certain curiosity about this one who had no intentions of staying past July and who had unspecified decisions to make. American women were supposed to be straightforward, uncomplicated. But this one came with plenty of mystery, potential proof that *she* might be different than her fellow countrywomen. Not that it made any difference to him. His dukedom needed an English rose, not an American Beauty with thorns.

## Chapter Four

River yachting at sunset was certainly different than sailing in San Francisco Bay. For one, it was tame, the water less precarious, although she was not naive enough to mistake the still waters for placid waters. Zephy regarded water the way she regarded sourdough, as something that had a mind of its own and must be respected.

'Well, what do you think of her? Is yachting to your taste, Miss Duval?' The duke had completed the tour of the yacht, bringing them back where they'd started—at the bow, where the spring dusk turned the waters a dark purple and the sky above lavender.

'I like it. The *Aquatica* is lovely.' She ran a hand over the smooth teak railing. The duke's pride in the yacht was evident from the polished wood and brass trimmings to the comforts on deck and in the saloon. The *Aquatica* was a seaworthy specimen of the highest order, complete with both sails and auxiliary steam to handle any condition. 'Is she just for the river, or do you sail in more open waters?'

The duke appeared to like the question. He leaned on the rail, looking out over the river. 'I do take her to Cowes in August for racing, and she is certainly capable of travelling the Channel. Is there yachting where you are from? I confess to not knowing much about San Francisco, other than it's a long way from here.'

A world away some might say. 'There is sailing on the bay. But with the winds, it takes a smart sailor to navigate the waters. Still, on a clear day it's good to be out on the water and see the city from a different, more peaceful perspective.'

She felt the duke's gaze slide in her direction. 'You miss home. I hear the wistfulness in your voice.'

'It's the only place I've ever been until now, if one doesn't count our summer outings to Napa Valley and finishing school. That's where I met Lulu Cameron,' she offered as an aside. 'I think it's natural to miss the only place one has known. But that doesn't mean I don't want to be here just now or that I'd rather be there.'

A crew member approached and offered them chilled Champagne from a tray. She took a glass and sipped, the cold beverage tart on her tongue. What luxury the duke lived in: French Champagne to enjoy on a private sail down the river at sunset. It was enchanting, and what a story it would be to tell back home. The Duvals had money, perhaps even more than the duke, but they did not spend it like this, did not live like this.

'Perhaps you prefer to be here just now because of the decisions that await you at home?' the duke asked after the crew member had moved off to serve Hale's brother and mother who stood out of earshot, deep in their own conversation. 'What sorts of decisions are they?'

She gave him a sharp but coy look. 'Aren't you supposed to be showing me the sights?'

He straightened and raised an arm. 'All right. Over there is Marble Hill House. It was built for the Countess of Suffolk, Henrietta Howard, a century and a half ago.'

'Oh, so one of your fairly new houses,' she quipped.

'Well, yes, I suppose you might say that.' He broke off with a laugh. 'You're teasing me.' He smiled and for a moment her breath caught. The smile transformed his face, crinkling his eyes at the corners, lighting their tawny depths so that they took on the shade of whiskey in a tumbler catching the light. He looked more human, less ducal. 'Perhaps that's your way of distracting me. I didn't forget what started this conversation. What awaits you upon your return? Or shall we make it a game of Rumpelstiltskin?'

She furrowed her brow, and he explained. 'If I guess your troubles you have to tell me, like in the fairy tale when the princess guesses Rumpelstiltskin's name.'

'All right, if you really want to work that hard, I'll let you, but only until we get back to London. If you haven't guessed by then, the deal is off,' she countered. This man beside her was more interesting than the duke she'd danced with last night.

'Guess number one,' he gave her a long look. 'Is it money problems?' She shook her head.

He rubbed at his chin and gave a little nod. 'Then, it must be love. Is there someone waiting for you at home?'

'That's two different things.' She prevaricated, but it was too late. 'How did you guess so easily?'

The duke—she wished she had something better to call him—shrugged. 'Money and love are the two most common motives in the world. Peasants, generals, kings, none of us are immune.' He gave a half smile. 'And you've come a long way from home. Perhaps you thought to outrun your troubles? People often make the mistake of thinking travel will get them away from their problems only to find their problems have come with them.' Lights were starting to shine on the shore, beaming out from mansion windows along the Thames. Inside those homes, people were going about preparations for supper, for evening entertainments, but here on the river, it was just them, in a world that existed between the Parkhurst garden party and the Rutledge card evening. Perhaps that was why she told him. Secrets were safe in this cocoon on the river.

'My father is eager to see me settled. He would like me to marry. Soon. He wants to know the family bakery business is in good hands for the next generation. I am welcome to make a match here or to accept his match when I return. Both choices have their limitations. Perhaps I don't want a match at all.' At least not for those reasons—business and expediency. She wanted a partner in life and in love. But that seemed a dream too far under the circumstances.

'It is not unreasonable for a man to want to see his daughter taken care of.' He was the duke again, and she already missed the man who'd beguiled her into sharing.

She gave a disappointed shake of her head. She'd expected too much from this man who, despite the lapse today, was exactly what he'd seemed last night: a priggish traditionalist. 'Of course you'd say that. You're a man,' Zephy snapped. For a moment there'd been hope for him. 'Why not let *me* run the bakery on my own, married or not? How hard is it to see that? I run the bakery now as it is. Widow Louise Boudin runs her family's bakery, and no one is pressuring her to remarry for the sake of the business. I don't *need* a man to guide me.'

'But perhaps you do need a partner,' the duke replied thoughtfully. 'There are things you can do and there are things that a man can do, places he can go that you cannot, socially.'

She grimaced. 'Now you sound like my mother.'

'Your mother sounds wise, so I will take that as a compliment.' He leaned against the rail and stared out over the water. 'Every man in Parliament knows he's only as successful as his hostess. Have you considered that? Diplomats know they won't be promoted without a wife beside them. Partnerships work both ways. Consider your American, Jennie Jerome, and her husband. His political success is because of her.' He slid her a quick look. 'Instead of saying a woman needs a husband to be successful, think of it as a husband needing a wife if he means to advance. No one can do it alone. Man or woman.'

'Louise Boudin does *not* need a man,' Zephy repeated. Had he not heard her the first time?

The duke held up a hand. 'This Louise Boudin you are so quick to champion may keep the books and run her bakery, but that is likely because everyone sees the ghost of her husband standing at her shoulder and that is enough. He is present enough to cloak her in decency.'

'Even a husband in absentia is better than no husband at all?' Zephy sniffed at that. 'Such hypocrisy.'

'Like that book in your pocket?' He was so damnably cool when he fired his darts. Not one of her barbs had riled him, while everything he said seemed to rile her. 'America vaunts its sense of democracy, but as soon as it can afford to, it sends its women back here to hunt titles, the very thing they revolted against.'

*In a revolution that was younger than the Countess of Suffolk's river house.* He didn't need to say the words out loud for her to feel them hovering in the air between them. He thought she was childish, her country was childish. She'd had enough of that. Enough time had been spent discussing why she'd been in the rose garden, but she'd not been there alone. 'Why were *you* in the rose garden, today? Who were you hiding from?'

He laughed. 'What makes you think I was hiding?'

'You were there alone, and dukes, I am given to understand, are never alone. They are too much in demand.' She could afford to be smug about it after what he'd put her through. 'Don't worry, Duke. Your secret is safe with me. Confession is good for the soul.' She flashed him a smile that said she knew she was right and she knew she had manoeuvred him into a corner.

That was a victory smile if he'd ever seen one: wide, confident, open and full of life. It lit up her face even in the darkness, and she was not hiding her enjoyment over having him on the ropes one bit. 'A gentleman *is* entitled to some privacy.' He'd let her decide if he referred to the privacy of his thoughts or the privacy of the garden.

'Shall I be the Rumpelstiltskin now?' She turned around from the rail so that her back was against it, her gaze fixed solely on him as the lights of London came into view behind her, making a fetching picture.

'If you like.' He wouldn't have to hold out against her very long. They were almost home, and what could she possibly know about him?

She gave a nod, her clear light blue eyes steady on him for a silent length until she said at last, 'You were hiding from Lady Julia Parkhurst.'

Well, damn. How had she gotten that on the first try? And yet he couldn't let her win that easily. 'Why would I be hiding from someone I spent the whole afternoon with?'

'For just that reason. You wanted some privacy. A rather odd thing to want from the person you intend to marry.'

She might as well have shot him at point-blank range. 'Lady Julia doesn't need all of my attention all of the time. That's not how British marriages work. We don't expect to live in each other's pockets.' Hearing himself say those words, even in defence of his position, made him sound like the prig she accused him of being.

'Separate lives. That sounds…fulfilling.' She let her tone communicate the opposite. He watched her think for a moment, considering. 'Is that what you grew up with? Parents who led separate lives?' There was no meanness in the question, only curiosity, and he found he didn't mind answering. She had a way of asking that made the question seem less intrusive than it might have been.

'It was more like different spheres in my home. My mother was in charge of the house, the staff, the children. My father was in charge of the estate. And yes, that often took him away from home for the better part of the year. He spent the autumns doing a progress of all the holdings. He spent spring and summer in London for Parliament. We were without him six months of the year. He would write, of course,' Hale amended quickly, not wanting to be disloyal to his father. His father was a duke: His life was built around responsibilities, and he had fulfilled those duties until his dying day. He'd been a duke without fault but a father with flaws.

'Still, a letter isn't a father. It must have been a lonely way to grow up,' Zephy pressed.

'I do not recall being lonely. My brother and I grew up at Glenmere, the family seat. It's outside of Brighton. It's a beautiful place with trees to climb, trails to ride, a river to fish in, everything a boy could want.' He smiled a little at the memory. 'It was special, though, when my father came home. He'd take me hunting. I treasured those days, understood the rarity of them.' Then he'd also been gone from Glenmere, off to school and university and those days all but vanished. 'What of your own parents? Surely they had their spheres as well?'

She gave a toss of her head and laughed. 'Heavens, no. My mother, my father and my *grand-père* all worked at the bakery. Every day from open to close. Hired labour eats at profits, so if you can do it yourself, then you do. For a long time it was just us and Pierre, our head baker. I grew up in the bakery, riding around on my *grand-père*'s shoulders learning the process. When I outgrew his shoulders, I got my own stool at the kneading table so I could work the bread with other women.' She fixed him with a wide smile. 'Have I shocked you?'

'No, it sounds different but delightful.'

'Delightful? Not always. It can be hard to find privacy, hard to be yourself. There's no time for anything else. We can't get away from each other. We're all underfoot every day, all the time.' The words were harsh and rushed. This, he sensed, was a point of resentment for her. She took a deep breath and slowed. 'At least that used to be the case. Last autumn, my father took seriously ill and wasn't able to go to the bakery. My mother stayed home to care for him. It was just me at the bakery then.' What a burden that must have been and a lonely one. He knew the burden of a sick parent, the burden to carry the load they'd once shouldered, the burden to do that effortlessly and without error. How interesting to have such a thing in common with this woman who was so different than himself.

She gave a shrug as if she could erase where the conversation had gone to—someplace far more personal than intended. 'We've gotten off-topic. We were talking about marriages and separate lives. I think you've overlooked a key contradiction. An arrangement of separation is contradictory to your earlier argument about partnership, about husbands and wives needing each other. If that were true, perhaps so many people wouldn't be miserable. Jennie Jerome's husband is not faithful to her, and rumour has it she's not faithful to him either.'

He suspected she was trying to shock him on purpose now. But she would be the one shocked if she went about in polite society saying such things. 'Young ladies aren't supposed to know such things let alone speak about them,' he scolded.

'I'd rather know such things now than later when nothing can be done about it. Do *you* intend to be faithful to Lady Julia? Or do you intend to doom her to a marriage of separate lives?'

The audacious question brought him up short. He supposed he hadn't thought about it one way or the other. He'd assumed he'd be faithful, but suddenly the idea of what that entailed—forsaking all others for the *rest* of his life for a pretty, brown-eyed miss who he knew nothing about beyond her family's connections and her skill at lawn tennis—seemed rather ominous. More ominous was the belated realisation he'd hesitated too long in making his answer, and Miss Duval had noticed.

'I see,' Miss Duval said quietly as the yacht turned towards its moorings. 'You are just like all the rest of your peers. I was beginning to hope you were not.'

He was not. He wanted to rail that *he* was not selling his title to the highest bidder. *He* was not mired in debt. *He* was not in her dirty little book of names. He wanted to shout that it was his *duty* to marry a marquess's daughter, to see that the dukedom survived the turn of the century. If she knew anything at all about him, she'd know that family was duty, marriage was duty, and he was merely doing his. Marriage wasn't a fairy tale or a love story. It was work. His parents had worked to build their lives, and her parents had, too. It was not work for the faint of heart. It was quite Darwinian at its core—survival of the fittest. Most titles didn't last more than three generations without dedication to duty. But he could say none of that. There wasn't time. Instead he said, 'And you are like all the rest of yours.' Saying it out loud dashed his earlier hopes. But there was no overlooking that she was opinionated, audacious, argumentative. And, unfortunately, she was completely unforgettable.

He should not find debating with her so stimulating. But he did. There must be something wrong with him to find disagreement so exercising. Part of him admitted to needling her just to see what she'd say next, right up to the point where he'd not liked what he heard, not liked what she reflected back to him about himself. Her perceived truth stung even if he knew better.

'I am not,' came her response, all the more strongly felt for the quietness with which it was uttered. The *Aquatica* bumped up against the dock. 'I was in the garden to avoid Lord Blankenship's attention and to verify I had indeed read the signs right, that he was hunting a fortune and his interest in me was purely financial. He's on page fifty-eight, if you're interested.'

He was *not* interested. 'I could have told you that much. Everyone knows Freddie hasn't a feather to fly with beyond his good looks. His stepmama holds all the financial power, even though he holds the title. It's not worth much on its own. His father's second wife's settlements prop it up.'

'Well, I didn't have you to consult,' she replied sharply. Her gaze drifted over his shoulder. 'Lord Leo, good evening.'

His brother. Timely as always with his intrusions, Hale thought dryly.

'Miss Duval, might I escort you to the carriage?' His brother offered a smile and his arm, both of which she took, taking time only to pierce Hale with a stabbing glance of her eyes. They'd not finished their conversation, but perhaps it was best to leave it as it was. Some discussions had no resolution, and this was likely one of them. It was also a discussion he had no business having with her to begin with. Men and women didn't talk of such things, particularly when they hardly knew one another.

Still, something niggled as he watched Miss Duval walk away with his brother, chatting and laughing gaily. Why hadn't she wanted Lord Blankenship? Wasn't Blankenship exactly what she was looking for, a quick, expedient exchange of money and titles to satisfy her father? Freddie was charming, light-hearted and, yes, something of a spendthrift and not incredibly responsible as a landowner, but good fun in exchange for those faults. What had held her back? If she hoped to make a match here, it was doubly confusing as to why she was avoiding Blankenship. Or, when the moment had come to own up to the trade, perhaps she'd not been able to do it? Was that just wishful thinking on his part because he wanted to be right, he *wanted* her to be different? Why would he want *that*? Why did he even care? He didn't have an answer except *Just because he did.*

## Chapter Five

She had no answer for her choices today. She'd disappointed Lulu and embarrassed Lulu's parents in front of people whose association they wanted to curate. Zephy sat stoically at her dressing table, letting the maid brush out her hair from its afternoon coiffure while she waited for the ominous knock on her door, the knock that would herald Lulu's arrival and gentle interrogation. She needed to have her answers ready by the time that knock came. Lulu deserved no less after how she'd acted today. Lord Blankenship had been hand-picked and delivered to her, and she'd scoffed at the gift.

There it was—a gentle rap followed by Lulu poking her head in first before entering. 'Zephy, may I come in? I wanted to talk over the afternoon.' Lulu smiled softly and shut the door behind her. She was already dressed for the casino evening at the Rutledges' in a beautiful emerald silk designed by Worth.

'You look like a countess, Lulu.' Zephy hadn't bothered to have the maid lay out a gown. She wanted to stay in tonight. She didn't think she could face down another room full of lords eyeing her fortune. The idea of marrying someone here in order to simply thwart marrying Mathieu Aubert hadn't been as easy to enact in reality as it had been in her head.

She'd failed today. She'd not been strong enough. She'd have to find the strength, though, or find another way through because she knew what awaited her at home if she didn't. Perhaps there was an unexplored middle ground she'd overlooked? What had the duke said—a husband in absentia was still a husband? Perhaps there was something there? A hopeful middle ground began to take shape.

Lulu's smile broadened at the compliment. 'You will look lovely, too. Have you decided what to wear?'

Zephy shook her head. 'I don't think I should go. I don't want to reflect poorly on you and your family. I think I did enough of that today. Perhaps if I stay out of sight I can also stay out of mind for the time being.' She might as well get straight to the point. She knew why Lulu had come to talk. There was no sense wasting time pretending otherwise.

'Perhaps Blankenship isn't the right one,' Lulu conceded, sitting gently on the edge of the big four poster bed. 'I thought you'd like him. He is charming. He was entirely dedicated to you.'

'He is clingy. He didn't leave my side the entire afternoon.'

'He is handsome,' Lulu tried again.

'He is vain. He checked his appearance in anything that could be used as a mirror. The silver punch cups, the lake, my eyes.'

'He was interested in you,' Lulu coaxed.

'He was interested in my money,' Zephy said flatly. 'If I hadn't had a fortune to my name he would not have looked twice at me if I'd gotten off the yacht naked.'

Lulu laughed at that. 'He'd probably have looked *more* than twice if that had been the case.' Then she gave a sobering sigh. 'Zeph, you knew it would be like that. Everyone in the game knows what the trade is. Your money for their title. You get to be a Lady, they get to be solvent, and somewhere in between, some of us decide to build a relationship with one another.' And some did not. Zephy thought of the conversation with the duke, of living separate lives, navigating separate spheres.

'Is it that way for you and Southford?' Zephy knit her brow in concern. Was that the kind of marriage Lulu wanted? A marriage of separate lives?

A faint blush that hinted at more than modesty stained Lulu's cheeks. 'I have reason to hope ours will be a marriage better than most. I want the same for you, and I thought you did, too,' she said meaningfully. 'Blankenship fulfils all the requirements.'

'In other words, he's entirely desperate.' Zephy sighed. He'd been a handsome, blond, obsequious puppy dog today at the garden party. Not at all like the duke who'd made it plain from the start what he thought of her. 'Is Southford desperate? Does he need your money that badly?'

'Money helps. I would be lying if I said otherwise.' Lulu gave a little smile, but Zephy caught the tightness at the corners. 'I like to think of it this way. The money brought us together. What we make of it is up to us.' She paused, and Zephy sensed her friend was growing exasperated. 'Blankenship was low-hanging fruit, Zephy, but we can find you another, if it pleases you.' Zephy heard the unspoken caution. She could not renege on the tacit agreement a second time. Such a snub would not be tolerated, and it would negatively impact those who'd arranged the introduction. Lulu's friendship was on the line.

'What *do* you want, Zeph?' Lulu asked quietly. 'Do you truly want to marry?'

'I don't know.' She was just as exasperated with herself as Lulu was. 'I thought I could do it, but when the moment came to encourage Lord Blankenship's interest, I thought about spending every breakfast with those vacuous blue eyes staring at me at the table, and I couldn't go through with it, knowing that he didn't know me, didn't understand me. He probably never would, and he probably wouldn't care. The not knowing wouldn't bother him.'

Which added further proof to the duke's words about separate lives. She didn't want that. Whenever she married, she wanted a partner, wanted a marriage like her mother and father's. 'Lord Blankenship has not baked anything in his life, hasn't built anything, hasn't worked a hard day managing hot ovens, temperamental dough and employees.' She'd never wanted to sink her hands into sourdough and lose herself in fashioning a loaf more than she did right now.

'No, he hasn't, and he certainly would not permit his wife to engage in those activities,' Lulu replied sharply. 'That *is* the price of the game, Zephy.'

'Then, I was right to turn aside his suit before it really got started. I couldn't possibly give up the bakery. In fact, the whole point of marrying is to help me keep the bakery.' The last tumbled out despite her earlier intentions not to burden Lulu with her problems.

Lulu's sandy eyebrows arched in concern. 'What are you talking about, Zeph?'

'I didn't want to tell you. You have so much to deal with concerning the wedding.' But now that the words had begun, she couldn't stop them. It felt good to share her burden with her friend. 'Father only let me come on the condition I find a husband or marry one of his choosing when I return so that he knows the bakery is secure once he retires,' Zephy explained.

'You think an English gentleman will go live in San Francisco with you and join you at the bakery?' Lulu couldn't keep the incredulity out of her voice. 'They have estates to run, families to manage. They can't be halfway around the world, Zephy. Nor are they made for such a life, as you just noted about Lord Blankenship.'

'Perhaps I don't need them to be.' She tried out the new plan that had been percolating in her brain since she'd left the duke at the yacht. 'Maybe what I need is a husband in *theory*, someone who will let me return to San Francisco with nothing but his name. He can stay here and oversee his estates, fattened up with my cash, and I can return home cloaked in the decency of being a married woman. We needn't bother each other.' It was the *idea* of having had a husband, the duke had argued, that made Louise Boudin accepted.

Lulu grimaced. 'I am not sure where we find such a man. He'd not have the benefit of a hostess if you were to leave, nor the benefit of an heir. Would you be willing to negotiate that? Perhaps stay a few years until an heir is acquired?'

'Good God, Lulu, you sound like a solicitor. No, I would not be willing to stay until an heir is produced. And then what? Leave the child behind? Do you think my father would stand for that? His grandchild is to be raised in the bakery. For that matter, do you think I'd tolerate that myself?'

'So you would need an older man who has already secured his succession. Or a second son who needn't worry about such things. Someone for whom money would be enough to brave the scandal?' Lulu mused out loud.

'I suppose so.' The conversation was becoming more distasteful by the minute. It wasn't Lulu's fault. Zephy had no one to blame but herself. She'd set herself up for this, and now she hadn't the stomach to go through with it. But if she didn't, she'd be married to Mathieu Aubert who would definitely be unfaithful, and who would get to be the face of the bakery, pushing her out over time simply because he was a man. Her life would become subsumed by his. By contrast, a marriage in half measures that at least allowed her freedom did seem better. She needed to remember that. Perhaps it would give her the fortitude to carry out her plan, but it wouldn't compensate for the emptiness of a marriage that was only a business transaction but was far from the partnership she desired. It left her saddened, resigned and having to admit that the duke was right. Maybe she wasn't as different as she thought.

'Do you have the book?' Lulu asked. 'I'll pick out some candidates while you change. Have your maid bring out the deep blue with the black lace. It's sophisticated. Mama has called for the coach at nine, so we only have a little time.'

'But I am staying in,' Zephy protested even as the maid hurried off to retrieve the gown. 'I thought we'd decided that would be best.'

'No, *you* decided that. I disagree. We must show everyone that you're interested in casting a wider net, that you're a discerning young woman unwilling to jump at the first lord who dangles a title in front of her.' Lulu had a talent for putting a decent spin on a potentially bad situation. She'd make an excellent countess, a superior hostess. Zephy hoped Southford appreciated that about Lulu. 'If anything, it will be Blankenship who won't show up tonight after being overridden by a duke.'

Zephy groaned at the reminder. The duke. She really didn't want to face him again so soon after their boat ride.

Lulu dog-eared a page and looked up from the book. 'Don't worry, casino nights aren't the duke's style. I doubt he'll be there. His brother will be carrying the family torch tonight at the Rutledges'.' Lulu's eyes lit up. 'Have you thought about Lord Leo Eberley? He'd be a prime candidate. Second son, no real need to secure the succession since his brother will marry before the year's out. He needs money but has no ambition that requires a wife.'

'I don't know that I'd want the duke for an in-law.'

Zephy held her hair up so the maid could finish the fastenings of her gown.

'Why would you care when you're thousands of miles away with everything you wanted?' Lulu shut the book. 'If you don't like Leo Eberley, I have three other names of gentlemen who will be there tonight. Happy hunting.' She smiled triumphantly, but Zephy didn't return the smile. Lulu's words echoed the duke's reaction all too closely—that the men in the book were little more than prey. If they were prey, she didn't like what that made her. She wasn't looking to trap, snare or ambush anyone.

She twisted around to see Lulu over her shoulder. 'Does the duke have a name?'

'Lord Leo's brother? It's Hale, I think. I saw it in Debrett's. No one ever calls him that, though. His friends call him Sunderland, and the rest of us call him Your Grace.' She heard the warning in Lulu's voice and would have laughed if she didn't know her friend was truly worried.

'I won't embarrass you again, Lulu.' She smiled her promise. 'Shall we go? I don't want to keep your mother waiting.' She would do her very best to have a good time tonight, to show the Camerons she could be on her best behaviour and the rest of London that she could play their game as well any other American. She would be the life of the party tonight, tomorrow night and the nights beyond because that was her mission, it was what she'd come to do. She had to marry someone. If that made her like all the rest in the starchy Duke of Sunderland's eyes, so be it. After all, *she* wasn't going to marry *him*.

'Sourdough Heiress Rises to the Occasion.' Good heavens. Would the bread bon mots ever stop? Hale laid aside first one newspaper and then another. One would think after two weeks of such punnery the well of witticisms would run dry. Two weeks was an eternity during the Season. One might soar to the height of popularity and fall from that very same pinnacle within that time span, replaced by one or even two fresher scandals. Zephyrine Duval hadn't fallen though, not yet. Although it *did* surprise him. She was a scandal waiting to happen. But she was propped up by her connection to the Earl of Southford and by the enormous fortune she was rumoured to have. Perhaps that made all the difference. She wasn't being allowed to fall. Society wanted her money to stay on England's shores.

'Ah, the papers. Did I make the Society columns?' Leo breezed into the room, looking perfectly pressed in bone-coloured trousers and a dark blue jacket, his blond hair with its unruly curl combed into submission. One might mistake his brother for an upstanding gentleman, dressed and up this hour of the day.

'No, thank goodness.' It was the first thing Hale

did in the mornings before reading the business and financial sections. He looked to see if Leo had made an ass out of himself the night before, had gambled away a small fortune he now had to cover or worse. Financial losses could be recouped. A woman's honour could not be. 'You're up early,' he remarked as Leo helped himself to coffee and eggs from the sideboard. Hale noted the food. Apparently, Leo wasn't hung-over either. Would wonders never cease?

'I am escorting Miss Duval and Miss Cameron to Knightsbridge today. We have an appointment at Tattersalls to look over some horses suitable for riding. Miss Duval hasn't a horse currently.'

'Does Miss Duval ride?' Hale asked coolly. He'd not seen the American miss since their ill-fated conversation on the *Aquatica*—proof enough that they were different people who ran in different circles with different priorities. While she'd been making the rounds of card parties, garden parties and balls, he'd been busy in Parliament seeing to important legislation and keeping up with estate business at a distance through a never-ending correspondence pile.

'Yes, she keeps horses at home in San Francisco and at her summer home, a château somewhere called Napa Valley.' Leo's reply was smug. 'She's a grand girl with so many interests and pursuits. Very active, these Americans. Did you know she's part of a cycling club, too? San Francisco is more progressive, more civilised than I thought.' That Leo had thought at all was an amazement in itself.

'No, I was unaware she was a cyclist.' He was not keeping notes on the American heiress who thought he was stiff-necked and old-fashioned. So why did it bother him—and not in an *I want to protect my brother* sort of way—that Leo knew so much about her? That Leo was taking her shopping for a horse?

'I've invited her to the Lords and Commons cricket match on Saturday. She's never seen one, and Southford is hosting a viewing pavilion. I told her you and Bilborough played for the Lords side, so don't let me down. Make it a good one.' Leo gulped down the last of his coffee as their mother entered the room.

'Have I missed both my boys eating breakfast together? Had I known, I would have come down earlier to witness this cosmic event.' Hale rose, and Leo held a chair for her.

'Hello and goodbye, Mother. I am off.' Leo pressed a swift kiss to her cheek, making her laugh with his attentions. But that was Leo, always charming, always the favourite.

'Should I be worried? Leo up so early?' she asked once he had departed. 'It seems too good to be true.'

'He's escorting Southford's Americans to Tattersalls.' Hale still wasn't over his sourness about the outing. Perhaps it was only that Tattersalls sounded like more fun than the morning with the estate ledgers that he himself faced.

His mother glanced at the papers. 'Yes, the Duval girl. He's quite taken with her.' She waited until the footman had poured her tea and stepped back before she continued. 'I can think of less productive ways for him to spend his time and efforts. It's been weeks since he's been in a scrape, although the fiacre fiasco was hardly a scrape.' Ah, she knew, then. So much for protecting her. 'He went too far with that one,' his mother went on. 'Lives were endangered. If Miss Duval has been a civilising influence on him, I am grateful. Leo's not a boy anymore. You cannot protect him forever, and he could do far worse than Miss Duval.'

'She could do far better,' Hale replied swiftly. What was his mother *thinking*? He wasn't sure who his defence was protecting in the moment—Leo or Miss Duval. 'My brother is not husband material.'

'Not yet. Most men aren't husband material the day they marry.' She smiled knowingly, a twinkle in her eye. 'Your father certainly wasn't. But he became an excellent husband with a little guidance. Just as your brother will. Just as you will.'

'*I* need guidance?' He chuckled. He'd been responsible for the dukedom since he was twenty-four. Surely, he could run a marriage and manage a wife—as long as she didn't contest him at every turn. An image of dark walnut hair and pale blue eyes flashed through his mind, the epitome of rebellion.

'All men need guidance, and those who are born to privilege and power even more. So you've decided, then? It's to be the marquess's daughter? I am the happiest of mothers to think both my sons might be married in the same year, and I could have two grandchildren to hold next summer.' She paused, her stare intent. 'You *have* decided?' She sought the confirmation he was unwilling to fully give.

'I am almost certain. I want to give us both time. She is still quite young. I want to be sure she knows her mind,' he prevaricated.

'Hmm.' His mother looked up over her teacup. 'And to be sure you know yours as well?' He wasn't expected to answer that. She turned her attention to the papers by his elbow. 'Anything good in the news? Probably not. It's always so boring when Leo isn't mentioned.'

He passed one of the papers down to her and returned to his reading. Ten more minutes, he promised himself with a glance out the big window letting in the morning sun, then he'd retreat to the office. Ledgers didn't balance themselves.

'You could always go join them. At Tattersalls, I mean.' His mother spoke without looking up from the pages. 'You were going to see about a horse for my new victoria. Now that the weather is better, I am eager to show it off in the park. But I can do nothing until I have a proper horse for it. I could send one of our grooms to make enquiries, of course.' She sighed.

He held back a chuckle. She was not being subtle. Perhaps she'd not meant to be. His mother knew him too well. He'd not spend the day away from estate business unless there was some other business he might conduct in its stead. He laid down his paper. 'I suppose I could take care of that for you today, Mother. Are you still thinking you want a chestnut?'

'Chestnut or a dark bay.' She smiled up from the papers. 'So you'll join them?'

He set aside his napkin, taking the hint for urgency. 'Yes, I'll leave at once.' At this rate he might get there before them. He ought not be looking forward to the outing as much as he was. He ought to be lamenting how his morning had been turned upside down with this new plan, bemoaning how he was chaperoning his brother again, this time to keep an eye on him because his brother had been *too* quiet, and already regretting the doubling of correspondence that would be waiting for him tonight because he took the morning off. But he was doing none of that. Instead, he was impatiently calling for his phaeton and already checking his watch, far too eager to be off to spend time with a woman he didn't like.

## Chapter Six

Zephyrine Duval was not his type of woman at all, a fact he was immediately reminded of once more the moment he spied her at Tattersalls. She was all animation and motion: Her face was in constant transition between nods and smiles and laughter, and her stride, as she walked beside his brother, was more athletic than graceful, eagerness and briskness in each step.

It was her energy that set her apart, Hale decided. It could not be disguised beneath the very appropriate carriage ensemble with its tight-fitting jacket in a spring-sky blue nipped at the waist and a tartan patterned skirt of dark and light blues that skimmed her ankles, revealing matching blue half boots the same colour as the small felt toque atop her dark hair. If she stood still and kept silent, she might pass as an Englishwoman. But given those two accomplishments were beyond her, there was no chance she'd be mistaken for none other than what she was—an

American abroad. Even Miss Cameron looked more English beside her. That ought to please Southford. Miss Cameron would have to be very English indeed if she meant to survive Southford's mother and Southford's own English peccadilloes, which included a long-standing mistress in Piccadilly.

Leo looked his way. Hale gave a circumspect nod of acknowledgement and made his way towards the little party. Southford had come, too, looking entirely like the devoted fiancé with Miss Cameron on his arm. For Southford's sake, Hale hoped the devotion was real. Too many of their associates had found marriage to an American to be a far more bitter pill to swallow than anticipated.

'Brother, you've decided to join us. What a surprise,' Leo greeted him, defensiveness leaping in his eyes.

'I realised after you left that I'd promised Mother to see about a horse for her new victoria. I do hope I am not intruding?' Which was not true. A little intrusion might be in order, based on his mother's comments this morning. Miss Duval in her blue tartan and his brother in his blue jacket made a striking couple—too striking. Such synchronicity would not escape their notice nor the notice of others. 'It seemed a missed opportunity not to come on such a beautiful day.' Sun poured through Tattersalls famed glass roof in testament to the good weather. A boy ran past distributing auction sheets. Hale took one and gave it a quick scan. 'Does anything look promising?'

'Basingstoke has brought some mares that should make decent steeplechasers. He's saving his yearlings for Tattersall's Newmarket paddocks. Everyone is saying he will challenge Sainfoin at the Derby this year with one of Warbourne's grand-foals.'

'I like number 36, Lady Jane, and quite possibly number 40, Marigold,' Miss Duval joined the conversation, offering her unsolicited opinion.

Hale glanced down the sheet and stifled a sigh. Of course she did. 'Those are Basingstoke's sister's horses.'

'Bred and trained by a woman? How wonderful. I like them all the more for it.' Miss Duval favoured him with one of her wide smiles. 'Is she here?' Miss Duval looked about the long show floor filling with people the closer it got to half past eleven and the beginning of the auction. 'I would love to speak with her about the horses. I saw them when the handlers had them out earlier. Splendid animals, both of them.'

'My brother can handle the transaction and any questions you might have,' Hale offered, trying to subtly redirect her. A woman at Tattersalls was still something of a rarity, although there were a few here today strolling the colonnaded gallery above. This was primarily a male stronghold. It would be beyond the pale for a woman to conduct her own business here, no matter the size of her fortune.

She turned cool blue eyes his direction. 'I am capable of purchasing my own horse, Your Grace, but thank you.' Then she turned a more charming version of that gaze on his brother. 'Lord Leo, do you think you might be able to inveigle Basingstoke and his sister to join us?'

Leo beamed at the commission, a chance to upstage Hale, no doubt, by performing a service for her. 'I am also eager to speak with Basingstoke. Let me see what I can do. Southford, brother, perhaps you might take the ladies up to the gallery, and I'll join you there with guests in tow.' That was quite commanding of Leo. In other circumstances, Hale would have applauded his brother's initiative. Now, though, he just found it worrisome.

The pairings were obvious. Southford already had Miss Cameron on his arm, which left Hale no choice but to offer the same to Miss Duval. Perhaps his brother knew how much the arrangement would irritate him. 'Miss Duval, the stairs are this way, if you please.'

'You disapprove of my actions.' She slid him a challenging gaze as they ascended the stairs.

'It's not disapproval per se. I think you are new here and do not know how to go about certain things,' he replied smoothly. 'You have champions and friends who are willing to counsel you. Let yourself be guided. Southford can be relied upon. He would not let you put a foot wrong, nor would Miss Cameron.' Mainly because it would reflect poorly on them, but still, it would be good advice. He could see immediately that he'd misstepped.

'Does Lady Julia allow herself to be guided? How boring that must be to tell a lady what to think only to have her parrot back those thoughts to you. It's like looking in a mirror and only seeing oneself. Where's the challenge in that? No wonder you gentlemen are such philanderers. You've become bored with your own creations when they give you exactly what you've asked for.' She fired off her argument in low, rapid tones as they trailed behind Southford and Miss Cameron.

'That is a rather biting indictment of the English gentleman.' At least she'd had the good sense to keep her voice down. He'd had to lean close to hear her, and the scent of fresh springtime caught his nostrils. She smelled of clean linen, sharp lemon and the softness of vanilla. That last reminded him of a warm kitchen with biscuits baking. Of course she smelled liked biscuits. She was a baker's daughter, although it was hard to remember that when she was turned out better than most Englishwomen, every feature of her toilette immaculate and expensive.

'Lady Julia knows her role,' he said in the absent

Julia's defence, but the other comments rankled. Lesley Greenwood and Ethan Tunney passed them, tipping their hats, and Hale found a polite smile for them, grateful they didn't want to stop and talk. He wasn't in the mood for their bonhomie, and he hadn't missed how their eyes had lit up at the sight of Miss Duval.

'Are you considering them? The young viscount's heir and the major?' he enquired, watching them go, off no doubt to purchase more polo ponies.

'Perhaps. They are entertaining and good fun. I was introduced to them at the Rutledges'.' She slid him another coy look full of challenge. 'Are you going to tell me there's something wrong them? They seem no worse than any other and better than some.'

'After your scathing commentary on an Englishman's character, I am rather surprised you'd consider them at all. Would you truly settle for a philanderer?' Down below, the auction had begun. It would be a while before number 36 was up.

'I am looking for something other than faithfulness in a husband. Thanks to you, actually.'

'Thanks to me?' That sounded ominous. She had all of his attention now.

'On the yacht, you pointed out that the difference between my acceptance in the business community in San Francisco and Mrs Boudin's is that she has the protection of a man's name even if he is dead, *the ghost of her husband standing at her shoulder* was how you put it.' Yes, he had said something to that direct effect.

'That's what I want, too.' She flashed him a smug smile. 'A man who will lend me his consequence through marriage and, in exchange for my settlements, will happily allow me to return to San Francisco with his name and a ring on my finger.'

'And your husband? Is he to follow you?' Hale was having difficulty keeping up with this madcap scheme of hers. She was talking about marriage and abandonment, two concepts that did not blend well together in his world.

She shook her head. 'No, of course not. That would defeat the purpose. I don't want him, just his name. He can stay here in England with his estates and his mistresses, and every time it rains he can look up at the ceiling of his great bedchamber and thank me that his roof has been repaired.'

'And you think such a man can be found in your scandalous little book?' he surmised. She probably could find one, which struck him as alarming. Her ploy was audacious and not entirely implausible, although plausibility didn't make it any less scandalous.

'Weren't you the one who said money and love were the two biggest motivators for our actions?' She laughed. 'I see I have shocked you again.' They stopped at one of the open areas between colonnades to look at the show floor below, where grooms were running a pretty bay filly the length to highlight her paces.

'Have you considered the scandal attached to what you propose? Can you imagine what Society would do to your poor husband?' It would also define who she could pursue. She couldn't possibly seek out an heir since she had no intention of securing a succession.

'He'd have money and financial security, and he's a man. Given enough time, his reputation will recover. He could seek a divorce and eventually remarry. Everyone would be in sympathy with him as long as he conducted himself well in the interim.' She gave a shrug as if those were concepts she tossed about on a daily basis. 'And he'd be wealthy. I think a second son living on an allowance would find himself in a better position as a result of it. Eventually.'

A man like Leo. A bolt of something uncomfortable shot through him. If she thought Leo would be amenable to such an arrangement, she'd have to think again. She'd have to get through him first. He would not allow his brother to consider it. 'Would nothing dissuade you from such a calculated course?' He wondered if she understood the ramifications of her plan? Reality was messier than words on paper. Such a cold course seemed at odds with her energetic, spirited nature. She was made for more.

He knew he was going to regret bringing it up, but it seemed no one else would. 'What about affection?

Companionship?' Southford and Miss Cameron were either ignorant of her plans or they were allowing her to run headlong towards disaster.

'Is the great Duke of Sunderland with his ancient bloodlines and his carefully selected fiancée talking about a love match?' she quipped. 'I sense some irony afoot. Don't tell me you are passionately in love with Lady Julia.' Her eyes danced as she baited him, damn her. She was enjoying turning the tables.

'At least there is the hope that such feelings will grow over time. We mean for our marriage to last.'

She settled her gaze on him. 'I know that you think my plan is despicable and that it violates every code you live by. Every time I think to set aside such distasteful mechanisations, I remember why I can't. I remember what waits for me at home if my plan doesn't succeed. Trust me, this is a far better course than a lifetime spent as the wife of Mathieu Aubert, where all I could hope for is that he dies early and sets me free.' The sharp conviction in her tone gave him pause, their eyes locking. He could feel the determined heat of her. She meant every bloody word of that.

'Surely your family would not force a marriage to a man who was *that* unsuitable,' he began.

'Surely *your* family would not rush your marriage simply to secure the succession of a title,' she parried, her words slicing into his argument.

'It's not the same.'

'Isn't it?' Obstinance flashed in the blue depths of her eyes, stark and relentless, the kind of obstinance he'd seen once before in the eyes of his father who fought his final illness with everything he possessed for the privilege of one more day, one more hour, one more breath. A no-holds-barred fight because there was no reason to hold back; because there was nothing left to lose; because the alternative was unthinkable. His father's determination had been fuelled by fear. And so was Miss Duval's. Behind the determined flash of her eyes, behind the sharp words and American bravado, she was *afraid*. If one looked deep enough into her eyes, it was there: fear along with the vulnerability he'd seen at Rivercross in the garden.

The realisation hit him as if he'd just been knocked for six on the cricket field. She hid it well. So well that even now when he saw the fear, he didn't quite believe it, so at odds was it with how he understood her. Perhaps it was a bold assertion on his part to think he could know someone after three meetings and yet he felt that he did know her. That was a dangerous feeling because it roused other feelings. It stoked his need to protect. He was good at protecting. He protected his mother, he protected his brother, his tenants, his father's legacy, all with dogged vigilance.

That same part of him wanted to reach out to Miss Zephyrine Duval and protect her, too, to take the fear from her eyes, the burden from her shoulders that was thrusting her down a reckless, unhappy path. Not that she would appreciate it. She might be scared, but she was also fiercely independent and highly competent—the sort of person who didn't take advice well from others. Someone like himself.

A wave from his brother below broke their defiant staring contest. Leo gestured for them to come down. The Basingstokes were eager to show off their horses. 'We can continue this discussion later.' Hale offered his arm.

'Why? I don't see the point unless you are going to change your mind,' she snapped, but Hale merely smiled. She'd be surprised to know her darts hit with less effectiveness now that he understood.

Down on the show floor, the Basingstokes stood off to the side with Lady Jane and Marigold. Hale let Leo make the introductions. Kenton Basingstoke was the Earl of Hartvale, a sporting gentleman in his early sixties who'd spent his life around the racetrack and hunt field, and his sister, Catherine, only a few years younger, was just like him. All the Basingstokes were horse-mad and talented as riders and breeders.

'These girls are from Warbourne's line. He was the original Basingstoke stud.' Catherine Basingstoke didn't wait to get to business, and Hale could see that Miss Duval was taken with the no-nonsense horsewoman.

'Warbourne? I don't know him,' Miss Duval said, running a hand down Lady Jane's shoulder. That was all it took for Catherine Basingstoke to launch into lines and lineage.

'Warbourne was my mother's prized Derby winner in 1817. She bought him at auction despite my uncle's objections. Pawned her jewellery for him, as the family story goes, all that she had left of her mother.'

Hale had heard the story before. The men moved off, giving the women their space with the horses. 'They'll be a while once Catherine gets going,' the earl chuckled appreciably.

'How is your mother?' Hale enquired. The Dowager Countess of Hartvale was a legend in the horse world. She was ninety-three, and rumour had it she still walked the stables every day and oversaw the yearlings. Her husband, Bram, had passed away twenty years earlier after a fall in the hunt field. Many had thought she'd give up the stud farm they'd run together for decades when he died, but she'd proved far more resilient than expected. Kenton and Catherine had been a big part of that resilience. They'd gotten her through, and she was still here today.

The earl grinned. 'Exactly how you'd expect her to be. Out to the stables every morning. I had to talk her out of trying to take her mare over a few jumps the other day. I said, "Mother, we agreed on flatting only, just walk, trot and canter in the arena".'

Hale smiled. 'How wonderful that she still rides.'

'How dangerous.' The earl grimaced. 'At her age, one fall and all her bones will disintegrate. But her mare is sure-footed and her seat is good, so if that's how she wants to go…' His words drifted off. 'Those horses are her joy. I think one night she'll lie down next to her mare and not wake up, and we'll find her in the morning. I think a lot of us would like to go that way.'

Hale nodded, his attention split between Hartvale and a vague sense of disquiet, of something being astir. Perhaps it was just the auctioneer rapping his gavel, or the commotion of leading out the next horse. But no, it was more than that. Something felt…off. He heard the hooves before he heard the cry. 'Loose horse!' Hale whirled about in time to see a frenzied chestnut pounding down the show floor, heading straight for where Miss Duval stood, trapped between the two mares and the thoroughbred racing towards her.

Dear God, she would be trampled. No! Hale did not think. He raced towards her. If he couldn't get her out of the way he could at least put himself between her and disaster. It was going to be close. At the last moment, he breathed a prayer and launched himself into the breach.

# Chapter Seven

She fell swift and hard at the last moment, the meeting with the soft dirt of the show floor knocking the wind from her as the thud of thoroughbred hooves thundered past, close enough to flutter the hem of her skirts. *Breathe. Breathe.* She had to breathe. Funny how it had never been so difficult to do it before. It might have something to do with the weight atop her. She fought for the tiniest of breaths and pushed at the hard chest pinning her to the ground. The body above her moved off, but breathing was not easier.

'I can't…' she managed the words on the weakest of wheezes '…breathe.' Panic followed. She couldn't breathe! She began to thrash in her horror.

The body that had been above her was now beside her, kneeling in the dirt, his voice low and steady as he raised her. 'Stop moving. You're always moving when you shouldn't be—rosebushes, horse auctions.' A warm chuckle followed the scold, and something in her terror-stricken mind eased. Sunderland was here with his imitable sense of calm, and surprisingly, she *did* feel some of the panic leave her.

'Inhale through your nose, exhale through your mouth,' he instructed in steady tones. 'That's it. Do it again, in through your nose, out through your mouth.' He was breathing with her; she could see the rise and fall of his chest, the chest that had crushed her, protected her, saved her. Her breaths were coming more steadily now, each one deeper than the last. Thank goodness. They were surrounded by people: Lulu and Southford, Lord Leo, the Basingstokes, Tunney and Greenwood were there and a few others she didn't recognise. This was not the kind of attention she wanted. Perhaps she ought to stand up, move out of the limelight. She began the struggle to stand but Sunderland put out a restraining hand.

'Not yet, there's no rush. Your diaphragm froze. It has been paralysed for a few moments. Let's give it and you time to regain full function,' he counselled. 'Just focus on breathing.'

It was hard to focus on simply breathing when her mind was starting to fill with questions. Perhaps that was a good sign. What had happened? Were the horses all right? One moment she'd been chatting with Lady Catherine and the next the horses had become jumpy. She'd turned and saw the horse bearing down on them even as the cry went up—too late to be much help to her. 'Please, I think I am well enough to get up.' This time Sunderland offered his hand and his gentle support, keeping an arm about her as he escorted her to a private tack room away from the crowd. Within moments, she could hear the sounds of the auction resuming.

'I'm going to miss the bid on Lady Jane,' she lamented, taking a seat on a wood settle. The room smelled of saddle oil and leather, a scent she found soothing and mellow in the moment. Now that the near disaster was over, she was feeling foolish for her panic and how public it had been. Everyone had seen it.

'It's no bother. Lady Catherine has withdrawn Lady Jane from the auction. She will sell directly to you. I am having Tattersalls take care of the details.' Sunderland took the hard chair across from her. 'I've sent for tea. It should be here shortly. There's nothing a good cup of English tea can't put right.' He smiled to cheer her, but it only served to make her feel more conspicuous.

'You're being nice to me. It must have been awful. I must have been awful.' She shook her head. 'I feel so embarrassed,' Zephy lamented. This was exactly what she didn't need now that she'd clawed her way back to respectability from the early misstep with Blankenship.

'Nonsense. Danger is not embarrassing. You've

emerged admirably now that we've dusted the dirt off your gown. All is intact. Not a tear or scratch in sight. We can all be grateful for that.'

'Thanks to you.' The enormity of what she owed him was just beginning to occur to her. Sweet heavens, he was good in a crisis: all calm and control. She was in a position to better appreciate his efforts now that she could focus on something besides breathing. He'd taken command of the situation from start to finish. When she'd frozen, he had not. When she'd been on the ground panicking for breath, he'd known exactly what to do.

'Anyone would have done the same.' He brushed off the thanks. She could not allow it. It was not often she found herself in reversed circumstances. Usually, she was the one who took charge.

'No one did, though. Only you.' She voiced the hard truth. Southford, Lord Leo, Lord Hartvale, none of them had surmised the danger quickly enough to launch a useful response, and when Hartvale had he'd gone for the horses and his sister. Understandable, she supposed. 'You might have been in danger more so than I. I can't believe Society would approve of your actions. A duke without an heir is not a worthy exchange for an American sourdough heiress if things had gone poorly.' As in, if his leap had not been in time to clear them both from the horse's hooves. As in, if those deadly hooves had struck him in the head before he could wed Lady Julia and produce an heir.

'Should misfortune befall me, there is always my brother. The dukedom is secure, relatively.' He offered another assuring smile as the tea tray arrived, silver pot and china cups rattling while the groom pressed into temporary service set it down.

'I suppose what I mean to say is that it was brave of you. You stepped between me and a runaway horse. There was nothing modest or humble about it. It was heroic.' She poured out the tea, lifting her eyebrow to query on the sugar. He shook his head. No. Of course not. No sweets for the duke.

That body had certainly been heroic: the hardness, the muscle pressed against her, wrapping her tight in the armour of himself, proof of just how close it had been, and he'd not let her go until he'd been sure the danger had passed. 'I was scared,' she said softly.

His gaze held hers as he took the cup, his fingertips brushing hers ever so briefly. 'I was, too.'

A hot flush took her at the intimacy of his confession. 'Then, thank you again, doubly so.' He'd been scared and had acted anyway—for her, a woman who he made no secret he disapproved of—which touched her unexpectedly and deeply. Who else would have done the same under those conditions, for *her*? Certainly not Mathieu Aubert, or Lord Blankenship, or Tunney or Greenwood. Prickly and traditional Sunderland might be, but there were definitely depths to this duke. Too bad she couldn't find someone like him to be a candidate for her scheme.

Those depths became more apparent over the next few days of shallowness and celebrity that followed. How had she not noticed those depths, *appreciated* them, before? Perhaps it had taken the contrasting parade of the ton's best and brightest—a term Zephy applied loosely—through Mrs Cameron's drawing room to show the duke's depths to advantage.

Word of the accident at Tattersalls had spread quickly, in part because of the participants involved. When a duke and a high-profile heiress faced-down a rampaging thoroughbred, it was interesting and it sold well. Newspapers dramatically trumpeted the event with ridiculous headlines, her least favourite being 'Duke Dives for Débutante'. Women had flocked to Mrs Cameron's at-homes, sons conveniently in tow, eager to use a polite enquiry about Zephy's health to advance notice of their sons. Ethan Tunney and Lesley Greenwood had been the first to arrive. They'd stationed themselves on either side of her like sentinels. They'd been there when it happened, after all, as they frequently pointed out to those who gathered around her, clamouring for a retelling of the episode.

'Weren't you frightened?' Miss Emerson, a coy blonde with a pretty, manufactured blush gushed, making a show of grabbing Major Tunney's arm in her shock, which Zephy thought was rather feigned. 'I mean, the duke is such a *large* man. He frightens me just by standing up to dance with him.' She fluttered her fan, her eyes wide as her gaze circled the group with a naïveté at odds with the implication of her next words. 'And *he* was *lying* on top of *you* for ever so long.'

'Until I was safe, until it was secure for both of us to rise,' Zephy countered the innuendo swiftly, feeling the heat rise in her own cheeks—in indignation of course, nothing more. She did not like the intended turn of the conversation. This not-so-innocent miss was attempting to transform the incident into something tawdry. She would not allow it. Sunderland would not forgive her if she brought scandal to him. He was not here to defend himself so she would do it for him. 'The duke was a hero and a gentleman. I owe him a great deal.' She fixed Miss Emerson with a strong stare. 'It is poorly done of you to suggest there was anything other than heroism on display that day.'

Tension rippled uncomfortably through the coterie around her. A few gentlemen shifted in their seats, uncertain how to respond. Spineless, every last one of them. Crumpling at the least provocation. A rustle and commotion at the drawing room door broke the strained atmosphere. Eager for rescue, eyes darted to the door, hoping for relief. Her own gaze shifted, too, to see the newcomer, or perhaps more aptly the latecomer. The at-home would end in just fifteen minutes.

'It's Sunderland,' Tunney whispered to Greenwood. 'Didn't think at-homes were his thing.'

'Maybe sourdough heiresses are, though,' Miss Emerson said slyly behind her fan, her eyes meeting Zephy's. 'He's coming this way. If heroism was on display at Tattersalls, what might you say is on display *today*? More heroism, or perhaps something else?'

This was exceedingly bad timing. His Grace's arrival in riding attire and tight-fitting breeches contradicted the neutrality she'd tried to convey. There was nothing neutral or blasé about the masculinity striding towards them. She intercepted a sly look between Tunney and Greenwood that Zephy would rather erase. Thanks to Miss Emerson's comments, there wasn't a person in the group who wasn't thinking about this masculine presence lying atop her, herself included. It wasn't helpful in the least. He was becoming a distraction, drawing her attentions away from the men she needed—men who would be useful to her plan, men who were desperate, attainable, malleable, available. The duke was none of those, and he never would be those things for her.

'Miss Duval.' The duke made a short bow. 'I've come to see how you and your new horse are faring.' He greeted the rest of the group with his gaze, confident and quelling, as if he knew his arrival had aroused speculation and he was eager to put it to bed. She bit her lip. That wasn't the best choice of thoughts. She didn't need to be thinking of anything being put to bed by the duke.

'We are learning each other, thank you.' She offered him a polite smile, while trying to communicate the danger with her eyes. For them to be seen together only added credence to the currently unsubstantiated rumours about the duke and débutante.

'I am glad to hear it. I thought we might try out your new mare together, put her through her paces in the park this afternoon now that your *obligations* here are satisfied.' In the span of one word, he'd relegated Miss Emerson and the others to the status of a duty to perform, nothing more.

'I would love to.' She was already rising, already moving past the envy in Miss Emerson's jealous green eyes and the sulky pouts of Tunney and Greenwood. 'Give me a moment to change.'

He smiled, coolly with perhaps a touch of smugness that was just for her. 'I'll send word to the stable to have Lady Jane saddled.' He made another short, polite bow as if he hadn't disrupted the at-home. 'Good day, Miss Emerson. Tunney, Greenwood, gentlemen, I am sure I'll see you at the clubs.'

They entered at Hyde Park Corner, the closest point of access from Curzon Street, already attracting glances in part because Miss Duval had chosen to ride astride. But it suited the situation. If Hale had had any worries about Miss Duval's ability to navigate the traffic in the short distance between the Camerons' townhouse and the park entrance, her equitation put him at ease. She kept a relaxed but firm rein on the new mare, her own sense of calm transmuting itself to the horse who showed no signs of nervousness amid the carriages and pedestrians. He'd expect nothing less of a horse trained by Lady Catherine, but it was still impressive. Miss Duval had not overclaimed her skill.

Hale slowed to let her come alongside him. The park was crowded at this hour, but compared to the press of the street, there was room to ride two abreast.

'We're near the South Ride. We can gallop there and see how Lady Jane goes.'

Almost immediately two gentlemen passed on their mounts, tipping their hats. 'Sunderland, Miss Duval. Good afternoon.'

He tipped his own hat, and Miss Duval offered a smile until the gentlemen were out of earshot. 'Do you think it's wise for people to see us together?' Miss Duval asked in low tones. The words had no sooner left her mouth than a phaeton passed. Hale recognised the driver and the young lady with him. Hats were tipped again, smiles exchanged.

'I had not expected to be recognised so thoroughly

or so often,' Miss Duval commented, Lady Jane walking companionably close to his own bay thoroughbred. 'It's one thing for the drawing room to be full of gossips. One almost anticipates that. It's another to be recognised out in public by people who are barely acquaintances.'

How interesting that the attention made her uncomfortable. In his experience, most young women craved a certain kind of attention during the Season, any advantage to stand out from the crowd of marriage-minded misses. 'Well, you *are* a celebrity of sorts and have been since your arrival. The incident at Tattersalls merely elevated the attention.'

'As are you.' She slid him a pointed look. 'Together, we attract quite an undue portion of attention. I'd hoped to avoid that by leaving the drawing room. I thought this ride might be a reprieve of sorts. But this has been more of a case of out of the frying pan and into the fire.'

'Reprieve? Did you need it to be?' He sensed he was missing a vital element of what was really bothering her. Had something transpired in the drawing room he was unaware of?

Her sea-mist eyes fixed him with a serious stare. 'Miss Emerson has felt free to share her interpretation of the Tattersalls incident publicly. She commented on what a large man you were, and I believe her exact words were "*he* was *lying* on top of *you* for ever so long". She did a fair imitation of Miss Emerson's guilelessly breathless tones. He barely suppressed a smile and would have laughed if Miss Duval's stare had not been deadly serious.

'Your Grace,' she scolded when he did not show immediate outrage—perhaps he'd not suppressed the smile as well as he'd hoped—'Miss Emerson was implying that you…that I…but mostly *you*—'

'I *know* what Miss Emerson was implying,' Hale cut in sharply when it seemed that Miss Duval would definitely go on to *say* the very provocative activity Miss Emerson had alluded to. It wouldn't do to have the implication breathed into life between them with words that could not be taken back; that he and the pretty American heiress who'd shunned Lord Blankenship had been engaged in a full-frontal press of bodies, with hips, thighs and a healthy ducal cock crushed up against the soft space between Miss Duval's legs long after danger had passed. It was bad enough that the image existed already in the privacy of his own head. 'She's a silly miss looking to make trouble since she hasn't been able to make a match of her own. You should pay her no heed.'

'I won't, but it's not me I am worried about. *Everyone* heard her. I defended you, most thoroughly, but I am not sure it did any good.'

'Why not?' Something warm unfurled in him at the thought of this outspoken American protecting *him*, as if a duke *needed* a defender and a mere débutante at that. But she'd not hesitated. How fierce she was! Would Lady Julia be as fierce on his behalf? That was poorly done of him. He shouldn't compare the two. They were apples and oranges. Lady Julia wasn't like Miss Duval in any way, a fact that ought to make him glad, *relieved*, and yet neither were feelings the thought generated, even though Miss Duval was challenging him.

'I fear your arrival mitigated the effectiveness of my argument that you would have done as much for anyone under the circumstances. It might have been best if you had stayed away.' She was arguing with him once again, a quality that ought to make her less desirable, and perhaps it would if he had to live with her, although that was not the case at the moment.

He gave a terse nod, not in agreement but in contemplation. After the first headlines had circulated, he'd thought much the same: that it would be best to give the incident some time and distance. If he wasn't seen with her, people would stop speculating and accept he'd simply acted as a gentleman and nothing more. Perhaps he could convince his own mind to accept that explanation, too—that he'd been motivated by chivalry and not by heart-pounding fear of watching the vibrant Miss Duval mowed down by a thoroughbred. Those had not been rational moments for him. It was something he ought to resist examining too closely. No matter what might be revealed or what conclusions were drawn, there was no point to it.

He'd given his plan four days. It should have been enough. But he knew when he stepped into the drawing room and spied her among her court, heard her laugh and saw her smile that it was not. Even with four days' distance from the event, the truth remained: He'd been desperate to save her. 'It's not unusual for a gentleman to follow up after assisting someone in a difficult situation.'

She arched a dark, slim brow. 'Like a doctor following up with a patient?' She gave a laugh. 'I don't think that argument will carry any weight. People see what they want to see.'

'We can't control others, only ourselves. I, for one, don't intend to let such baseless speculations decide who I will associate with or when.' His grin gave credence to his words. He wasn't going to waste another moment on Miss Emerson's thoughtless words, and Miss Duval shouldn't either. Although, he might just have a word with Tunney and Greenwood at the club to make sure no one else did either. For now, he'd had enough of drawing room politics.

'Are you ready to gallop? This will take us all the way to the Serpentine Road.' They'd reached the South Ride, which ran the southern length of park.

'Shall we make it a race?' She flashed him the wide, laughing smile he'd come to associate with her.

That was better. He far preferred that smile to her scolding tongue. 'On my mark?'

Hale adjusted his reins. 'Absolutely. Say when.'

Her eyes danced. 'Go!'

They were off, and for a little while, all was right in his world.

## Chapter Eight

It was hard for anything to be wrong in the world when galloping full tilt, the wind in one's hair, the earth flying beneath a confident horse's hooves, and a reckless woman eagerly embracing that freedom beside him. As fast as he and Apollo were going, Lady Jane and Miss Duval were matching them stride for stride. She glanced over at him and laughed—the same loud, vivacious laugh he'd heard that first night in the ballroom, only now he understood what he was hearing: joy, life. How could those things ever be voiced quietly?

They reached the end of the Ride and slowed their horses, both steeds blowing hard. 'I declare a tie.' Miss Duval blew out a breath of her own and patted Lady Jane's heaving shoulder. 'She is splendid. I must write to Lady Catherine and tell her how pleased I am.' She was all smiles and fresh air. If vivacity had a look, Hale thought, this would be it: a dark-haired miss in a blue riding habit, hat slightly askew, eyes sparkling with joy, cheeks flush with life, and that mouth—oh, that mouth with its smile was positively intoxicating, tempting him to be as reckless as their ride, to lean over and claim a winner's kiss even though he hadn't won. She was right: It had been a tie.

'Let's walk them a bit.' He circled Apollo and began the return journey to Hyde Park Corner, more slowly this time. 'Do you always ride *en cavalier*? Astride, I mean?' he clarified.

'Yes, it's much safer. There's a park in San Francisco like this one.' She gave a toss of her head. 'It's called Golden Gate Park. It's a large space like this where people can drive their carriages and enjoy the views. But gentlemen like yourself,' she arched a teasing brow, 'who enjoy going fast would dash around the carriages until it became a safety concern. So a few years back, a group of wealthy citizens persuaded the park commission to put in a straight gallop like the South Ride.'

'I do not *dash around carriages* endangering young ladies. I leave that to my brother.' He chuckled. 'I didn't see you taking it slow. I trust you made good use of the flat track back home?'

'Yes, it is one of my favourite places in the city when I want to get away from the bakery. One can't think about bread or anything else when the world is flying by. A good gallop requires all of one's attention. There's no time to think of anything else.'

'I couldn't agree more.' He rubbed Apollo's shoulder. It was somewhat gratifying and yet unnerving to hear his own sentiments echoed so thoroughly.

'Something we agree on—how novel.' She gave a teasing smile. 'I shall have to make a note of it.'

'Please do,' he teased in return. When had it become so easy to *be* with her? So easy to set aside the proper mantle of manners he wore as the duke and simply talk like a regular person? Was it merely part of the American charm, or was it her that made such ease possible? 'Perhaps there's something else we might agree on? Ices at Gunter's before we go back?' His mind cringed at the suggestion. This was daring fate. But his heart disagreed. She was not for him; there was absolutely no risk at all in prolonging this delightful episode. You ought to resist, his mind fired back. But what was there to resist? Resistance assumed there was something to withstand.

'I would love to go. We've been so busy between the Season and the wedding plans that we haven't gone yet.' Her eyes lit up, and he felt an illogical burst of pleasure at having pleased her with the simple suggestion.

At Gunter's, they found a boy to hold the horses while they strolled Berkeley Square and ate ices—

lavender for her and chocolate for him—another rare indulgence. Today seemed to be full of them.

'We'll have to come more than once. There are so many flavours to try I could barely choose. I want to try parmesan next time. I am not hopeful, though, that cheese makes a very good flavour.' She made a face and slanted him a look. 'Unless of course there's a rule about coming twice? Like dancing?'

It took Hale a moment to realise she was teasing him. He chuckled. 'No, there's no rule about how many times we can visit Gunter's.' Although, people would probably notice if he took her out too often. 'My brother would bring you if you asked.' He wished he hadn't said that. He suddenly felt territorial. This was *his* afternoon.

'I am sure he would,' she replied with a sigh. 'I am sure they all would.'

'Is that disinterest I hear?' He didn't want to imagine Leo buying her ices and making her laugh. He didn't want to imagine any of them buying her ices. Not Tunney, not Greenwood, none of them. And yet it was unfair to wish for such a thing, to monopolise her time with his company when she had to choose one of them.

'It's just that a desperate man is easy to find. There's no challenge in it. They're just falling over themselves, fools every last one of them. They haven't your depth.' She paused and blushed. 'Your brother excluded, of course.'

'Of course.' Hale laughed. 'You needn't worry for my feelings. I won't say a word to him. It will be our secret.' It was his turn to pause. 'You think I have depth? I believed you thought I was quarrelsome and traditional, a general dried stick.' They'd stopped beneath a big, leafy shade tree.

'Can't all those things be true?' she teased, giving a thoughtful lick of her spoon that had his eyes riveted on her mouth. Again. Dammit. Staring at her mouth was becoming a hard habit to break. 'And yes, you have depth. I hope my confession doesn't go to your head.'

'Don't worry, I won't allow it to,' he assured her with mocking seriousness. She was a merciless tease. He liked it. No one ever joked with him. Miss Parkhurst certainly didn't joke with him. Society found it hard to joke with dukes. But Miss Duval didn't let that stop her. No, he needed to stop the comparison right there, and he must stop comparing the two women altogether. He was not going to measure one against the other. Besides, his conclusions wouldn't matter. The exercise was just as pointless now as it had been earlier, but the reminder was carrying fewer teeth than usual.

Her head was tilted, looking up through the leafy

canopy. 'What kind of trees are these? At first I thought they were elms, but they're not.'

'They're plane trees. They're actually a cross between the American sycamore and an oriental plane. They've been here for nearly a hundred years.' He gave her a smile. 'Another American in London. One might say you have something in common with them. They have unique roots that have the ability to navigate around obstacles. It allows them to search out water. They're fighters. They know what they want, and they go after it.'

'There's a compliment in there for me, I'm sure, if I hunt for it.' Her dancing eyes sobered for a moment. 'And perhaps a cautionary tale, too?'

Something shifted between them, the levity of the moment giving way to seriousness charged with new awareness. His need to protect surged. Every ball, every party, she was navigating a veritable battleground, waging her dangerous campaign for something she thought she needed. The London Season was not to be taken lightly despite its outward appearances. 'Miss Duval, at the risk of sounding like the traditionalist you accuse me of being, allow me to share some wisdom. Consider it the moral to the cautionary tale.' The public square had suddenly become private. Their voices had dropped, the space between them had closed as they stood face-to-face, the remnants of their ices melting, forgotten.

He was cognizant of her gaze on him, her own eyes matching his in sombreness. The tension in her posture suggested she'd felt the shift between them as well. 'The Season is a whirlwind, spinning us into more activities than can be reasonably jammed into any given day. I think it's designed that way on purpose, to drown us in fun and frivolity in order to obscure the very serious intent of what we're here to do and, if we're successful, what that will mean for the rest of our lives. Society would like us to forget the enormity of our undertaking here because if we think on it too much, we might be overwhelmed and falter.'

He set aside his melted ice on a bench and gripped her hands. 'And yet, Society will expect you to choose at the end of this. *That* is the price of the Season, that you *will* choose. Only a few rare birds get to play for free, Miss Duval.'

'I know.' The breathless whisper of her words nearly knocked him over. Of course she knew. It was part of her plan, and yet he'd felt the desperate urge to impress the enormity of these weeks upon her in case she thought to renege at the last.

'I must choose one of them. And so must you. It's why we're all here. It's the contract we signed by showing up, by accepting invitations. I know what I am doing.'

He gave a slow nod. 'The Season wants you to believe it's a careless, spirited gallop, but it is not. You get to choose—but only once. Choose wisely, Miss Duval.' *Choose me.* The unbidden words formed recklessly in his mind even as regret coursed through him, regret that things couldn't be different, that *they* couldn't be different, for themselves, for each other. Even if she chose him, he could not choose her. He'd always known that, but never had it been accompanied with regret before.

He had no need of an American heiress in his life, in his dukedom. For that, he needed Lady Julia Parkhurst with her quiet beauty and elegant lineage. She might not know him, but she knew his life and the life they'd be expected to lead. He did not need a woman who rode astride neck or nothing, who laughed with her mouth and her eyes—eyes the colour of the sea on a foggy, misty day, eyes as full of mystery as they were of provocation. He did not *need* a woman who dared him, who argued with him, who had no intention of bending to tradition, who did not understand the life he led. But in that moment, that was the woman he *wanted*, and suddenly there was something to resist after all: the folly of allowing feelings to enter into the decision of marriage. He would resist…later. But not right now, not on this sunny spring afternoon beneath the plane trees in a deserted Berkeley Square. Instead, he would seize his moment before it passed.

Hale leaned close, watching her eyes briefly go

wide in surprise, then darken with acknowledged want. Her head tilted, her lips parted, the tip of her tongue whetting her lips in quiet invitation—an invitation he accepted against all judgement, better or otherwise. Then his mouth was on hers, and all else was reduced to the taste of her—all creamy floral sweetness—on his tongue, and even sweeter forgetfulness. He forgot he was the duke, forgot his choices were not his own, forgot that Zephyrine Duval was not the woman he was looking for.

She forgot she was in an empty but public square, forgot the bakery, forgot the duke was not the kind of man she was looking for, quite the opposite in fact. It was an easy fantasy to give herself over to. The duke kissed as if he had all the time in the world, as if he had nothing else he'd rather do with that time. She let herself be lost in the moment, in the kiss, in him. *All* of him.

Her senses were captivated by him. He *tasted* like the early promise of springtime. Earthy cocoa teased her tongue as their mouths played, explored, lingered. And when she *breathed* him in he smelled like hope, the woodsy masculine scent of bergamot and citrus hinting at the vitality of life renewed. Her arms were about his neck, her fingers buried in the silky midnight depths of his hair where her hands *touched* him.

A little sigh of delight escaped her lips. Somewhere

in the distance of another world far from this cocoon of sensations, a horse whuffed, and she felt the duke let the kiss go, let *her* go. He touched his forehead to hers before they parted, perhaps a sign that he was just as reluctant as she to step back into the real world where things made less sense than they had a few moments ago.

'The horses are getting restless,' he murmured. She would accept the explanation. It was better than an apology or some nonsense about the kiss being a mistake when it was clearly anything but that. He gestured for the boy holding the horses to bring them over. He turned to her. 'I'll help you mount, Miss Duval.' It was meant to be a gentlemanly gesture, but the idea of mounting came out sounding entirely too intimate to her ears after that kiss. She felt her cheeks heat even as he cleared his throat.

'I can mount myself, Your Grace.' That didn't sound right either.

'I am sure you can. But please, I insist.' He cupped his hands for her boot—hands that had held her, touched her. She'd never look at those hands the same way again. That was going to be problematic.

'Only if I may insist on something as well. Perhaps now we might move beyond formal address. Perhaps you might call me Zephy as my friends do, or Zephyrine if you prefer. And I might call you Hale. Americans are far less formal.' She needed the concession for herself. She could not think of him as merely *the duke* or *Sunderland* after that kiss. *Duke* was a title. Sunderland was a place. But she'd been kissed by neither. She'd been kissed by a man, and he'd been kissed by a woman, not an heiress, not by the embodiment of a fortune.

'Friends? Is that what we are now?' There was some of the old banter returning to his tone.

'What else might we be?' she challenged with a coy half smile, putting her boot into the cup of his hands.

He answered with a wry grin of his own as he tossed her up. 'You'll call me Hale when we're alone? Do you think we'll be alone again? It is highly improper.'

He was not wrong, and if today was an indicator of the kinds of things that might happen when they were alone, they'd best avoid the circumstance. She threw him a saucy look as she settled her reins. 'I like to prepare for any eventuality.' She tried not to watch him unduly as he swung up on his own mount—*steed*, *horse*—she really needed to use a different word than *mount* at the moment. But it was hard to ignore those thighs encased in tight breeches or the peekaboo flex of buttocks beneath his jacket as he settled in the saddle.

'So *Zephy*.' He smiled at her as they began the amble down Charles Street towards the Camerons' townhouse. 'Tell me about your name. If I am to use it, I'd like to understand it. I know it's French, but that's all. It sounds very modern.'

She let out a deep breath. It seemed as if the kiss was comfortably behind them, which felt both good and bad. She didn't want to forget it, but neither did she want to dwell on it. That would only hold them back, perhaps make things unnecessarily awkward. Dwelling on it wouldn't change anything. Different paths called them.

'It is somewhat modern, part of the French preference for names from literature and plays and nature. You probably recognise the Greek root for *wind* in it.' He nodded, and she continued with an impish grin. 'But it's old, too. There's an early first-century Catholic saint by that name, and there's been a French princess, Marie Zephyrine, who died young.'

Hale offered her a considering look. 'I am not sure it suits you. A zephyr is a gentle wind. You may be wind, but you're not a gentle breeze.'

She laughed. 'Are *you* teasing *me*, now? I thought I was the one who did all the teasing. I must say this a delightful change. See what magic can happen when we move away from formalities? Names humanise people as much as titles dehumanise. You have to admit my suggestion was a good one. It's so much more fun to be Hale and Zephy. Do you agree?' They were nearly to the townhouse. 'As for my name, it can also mean a fresh wind, not just a gentle one. I prefer to think that particular interpretation suits me.'

Hale gave a nod as a groom came out to help with her horse. 'I will concede on those grounds, and on that note I will bid you farewell, Miss Duval.' Their eyes met, a quiet, secret message passing between them. They were in public now. First names were to be safely stowed away for the next time they were alone. And perhaps kisses, too, although that was likely a fantasy. They'd not spoken of it: They didn't need to. She couldn't realistically entertain any hope of those kisses repeating. Nor should she be wishing for such a thing. She needed a different sort of husband, and Hale was all but pledged to another woman much more suitable for him. If he'd been formally betrothed, she'd have not allowed the kiss, nor did she think Hale would have attempted it.

Hale was not for her any more than she was for him. But that did not change the fact that there'd been passion and heat in those kisses today. On those grounds, they were proving hard to dismiss. It was a dangerous, reckless frisson of excitement that skated its way down her spine as Zephy watched Hale ride away—properly erect on his mount. Another extremely poor choice of words, but perhaps not untrue given the events of the afternoon. The improper thought would not be dislodged as she went inside to change for supper and prepare for another evening at the eye of the whirlwind.

## Chapter Nine

Zephy cast an experienced San Franciscan eye skyward as she and Lulu took their seats beneath Southford's white-canopied pavilion along the sidelines of the Vincent Square cricket field. 'I think it's going to rain,' Zephy said cynically. She and Lulu had been debating the merits of the weather on the carriage ride to Westminster, and she was sure of it now. The April sky was overcast, heavy with ominous clouds. It was definitely going to rain. It was just a question of when and where *she'd* be when it happened. She wasn't putting a lot of stock in Southford's pavilion to fend off rain. His pavilion seemed designed more for protection against sun with a roof overhead but no walls.

Southford rose as they approached. 'Welcome, ladies, Mr and Mrs Cameron. Your timing is perfect. The cricket game is about to start. We have a cold collation laid out, and there's Champagne chilling.'

He took Lulu's hand with a smile. 'And chocolates for my sweet.' Sometimes Zephy wondered if Southford wasn't too smooth. When things looked too good to be true they usually were, and Southford did have that look about him. The earl gestured, and a footman circulated with a tray of Champagne. No one could say Southford didn't know how to entertain. This was quite a picnic. Zephy slid a glance towards her smiling friend. This time next year, Lulu would be the countess of all of this. She hoped it would make her happy.

Zephy took a glass of Champagne and sipped, her gaze moving out to the field where men dressed in white shirts and trousers milled on the green. She spied Hale immediately, taller than his teammates, his dark hair gleaming. Lulu moved to her side. 'The duke cuts a handsome figure in his cricket whites,' she murmured over her flute. 'Don't tell me you haven't noticed. You wouldn't be female if you didn't. Every woman here is noticing him.' She dropped her voice. 'My mother thinks there's something between you and the duke. Is she right?'

'Why does she think that?' Zephy tried to keep her voice neutral with no hint of alarm. She'd been careful not to give anything away the day she'd come back from the ride, and she'd spent the interim scolding herself for the lapse in judgement.

'Well, he was *quite* commanding the day of the at-home, swooping in and whisking you off to ride.

Then, when you came home, you hardly said a thing about being gone for three hours with him.'

'We were in public the whole time,' Zephy countered. 'On horseback, moreover. You can barely conduct conversation on horseback let alone anything questionable.' All true except for when they'd strolled Berkeley Square, eating ices, talking and…kissing. She'd thought of that kiss far too often in the intervening days.

A knowing smile teased Lulu's mouth. 'If you say so, Zephy. But I think just now you protested too much.'

Zephy sighed. Lulu wasn't going to leave this alone, and she had to discuss it with someone: It might as well be her best friend. 'All right, if you must know, I kissed him, or he kissed me,' she confessed in a rushed whisper and then added, 'You *cannot* tell your mother.'

Lulu choked on her Champagne. 'You *kissed* the duke?'

'*Hale*,' Zephy corrected. 'I kissed Hale, and it doesn't mean anything, Lulu. It was just a moment beneath the trees on a spring afternoon.' A much finer spring afternoon than this one.

'*Hale*?' Lulu repeated. 'A first name *and* a kiss. I don't know which one is more dangerous. Both are quite…intimate. I don't even call Southford by his first name.'

'It means *nothing*,' Zephy said firmly, for both their benefits. She needed the reminder as much as Lulu did. 'You know my plan, and he does not suit it. Besides, he's going to offer for Lady Julia, and I can't be a duchess. I can't stay and be what he needs.' It would cost her everything she'd come here to protect, to fight for. She'd be failing her family and the business. The bakery needed her. She *had* to go home in July. Up until that kiss, she'd only understood the cost of that choice in theory. 'It was just a moment's foolishness.'

'That's good, because his brother is coming this way and he's looking like *you* might be *his* moment of foolishness,' Lulu murmured, drawing her gaze just in time to see Lord Leo Eberley striding towards them, impeccably turned out in white linen and flashing a dazzling smile that summed him up in toto—energetic, fun and recklessly exuberant as if he had the world by the tail. This was the brother she ought to be stealing kisses with, the brother who could give her exactly what she needed. But Lord Leo raised nothing in her except the gladness of meeting a friend. Maybe Hale was right and she really was contrary. She'd have to try harder.

'Ladies, you look lovely.' Lord Leo bowed over each of their hands but held onto Zephy's, tucking it through his arm. 'I've arranged for a chair next to yours, Miss Duval, so I can explain the game as we go. Southford told me it's your first cricket match. Come sit. Hale's team is taking the field. They'll bowl first.'

'The Lords' side should win today,' he began his commentary immediately as he saw her settled in one of Southford's canvas camp chairs. 'Hale and Bilborough are the Lords' main bowlers for the match. They've been bowling together for years, ever since their schooldays. It's how they became best friends. One of them is a spinner, and the other is a pacer, so it keeps the batters off balance.' He flashed her an easy, confident smile, and the realisation hit her all at once: No matter what Leo did, no matter how well he ingratiated himself, Hale would always come out ahead by comparison. Not because Hale was a duke but because Hale was a *man*, responsible and loyal, someone a lady could rely on for more than a good time. Zephy suspected Lord Leo would always be a boy regardless of his age. Such a person had no bottom when there was trouble.

*Exactly what she was looking for.*

Leo leaned close, keeping their conversation private so as not to disturb those around them. 'Watch Hale. He beats a batter on account of how fast he throws. Batters can't keep up with the speed of the ball.' Leo sat back, pride in his brother evident in the beaming smile on his handsome face.

'Are you and your brother close?' It seemed to her

that they were, which didn't make her job any easier. Hale had intervened at the ball on his brother's behalf—a protective older sibling.

The smile dimmed. 'We used to be. Until my father died. His death, the title, they changed my brother. He became a lot less fun.' Leo gave a shrug to minimise the import of the comment but not before she heard the disappointment beneath. 'Perhaps it was bound to happen anyway. Maybe I was lucky it just didn't happen sooner with a six-year age gap between us. That can be a very large chasm when you're eighteen and your brother is a twenty-four-year-old duke. We used to climb trees. Race our ponies together. We even built a tree-house one summer.

'When I was younger, he was a good older brother. But somewhere along the line, he decided he had to be my father, my duke, more than being my brother. Now he's stifling, overprotective. He forgets that I grew up, too, that I'm not eighteen anymore.' Leo gave another shrug, but Zephy didn't miss the hurt in his words. 'I have the best of both worlds. My brother has neither. Sometimes I feel sorry for him. I, for one, am glad I have no title to inherit. I am quite content to be me.' His beaming smile was back, disguising the loss he felt. 'I have all the fun, none of the responsibility.' He nodded towards the field, clearly done with this glimpse into his deeper emotions. 'Watch this. I bet Hale will get this batter out.'

The next batter swung and missed. The crowd cheering for the Lords clapped their approval. 'What did I tell you? He's fast. By the time the batter realises what's coming, it's too late.'

Yes, that was definitely true of Hale Eberley, Duke of Sunderland, Zephy thought wryly. He was apparently gifted at taking people unawares. By the time she'd seen his kiss coming, there'd been no thought to evading it, no *desire* to evade it. Now the damage was done. That kiss could never be repeated. There was Lady Julia to consider, there was Leo to consider, her family and Hale's. Her business and his dukedom.

Why couldn't she make this easy on herself? Lord Leo lounged so comfortably beside her, talked so easily with her—with anyone really. He was truly gifted at small talk and could put even the shyest of wallflowers at ease. He made himself the perfect companion effortlessly. And he made her choice so simple. He was available, an easy conquest. All she had to do was smile at him, bring him up to scratch. It would be easy to convince him the arrangement she wanted was in his best interests. It could give him freedom from his stifling, overprotective brother. It would give her freedom, too. She could have everything she'd come to England seeking: her freedom, her bakery, a marriage to satisfy her father's concern. And who knew how it might turn out? Maybe better than she'd hoped.

Leo had no ties to England, no estate to worry

over. He might come to San Francisco for a while, long enough to satisfy wagging tongues. He was a handsome, easy solution to a difficult problem. And yet...all she could think about was Hale. Any scandal that affected his brother would affect him. Of course there was more to it than that... There would always be those kisses between them, reminders of what they couldn't have.

'Is there something on my face?' Leo touched a hand to his cheek. 'You're staring, my dear.'

It wasn't hard to summon the good grace to blush. She cocked her head and covered her faux pas with a winsome smile. 'I was thinking how different you and your brother are.' It wasn't a lie. 'You're blonde, and he's dark. You're fun, and he's so serious, as you pointed out.' And beneath all of Hale's reserve, there lurked fiery passions. Leo wore his passions, superficial and fleeting as they were, on his sleeve. On one hand, Leo had an open honesty to him. But on the other, there was no thrill of discovery, there was only the thrill of living in the now.

He reached for her hand and gave her knuckles a playful buss, fun glinting in his eyes. 'You're different, too, Miss Duval. I like that.' Oh yes, Leo was a simple conquest right there for her taking. She should seize the opening to deepen the conversation, but instead she turned her gaze back to the field and took the safer road. 'Oh look, Lord Bilborough is bowling now, from the other end. Why is that?' She didn't particularly care, but her questions would keep Leo occupied with conversation for a while, another reminder that he might be twenty-eight and he might wear a man's fine fashions and enjoy a man's pursuits, but he was still very much a boy, and like many boys he was easily distracted by a ball and sparkly things.

Could she do it? Marry Leo? She pondered the question while he explained the spinning art of Bilborough's bowling and why bowlers alternated on the ends of the pitch. Could she imagine life with Leo, such as it would be, given her circumstances? Could she imagine kissing Leo without thinking of Hale? It seemed unfair to Leo for her to harbour such secret, disloyal thoughts. Kissing Hale had been like nothing else she'd experienced. Before Hale, kissing had been a neutral, disappointing transaction consisting of nothing more than the press of lips, a brief, unemotional tangling of tongues at best and an inexperienced devouring of mouths at worst. Hale's kiss had been a glimpse into the soul of another, a step across a portal to other pleasures, and a reminder of what her deal with her father required her to forego. She didn't have time to find love, to fall into it. Expediency was the nature of her quest. Until that kiss.

Perhaps it didn't have to be Leo? There was time to pick another. There were other handsome, financially distraught men eager for her fortune and desperate enough to accept her terms. That was another simple solution. But who? She'd not found any gentleman that remotely appealed, no matter how often she combed through her book of names. Not that likeability should matter. She wasn't going to live with them, wasn't going to make a life with them. But it did matter. She was coming to see that.

Whoever she married, she needed them to be on her side, to be in on her plans *with* her. It would take a man with a certain level of selflessness to go through with it. She could not afford to have a husband who was in the scheme only for himself, who had no intentions of being her ally, no intentions of protecting her if need be.

She'd not recognised that condition until recently. That was Hale's fault, too. He'd been on her side in terms of the fallout from the incident at Tattersalls. He'd come to her rescue in the Camerons' drawing room unbidden, knowing instinctively what she needed, even if his timing could have been better. He'd not abandoned her to the gossips. They'd been in that together.

Out on the pitch, Hale was stepping up to bowl again, his cricket whites catching the eerie light of the grey sky. It gave her an excuse to look at him without feeling guilty. Where would she find a man like Hale? A facsimile was the best she could hope for. Because it couldn't ever *be* him. They were too intemperate together, and their lifestyles were at odds, even if their personalities somehow aligned—which they did not. Superb kissing changed nothing, overcame nothing.

The first clap of thunder took Zephy by surprise, and she leapt in her chair, reflexively grabbing for Leo's arm, a gasp of shock escaping her at being so thoroughly startled from her thoughts. Leo laughed, and she laughed, too, at being caught out. It was funny for a moment, until lightning split the sky and clouds opened as if ripped asunder, spilling their contents in a gushing deluge. There were surprised screams and chaos. Coachmen raced to put up carriage hoods and retrieve umbrellas from under carriage seats. But Zephy was oblivious to all of it. Her gaze was riveted on the bowling end of the pitch where Hale stood with Bilborough, his dark hair plastered to his head, his white shirt painted to his body. Her breath caught at the sight. He was very much the duke unleashed. He lifted his head to the sky, letting out a very unducal crow as primal and fierce and as sudden as the spring storm drenching him.

'Miss Duval.' Leo was tugging at her arm, intruding on the scene. 'Come stand in the centre of the pavilion. There's more protection from the elements there. We'll have you and Miss Cameron to safety soon,' he said with an urgency that suggested the deluge interrupting an afternoon of Champagne and cricket was of natural-disaster proportions.

'Yes, of course,' she murmured, but she spared one final glance at Hale standing on the pitch, soaked to the skin, his eyes clashing with hers, sending a lightning bolt of hot, sharp awareness sizzling through her. That glance was a mistake.

Leo's eyes were on her, filled with an awareness of his own. In a quick motion he shrugged out of his coat and settled it about her shoulders. 'You're getting wet, Miss Duval.' She might have mistaken the gesture for chivalry if his gaze hadn't flashed out to the pitch and his expression gone grim with secret knowledge.

'I think your brother is the one who is in danger of catching a chill.' She tried for a smile to mitigate her error. She'd not meant to give herself away.

'My brother can take care of himself. The umbrellas are here, Miss Duval.' Leo took one from a footman and held it for her. 'Let's get you to your carriage. Miss Cameron is already inside.'

It was a rather cold leave-taking for the usually warm, energetic Lord Leo. She feared she'd inadvertently hurt his feelings. 'Thank you for your attentions today. I was honoured by them and by you,' she assured him as he handed her into the landau with its roof up. Her words did earn her one of his smiles, and she smiled back trying to repair her lapse. 'Will you be at the Southford house party?' In a few days, they would—as much of the ton would—be removing for the post-Easter retreat to the country before coming back for the height of the Season.

'Would you like me to be?' Lord Leo asked with a return of his boyish, flirty charm, but there was a nuanced message beneath the question this time. Perhaps there was more subtlety to Lord Leo than she'd given him credit for.

'I would, Lord Leo. I would look forward to sharing some more time with you. And I can return your jacket. Thank you again.' She smiled as he shut the carriage door and sent them off.

'What was that all about?' Lulu asked as the carriage lurched into motion.

'I'm moving forward with Lord Leo,' Zephy said firmly, her fingers busily pleating the folds of her damp skirt.

'It looked more like backwards to me,' Lulu surmised astutely. Her parents were riding with Southford and his mother, and they had the privacy to speak freely, something Lulu seemed bent on taking full advantage of. 'You couldn't keep your eyes off Sunderland. Lord Leo noticed, and so did I.' Ah, so she'd not imagined the proprietorship behind Leo's sudden gesture with the coat. That made it all the worse.

Lulu sighed. 'You know it's impossible with the duke, don't you? He can't give you what you want.

He *won't*. He'll never consent to a wife who intends to leave him, let alone an American. You are reaching too high, Zephy.'

'I am not reaching at all, Lulu. It was one ill-advised kiss. It doesn't mean anything. It certainly doesn't mean I am willing to throw over my plans or my family's needs for a man I've only just met.' Good. That sounded firm and certain. And logical. She was proud of herself. 'Hale's family isn't the only one that needs considering in all of this. My family has expectations of me as well. Hale does not suit them any more than I suit his. But Lord Leo needs me. He does suit my situation, and I believe he'd be amenable to my conditions once I explain them. I hope the house party can be a chance to settle things with him.' Yes, this was right. She was getting things back on track.

'Perhaps you should stop calling the duke by his first name then, if you're so sure,' Lulu advised softly.

## Chapter Ten

Hale wasn't sure what had prompted him to act like that, to stand there in the rain until his shirt stuck to his body, to raise his head to the sky like an exultant madman, to look her way, to acknowledge that he'd felt her eyes on him.

He wrestled out of his wet shirt and took a towel from Bilborough, rubbing himself down briskly, warmth seeping back into his bones. The clubhouse was empty. The others had packed up quickly and departed.

'Do you want to talk about what happened out there between you and the American? The American, I might add, you had no use for a month ago.' Bilborough passed him another towel for his hair.

'No, not particularly.' Hale pulled on a clean shirt.

'Then, perhaps you might want to talk about that ride in the park, or the event at Tattersalls, or the yacht ride. For a woman you've sworn to dislike, you seem to be finding yourself in her company quite often.' Bilborough pressed the issue, taking a seat on one of the long benches. 'Don't waste your time telling me it's about watching over your brother. That look out there wasn't about protection, and *he* noticed.'

Probably more people than Leo had noticed, and that was unfortunate. Hale sat down beside his friend. 'I can't explain it. It would be easier to understand if I could. There is an attraction between us, a most unsuitable attraction.' Saying the words out loud made that attraction damnably real and all that much worse.

'What kind of attraction are we talking about?' Bilborough asked carefully.

'The worst kind. She's entirely wrong for me, but I *want* her. I *hunger* for her. She argues with me, challenges me, makes me see things in a new light... She makes me *feel*, Bilborough. She's a very disquieting woman. Not at all like Lady Julia.' Who didn't make him do or feel anything uncomfortable. That ought to recommend her to him more highly, but it didn't. Lady Julia didn't make his blood race, didn't make him act recklessly in Berkeley Square.

'What do you mean to do about it?' Bilborough asked.

'*Do* about it?' Hale echoed. 'There's nothing *to* do about it but carry on.' Hale sighed and slapped the towel against his thigh in frustration. 'It's why I haven't talked about it. There's no point.' He furrowed his brow. 'What did you think there was to do about it?'

'Well,' Bilborough spoke slowly, cautiously as if each word breathed treason to life, 'you're a duke with money. You can do as you like. She has plenty of money, enough to render such a match understandable to Society, given it's what everyone is doing if they can.'

'My father would surely disapprove,' Hale began. The Sunderland dukes had a long history of making grand English marriages.

'Your father is dead. He is not looking over your shoulder, managing your life, your marriage. You can do as you please. You could marry her, if you wanted to.'

'I can't marry her,' Hale answered softly. Let Bilborough assume the reasons were tradition and Lady Julia's expectation of a proposal. He knew better. Even if those things were out of the way, he couldn't marry Zephyrine Duval. He could give her none of what she needed: It would compromise the dukedom and himself and bring scandal to his family. And yet, to deprive her of the things she sought would be selfish and unfair.

'So you will suffer?' Bilborough surmised.

'I will endure.' And he would resist. No more kisses, no more galloping races or the answering of hot looks. No more giving in to the moment.

'Is that what you want?' Bilborough threw him a long look.

'It is what must be.' Hale rose and collected his clothes. Dukes didn't get to want things. The man was subordinate to the title, always. That had been another lesson of his father's and one that Hale had fully embraced when he'd taken on the mantle of Sunderland. But it had never been so difficult to subdue his desires before. There'd never been someone like Zephy, and he'd never been so sure of what he wanted before.

'Are you sure this is what you want?' Hale fought hard to keep his tone neutrally enquiring. It was a monumental effort, given that inside he was pieces of every emotion imaginable ranging from surprise and incredulity to something akin to rage and jealousy. None of those emotions were helpful at present, and he could understand why Leo had waited until they were on horseback, covering the last three miles to Southford's estate, before bringing the subject up. This was volatile ground indeed. To bring it up earlier would have turned what had been an enjoyable brotherly journey to Southford's estate into a difficult, uncomfortable ordeal.

They'd left this morning from Victoria Station on the Brighton South Coast train, passing a pleasant hour and a half in the first-class car in conversation between themselves and occasionally other passengers. The remnants of Saturday's spring deluge had passed. The skies were clear and blue, and Hale's spirits had been lifted by the good weather. At the station their horses, which had been sent ahead a few days prior, were waiting to make the short journey to Wheaton, Southford's estate, which lay between Woodingdean and Brighton.

Wildflowers were blooming, and the land was alive—all signs of a good spring planting, and that was important to a duke. It meant people would be fed, rents would be paid, and the village would thrive. It was a beautiful day for a ride, or at least it had been until two minutes ago when Leo had gently presaged the dropping of his news with the ominous words *There is something I'd like to discuss with you* before surprising Hale with the worst news possible. 'I am going to propose to Miss Duval this week. Of course, I'll speak with Mr Cameron when the time is right since he is her nominal guardian while she's here.'

Leo wanted to marry Zephy, the woman he'd kissed outside Gunter's beneath the plane trees, the woman who had roused him beyond good sense on multiple occasions now. The thought had rocketed through him, ricocheting off the edges of his heart and the corners of his mind. It had taken Hale a long moment to gather himself and make the proper response.

'Yes, this is what I want.' There was a firmness in Leo's tone that Hale had not heard perhaps ever. It was not the insistent firmness of a quarrelsome adolescent who had not understood why he couldn't have a new horse. Nor was it the sulky adult who was angry over the strings that came with what he believed was his too-small allowance.

Hale reached for the usual counters to cover the emotions roiling within. He simply couldn't allow the match to move forward. He led with his best argument. 'You've only known her a month.'

'That's an eternity in ton time during the Season.' Leo shook off the brevity of the association. 'I have the rest of my life to discover her. I don't need to know everything upfront.'

*No* to the first and a hearty *oh yes, you do* to the second, Hale thought. But those were words he kept to himself. He was in a damnable position here. Zephy had confided her intentions to him about her plans for an unconventional marriage that would end in the most unorthodox way. It was not something he was meant to share with anyone else, not even his brother. At the time, it hadn't mattered. Leo wasn't involved, and there hadn't been those passionate kisses between them.

But that had been a month ago, and Leo was right: A month was an eternity during the Season where people made matches on two weeks' notice and weddings ran riot. Much had changed. Now Leo was talking about marriage to the Sourdough Heiress, and

Hale's own feelings had gone from being merely irritated by her presence to something more complex. *Hunger.* That was the word he'd used with Bilborough, and it was far too accurate.

'Perhaps the haste would not concern me if she were an English lady,' Hale pressed his argument. 'You know English women and they know you, and what it means to be the wife of a duke's brother. You are my heir presumptive until I have a son, Leo. You are a duke's son yourself. You cannot be reckless.' Although it seemed pretty late to be teaching that lesson. Leo had always been reckless.

Leo gave him a hard stare. 'Do you object because she's American?'

'I suppose I do. She comes from a different place. If we reduce it to the bare foundations, she is an artisan's daughter, Leo. Her family bakes bread for a living. She knows more about flour than formalities, more about pies than precedence.' Even as he said the words, it felt disloyal to Zephy to slander her like that. He sounded like a prig and a snob, although he knew there were families in the ton that looked at her as such. Still, he was her...friend, and friends defended each other, not tear each other down. He wasn't acting like much of a friend at the moment, or an honest brother. He was acting selfishly.

'I think they just bake bread, brother,' Leo broke in with the stern correction. 'I would appreciate it if you didn't demean my future wife.' That was new, too. Leo might stew and stomp when they disagreed, but never had he contradicted Hale outright before.

'Look around, Leo. Do you see many happy Anglo–American marriages? I don't. I see unhappy men who took a short cut to financial salvation at the expense of their happiness. Now they are married to women who don't quite know how to go on and don't quite fit with their new families or new society.' Leo would fall into that category as well. She would divorce his brother unless Leo could convince her otherwise or unless Leo simply went with her to San Francisco. That option was untenable as long as Leo was heir presumptive.

'She's a jolly good girl, Hale. We have fun together. We laugh, and she's easy to talk with. I don't think any of the chaps you're referring to had that.'

'You need more than laughter to build a marriage.'

'Do you? I disagree, but we would have more than laughter. We'd have money.'

At last, there it was. 'She does have a lot of it. Is that why you're marrying her?' Normally, he'd feel the need to protect an heiress from a fortune-hunter, but not this one. She could defend herself, and at any rate, she was dangling that fortune like a great golden carrot in front of the ton's gentlemen, daring them to take it. Dear, darling, perhaps overly simplistic Leo was the first to bite.

'The money is nice. It would cut me free of your leading strings,' Leo replied, and the truth stung. He'd not meant to stifle his brother but to protect him from his own recklessness.

'You were eighteen when Father died, barely off to university, barely beginning to sow your oats. It was a hard time to be both your brother and your father.' It had been a huge adjustment for all of them, even Hale, who, at the age of twenty-four, had to go to town to sit in Parliament, to discuss legislation instead of just making the social scene as a young buck. He'd been immediately catapulted into several roles he'd thought to take on gradually over the next ten years instead of all at once. He'd had to grow up fast, and perhaps he'd expected Leo to do the same.

'You have to let me go sometime. I am tired of being protected, scolded like I am a child.'

'You want to be an adult? You want to have a part in the dukedom and prove yourself? Then, take up the estate in Hampshire. I've been after you for years to take it on and make it your own.'

'I've been after you for years to just be my brother like you used to be. Can *you* do that?' Leo snapped.

Hale opened his mouth to respond and then shut it again. What was there to say? He couldn't be that brother again, too much had changed.

'That's what I thought.' Leo slanted him a strong look, their horses gently bumping shoulders as they rode. 'Honestly, I thought you'd be more pleased by the announcement. You've been wanting me to grow up for years, take my life seriously. Now that I have, you are stonewalling me.'

'And you have taken me by significant surprise so I rather think it is fair play. I was not expecting this.' The gatehouse with its brick arch came into view. They were nearly there.

'Not expecting this or not expecting it with *her*? Would you have been more approving had it been with someone like Miss Emerson?'

Hale's mind exploded with words he couldn't voice. *Yes, dammit. Because I haven't kissed the likes of Miss Emerson and burned for days afterward. I haven't quarrelled with her. I haven't been challenged by her, and I haven't felt her eyes on me as I stood soaked to the skin on the cricket pitch.* They passed beneath the arch heralding entrance to Wheaton. He had only a few minutes left to make his case without giving anything away. 'I just want you to be careful. Take time this week and get to know her. *Think* about what life after marriage will look like. Where will you live? How does her San Francisco life fit with your life? Make sure you understand her conditions. American girls are different than our girls here. They have a say in their settlements and how they're meted out and controlled.' This counsel was the closest he could come to offering a warning and an olive branch. Now he could only hope his brother would heed it.

The big Elizabethan manor with its Tudor windows and blue sandstone façade appeared at the end of the leafy oak drive. He wanted peace with Leo before they dismounted.

'Thank you for the advice. I *will* do that,' Leo said curtly, but Hale wished his tone had sounded more conciliatory. Leo paused. 'Are you sure that it is concern for me that motivates your reluctance? That there is no personal agenda behind your advice?'

'Why would you think that?' Hale asked in measured tones, a lead stone landing in his gut, his mind flashing with those last scenes from the cricket game: Zephy standing at the edge of the pavilion oblivious to the rain spattering her skirt, her gaze locked on him; Leo wrapping his coat about her shoulders. In retrospect, that now seemed more like an act of possession than politeness.

'I saw how you looked at her at the cricket game and how she looked at you. If I don't strike now, I think I will lose her altogether. I must make my case while I still have a chance, while she still finds me more interesting than my brother the duke.' Leo threw him a piercing stare, daring him to deny it.

'I don't know what to say,' Hale replied solemnly, wanting to treat his brother's words with the seriousness they deserved. He understood, at least in theory,

Leo's resentment at being overprotected, feeling stifled to the point of rebelling with outrageous stunts. He'd never meant to be in competition with his brother over a woman.

'Say that you'll leave her alone. She doesn't suit you. She's not duchess material. You have Lady Julia, you have everything.' Maybe. Hale privately debated the truth of that. Despite them both being in town, he'd not seen Lady Julia in over a week, and she'd not replied to his note telling her of his plans to go to Wheaton to support Southford in his last entertainment as a bachelor.

Leo tossed him a grim stare. 'Let me have this. Let me have her.' With a final glare, he chirped to his horse and rode off ahead. Hale let him go. They both needed time at the moment. Words would only do damage.

'I want her, too,' Hale whispered to the air. He needed her in ways that were different than Leo's. He didn't need her money or any of the tangibles she would bring to a marriage. He needed her spirit, her passion. The difference was, *he* couldn't have her. He could meet none of her conditions, and she could meet none of his. For the first time, he'd found a woman who he could not make happy. He could not give her the things she wanted. The solution was obvious. He had to give her up. So why did that leave him with dread in the pit of his stomach?

\*\*\*

Zephy stationed herself on an ottoman beneath an oak near the barbecue pit on the east lawn—the pit was Southford's homage to his American betrothed—having deduced that it would be far better to have a circle about her than to limit herself to only two sides. If she meant to play the game, she needed to keep up appearances and surround herself with as many suitors as possible. With luck, she might find someone else besides Lord Leo and be able to put a wall of people between her and Hale.

And her strategy had worked. Up to a point. The young men had gotten their portion of the roasted pig and flocked straight to her beneath the oak, plates and all, grinning and jockeying for her attentions. They were easily pleased with a laugh, a smile, a bon mot from her. It was not much different than wooing customers at the bakery or managing the businessmen the bakery allied itself with or sat on city commerce councils with. But her strategy had not revealed a new contender. Lord Leo arrived late, but his arrival clearly elevated the tenor of the group, proving he was the best she could hope for.

Her strategy had also worked in providing a much-needed wall. Where the young men were, it stood to reason the young ladies would follow, and they did. It had not taken long for the young ladies to gather about her as well, perhaps also hoping to shine from the borrowed light of her popularity. Zephy didn't mind. She was more than happy to share. But the wall couldn't stop her eyes from drifting over heads out into the rest of the party, searching for Hale. Surely he'd come? Or perhaps he'd gone to a different house party. There were several to pick from, and Lulu had told her the Parkhursts were hosting one at Rivercross. Zephy told herself it didn't matter if Hale was here or at Rivercross. It made no difference. But when she caught a glimpse of his dark head and broad shoulders standing with a group about Southford, her breath caught anyway, and she knew her logic had failed.

'Miss Duval, might I say how lovely you look today?'

She turned her head to smile at the gentleman with the compliment. 'Major Tunney, how kind of you to say so.'

'You look like a piece of Wedgwood china in that shade of blue.' Mr Greenwood, the viscount's heir and Major Tunney's inseparable friend, upped the stakes with a grin. Suddenly, it was hard to breathe. She pressed a hand to her stomach, feeling as if she was laced too tightly or had eaten too much when neither was the case. She'd barely touched her plate. The wall of people she'd built for her own protection seemed to be turning against her, closing in. Panic was rising. This was not her. She was not a flirt chasing compliments or men. She was a level-headed daughter of a baker who ran a bread empire, who worked hard every day. Who did not dally beneath oak trees smiling false promises. And yet, the woman she knew she was on the inside needed her to be this other unlikely young woman in order for her *real s*elf to survive. But this was not her, and it frightened her that it had only taken a few months to drift so far from home. Perhaps this was what her father had feared in letting her go abroad.

Leo had inveigled his way forward and was at her side. 'Miss Duval, may I show you the lake? There's a lovely promenade and viewing pier.' His voice was low, his gaze insistent, conveying that he'd seen her distress and had moved to extricate her.

'Yes, please. Southford has shared so much about it that I've been eager to see it for myself.' She made a plausible response and rose, taking his arm, her breathing slowing at the thought of escape. 'Thank you,' Zephy murmured as he guided her away from the crowd. 'I was feeling...overwhelmed.'

'I imagine you were. You are on the brink of making an important decision that will shape the rest of your life.' He offered her an easy smile. 'I feel that way, too.' For a moment Zephy feared she'd gone from the frying pan and into the fire. She sent up a fervent prayer that Leo did not mean to propose right now, that he'd not rescued her only to push his own case.

To her relief, Leo merely let them walk in quiet peace. She would have to remember to thank him for that.

The lake worked its soothing magic with its light breeze and strolling couples who kept their distance from one another. At the lake's edge, Leo stooped to scoop up a handful of pebbles. 'I find tossing rocks helps me sometimes when I'm engulfed, when the world feels too big.' He put a few in her hand and turned to toss his own.

The pebbles did help, and it was fun to compete to see who could throw farthest or how many ripples a pebble could generate, but what she truly wanted was to sink her hands into the dough of her sourdough starter and bury her thoughts in its depths. Her simple visit to London with its straightforward goal had become a complication entangled with consequences for others. She'd never intended for that to happen. Her intentions, however, had been naive. Of course others would be affected. She was like the single pebble thrown into the water of the Season, and her presence had caused ripples in the pond of Society. She was getting fanciful now, further proof that she needed to get back to the basics, back to bread.

## Chapter Eleven

Zephy sunk her hands into the soft dough and let out a long exhalation, a centring sigh of relief, of homecoming. She breathed in the tangy, yeasty smell of the dough. Oh, how she'd missed this! With her eyes closed, she might very well be back in San Francisco in her father's bakery instead of a few thousand miles away working covertly in the Earl of Southford's darkened kitchen while the rest of the house party was abed. Lulu had laughed when she'd unpacked her sourdough starter along with her gowns upon arrival in London. Zephy had fed it without fail on the crossing, at the Cameron townhouse, and she'd brought it with her to Southford's even though the Camerons' cook had promised to look after it. But Zephy wouldn't hear of it. Thank goodness she'd not been dissuaded by Lulu's teasing or the cook's insistence. She'd needed the dough tonight. The inadvertent pun brought a brief smile to her face but it didn't last.

This evening, she was entirely serious about the dough. She'd waited until the house was quiet, the kitchen empty and the servants asleep before she'd crept down to mix up the dough—starter and flour and water. Three ingredients that, when combined, created life-sustaining bread, created her identity. Bread was life. Her life. She *was* a baker, and it was good to remember that.

Convinced the flour was worked in well enough, Zephy covered the bowl with a damp towel and set it near the hearth where there was still warmth from the day's cooking. She wiped her hands on her apron. Good heavens, that had felt good, and she felt more like herself than she had for some time now.

'What are you doing down here?'

She jumped at the low male tone invading her borrowed sanctuary. She'd not been expecting anyone, and the intrusion came as a double shock. She turned from the hearth, and the shock tripled. Her intruder was no mere servant but the Duke of Sunderland without his jacket, his broad shoulders on display. 'I think the real question is what are *you* doing down here, Hale? I didn't think dukes knew where the kitchen was,' she quipped. The last time she'd been with him, he'd been soaking wet on a cricket field, there'd been that unaddressed gaze between them, and the unaddressed kiss between them at Berkeley Square before that. There was starting to be a lot of unaddressed business between them.

'I'll tell you what I am doing down here if you'll tell me what you're doing,' he answered with some teasing of his own, something that she was sure he only did with her. She was starting to wonder if he wore his politeness like a mask, a way to keep a barrier between himself and everyone else in public. 'Milk.' He rummaged in the icebox and held up a glass bottle. 'I was hoping milk might help me sleep. Your turn.'

'Bread. I needed to bake.' She gestured to the bowl and its damp towel by the hearth.

He knit his dark brows, momentary confusion on his face. 'Surely the cook can do the baking if there's something you wanted? You only needed to request it.'

'No, I *needed* to bake,' Zephy repeated, grasping for the words to help him understand. 'I *needed* to make dough, to bury my hands in it, to remind myself of who I was and of who I still am.'

He brought the milk to the worktable and pulled up a stool. 'Did it help? Did you remember?'

She took a stool opposite him and leaned on her elbows. 'I did. Baking sourdough is simple. It's three ingredients, and from those three ingredients comes food, nourishment. It doesn't have to be complicated, but perhaps I've been making it that way.'

He poured the milk into two mugs and pushed one towards her. 'Here's to a simple life.'

She took a long swallow and studied him. 'Why can't you sleep?'

'Same reason. Complications. Entanglements.' He gave a wry half smile. 'A duke's life can be straightforward, like your bread. A duke must do three things: ensure the succession, secure the estate and occupy his seat. Beyond that, everything else is optional. My duties are clear, and yet I cannot sleep at night because of *everything else*, all the optional items.'

'Love. Romance.' Zephy stared into her mug, gathering her thoughts, choosing her words carefully as those thoughts assembled themselves. 'They are optional items. For me, too. No one is asking me to love Mathieu Aubert. No one is even considering if those are things I want.' The darkness and warmth of the kitchen was weaving a potent spell, an intimate spell.

'Do you want those things?' Hale asked, the soft enquiry of his voice lending its consequence to the spell. She understood the source of the question. Outside of Lulu, only Hale knew what she intended should she find a husband here. Love and romance did not figure into those plans.

'I didn't think I did but now that the time has come to act, I am starting to see what life would be like without them, and it's a dark, lonely existence with no one to watch my back, not even the man I marry.'

She let out a sigh. 'I see now that my plans were predicated on the idea that whoever I chose would be in the scheme with me, caring about me, caring about me being able to get what I want, helping me to stay safe amidst the gamble. But without love, there is no guarantee of any of that, no trust. That scares me, greatly. My whole plan could explode, backfire against me without that, and all I would have done is acquired an enemy.'

She was aware of his eyes on her, glowing with amber intent as he asked, 'What will you do now? Will you still go through with it?'

'I don't know what else *to* do. I'm running out of time. I have to go home, but I can't marry Mathieu Aubert. So I will take my chances.' *With your brother...*which seemed like one of the worst ideas in the world at present with Hale sitting across from her, waistcoat unbuttoned, shirt sleeves rolled up, tanned forearms sprinkled with dark hair on muscled masculine display. And yet, an idea even worse than marrying Lord Leo was thinking she could fall for Hale and emerge unscathed. Hale was the exact opposite of what her plan required.

'What about *your* complications?' she asked, hoping to move the conversation in a different direction.

'I must be patient. They will resolve themselves in time, and then life will go on. I will go on.' Something shuttered in his eyes, and she felt a sense of loss followed by a keen stab of knowledge that *she* was his complication, and that perhaps he guessed he was hers: two opposites that had attracted, to the detriment of both. This attraction they felt was an illusion. They could only make one another miserable.

She made the excuse of needing to check the bread, aware that she was rambling. 'The dough is in autolysis now. That's the first resting period. It's important the bread is put someplace warm at this point. This accelerates its ability to grow.' Zephy brought the bowl back to the table and uncovered it. 'Now I'll transfer it to a new bowl and cover it again with a dry towel so it can fully rise. Sometimes we call this *bulk rise*. And that's it. There's nothing more we can do for it now except wait. It will be ready for baking in the morning if I can convince Cook to spare me some oven space. I thought I would use the bread for sandwiches in the basket for the lake tomorrow.' Their hosts were recreating a country picnic complete with a basket auction, all funds going to a school project Southford and Lulu were sponsoring in the village as part of celebrating their wedding.

She untied her apron, as if taking it off would encourage her to leave the kitchen, to break up this dangerous midnight tête-à-tête. She had no excuse to linger now with Hale, no bread to work, no milk to drink. Dammit. The apron strings tangled in a knot.

Zephy twisted, trying to reach around to better grasp the knot, but Hale was faster.

'Let me see.' He stepped behind her and went to work on the ties. 'You are forever getting caught in knots.' He laughed, his breath skimming her neck, his fingers brushing her back as he worked. She could feel the heat of him, smell the scent of him—all bergamot and citrusy male in the warmth of the dim, yeasty kitchen. Those were heady scents to a woman who found pleasure in baking and peace in the homely feel of bread dough beneath her hands.

'There.' He murmured the word at her ear. She was free. Free to step away, free to seek the sanctuary of her room. But she did neither of those things, nor did he. Hale did not step back and did not drop his hands but let them linger at her waist. 'I should not have kissed you, Zephy.' His voice was a low rasp, like the sound of a match striking flint. His hands tightened at her waist.

She turned, facing him, her arms about his neck, her hips pressed to his. Why did it feel so good to stand so close to him? Was she that lonely? 'That's not quite an apology.' She was provoking him, *them*, teasing herself as much as him with her closeness. His eyes had gone dangerously dark. She knew better, and she simply could not do better. She was choosing to kindle the fire, even after the less-than-subtle conversation about straightforward paths and complications. She whet her lips, and the flames leapt higher.

He was burning. His veins were filled with the heat of molten lava, moving through him with the same inexorable intensity. He wanted to devour her the way a wildfire devours a tree, stripping away the externals before sinking itself into the tree's core. 'You're right, it's not an apology. I save those for things I regret.' They'd become each other's complication. How had that happened? *When* had that happened? Why had he allowed such folly to rage uncontained? Why had he foolishly thought he could control it when the time came? Or that he'd *want* to control it? He didn't. He sealed his mouth over hers, wanting to ravage like a fire, plunder like a pirate, to take and take, and so did she. For every inch of her he claimed, she claimed two of him, answering him stroke for stroke so that they might burn together.

He lifted her to the surface of the worktable, setting her on the edge, her arms wrapped tightly about him as he stepped into the *V* of her legs. Yes, this was better, so much better. The hardness of him could feel the heat of her, and his desire ratcheted, his need escalated.

'I'm burning, Hale.' She gave a long sighing moan beneath his mouth, her neck arching in invitation, and his mouth moved to accommodate.

'Burn away. Fire cleanses, it obliterates the old, clears the way for the new.' He made his argument against the column of her throat, his own voice rough with all that had been pent up in him and had broken loose at last. His hips pressed into her, and she gave a strangled cry, answering with a hard press of her own, her body starting to writhe, starting to search instinctively for more.

'Hale.' His name was a plea on her lips, a desperate moan purling up her throat.

He answered with his hands, pushing up yards of fabric past slim silk-stockinged legs and lacy garters until he reached the caldera of heat between those thighs and slid his fingers into the damp warmth of her that managed to both slake and scorch him, his own ability to speak reduced to God-invoking gasps of guttural pleasure.

It was intoxicating to watch her so openly take the pleasure, so candidly claim it. She leaned back on her elbows, her thighs wide for him, her head thrown back, her neck arched to the ceiling, her eyes shut tight as she immersed herself in his touch. There was no artifice here, no false modesty, no holding back as she answered to the stroke of his fingers, the press of his thumb. Her response made him feel like a god: immortal, powerful, an almighty Zeus, a provider of an extraordinary gift that was desired by the receiver as much as offering it was desired by the giver. Her breathing shuddered, and the muscles of her abdomen tightened, her body beginning to gather itself.

'Let it come,' he found the wherewithal to coach her, to prepare her with the hoarse rasp of his voice and encourage her, coax her with his hand. Climax came over her like a wave, growing, swelling until it reached its apex and crashing in the long release of a sigh when it could no longer sustain itself. And he devoured every beautiful second of watching it happen, of watching *her* happen to herself.

She did not open her eyes until the wave had retreated and the tide of her passion ebbed. When those blue eyes did open, they mirrored his awe in the act and recognition in the pleasure. His Eve had eaten from the tree of knowledge and he had fed its fruit to her. Who did that make him in this scenario, exactly? Pride warred with guilt. Pride at what they'd accomplished together. Tonight they had burned and been like two phoenixes rising from the ashes of their chains, reborn to a new life if they so wished. But there was guilt, too. Guilt that they were pledged to other trajectories that would involve other people, other commitments. He'd had no business pursuing these moments with her, and yet he'd been helpless to do anything else. The knots of complication tightened. He ought to feel remorse. He did not. He felt only elation.

She sat up, her eyes still sharp, a smile playing her

lips. 'Oh my. That was…spectacular. I had no idea.' She gave a breathy laugh, and he bent his head to hers, their foreheads touching as he laughed with her.

'*Spectacular.* That's quite an accolade.' His own heart rate was finally beginning to slow. Her pleasure had become his, and although he'd not found physical release, his body had responded as if it too had been in the throes of lovemaking. He drew a deep breath and let it out, willing his mind, his body to centre itself in the moment. 'It was good for me, too.' He wanted to say more. He wanted to tell her there *was* more. That this was just the tip of the pleasure two people might explore together. But what was the point? If uttered, those words would become a source of torment for them. They could not explore that pleasure. That pleasure went even further beyond the bounds of propriety, that pleasure required promises neither of them were in a position to make, no matter how thoroughly their bodies argued to the contrary. Even the pleasure tonight could not be repeated.

His conscience mocked the idea. That kiss in Berkeley Square was supposed to have been unrepeatable. But that had not been the case. They'd repeated it and more tonight, proving that anything was possible. Boundaries meant nothing. That was the territory of anarchy, and he'd stepped over its borders with this midnight madness. They needed to leave this space before they were discovered by a sleepless maid or early-rising housekeeper. 'Shall I light you up to your chamber?' he murmured.

She lifted her head and gave it a small shake. 'No, I should go alone. Just in case.' She slid off the table, her body skimming the length of his. He refused to step back, refused to give up the opportunity to touch her. She looked down and reached a palm between them, pressing against the length of his trousers. 'We should do something about this.' His breath hitched. When had her boldness become an aphrodisiac instead of an annoyance?

He gently brushed her well-intentioned hand away from his unsatisfied erection. 'I can take care of that myself.'

'This time. Next time, it will be my turn.' She offered a wicked smile.

'There won't be a next time, Zephy. You know there cannot be.' He made sure to school his features, to show her that he was in earnest on the subject.

Her own gaze sharpened to blue flints. 'Is this where you tell me you wish it hadn't happened?'

'No. Just because it won't happen again doesn't mean I didn't like it. It just means it's impossible.' He'd meant for her to leave first, but perhaps it would be best if he was the one to go. Hale made her a short bow and departed. Sometimes the only way to end a discussion was to exit the room. If only he could leave the memory behind as well, but he very much feared *that* was seared into his mind in the most permanent of ways and would haunt him for better or for worse all his days, a secret pleasure he could share with no one—not even the people he was supposed to be closest to: not his brother, nor his future wife. They would never forgive him. But even worse than that—they wouldn't understand.

## Chapter Twelve

Lulu wouldn't understand. Not this time. Not about Hale and what had happened in the kitchen last night. Zephy barely understood it herself, only that it had been heated, wild and she'd wanted it desperately *with Hale*. And all of those realisations had left her mind in a jumble.

It would have been nice to talk it through with her best friend. But for the first time ever, Zephy felt entirely alone, which was a ridiculous feeling when she thought about it. She was surrounded by people on all sides, people chattering and laughing beneath blue skies as they walked to the lake. Everyone's spirits were high, buoyed by the gorgeous weather and the distance from the formality of town. Away from London, they might dress more comfortably, act more freely, and it seemed most people had taken that opportunity today. The men wore loose sack jackets in cool fabrics, and the women had chosen light cottons and pretty sprigged muslins. Parasols twirled, and bonnet ribbons floated on the breeze beside the laughter. Lulu was following behind in the last carriage with Southford and his mother to ensure everyone and everything found their way to the day camp set up by the lake. The picnic baskets that would be part of the luncheon auction had been piled into a wagon earlier, Zephy's included.

She'd gotten up well before breakfast was laid out for the guests to get her bread scored and in the oven and still have time for it to cool before being wrapped in a cloth and packed. She stifled a yawn behind her hand. Getting up had been the easy part since she'd not truly gone to bed, at least not to sleep. Her body had been too alive for sleeping and her mind too overwhelmed to settle down. What did such intimacy mean to her? To Hale? Had it been a game to him? She did not think it was. He had never once struck her as the type to play games. Mathieu Aubert played games, and Hale was nothing like him. But what else could it be? Because it *couldn't* be serious.

Hale had made it clear what he thought of title-hunting Americans, and she'd made it clear what she was looking for. Hale met none of her criteria. And yet last night they had clung to each other, devoured each other, burned for each other in ways that defied understanding, in ways she would like to burn again with him given the opportunity. Theirs was not the response of two people who despised each other. This was another complication. How was it that two people could need each other so desperately and yet could not fulfil each other's criteria in a life mate? It seemed the height of cruel irony that such a thing was possible.

She caught a glimpse of Hale, walking up ahead with a group at the front of their sprawling cavalcade. Today, his dark hair was hidden beneath a bowler done in ivory straw, but that didn't stop her fingers from remembering how his hair had felt beneath their tips. Would he bid on her basket for lunch? Winners got to eat lunch with the basket's owner. She'd packed that basket for him, although she hadn't realised she'd done it until it was too late.

Rapid footsteps sounded behind her, followed by an enthusiastic greeting. 'What are you doing walking alone?' Leo fell into step beside her, his golden head hatless, his bowler in his hand. 'I thought for sure every gentleman would be fighting for the honour of escorting you down to the lake.'

'I wanted a moment to myself. I hung back on purpose.' Long enough to be aware that there wouldn't be a place for her in the Southford carriage. Southford's mother had made it clear she wanted Lulu all to herself. All the better to separate her son's soon-to-be-wife from her questionable American associates as the wedding drew closer. Zephy did not envy

Lulu her mother-in-law. There would be no more riding Lulu and Southford's coattails. Even Lulu's own parents had been evicted from the carriage.

'Am I intruding?' Leo's smile faded, and she was reminded of the man in him she'd glimpsed momentarily at the cricket game. He might be boyish and fun on the outside, but there was a certain steel to him when he chose to exercise it. He wasn't entirely spineless like the others. Another reason she ought to pick him and be done with it. Except that meant never getting away from Hale. It meant making Hale a part of her life forever and never being able to act on last night again. It meant thinking about last night every time she looked at him.

No, she was taking it too far. She had to remind herself that this wouldn't be a regular marriage. She wouldn't be looking at Hale across the table at family dinners. She wouldn't be seeing either of them. She'd be home in San Francisco running her bakery, and in time they would entirely disappear from her life. 'Please stay. Some company would be nice. Too long with one's thoughts can be dangerous.' She flashed him a smile to assure him of his welcome and looped an arm through his.

'I have your coat upstairs, all pressed and brushed.' She'd not seen him since the cricket match. 'The Camerons and I came early with Lulu to help with preparations. I was able to have my new mare brought as well. She's enjoying the countryside as much as I am.'

'England agrees with you, then?' His gaze was studying her. 'Do you think you prefer the country or the city?'

'Why choose? Why not split one's time between both?' She prevaricated with another smile—he seemed to like those. Smiles made him feel more confident. She'd learned that early about him. Not that her answer mattered. She'd not be splitting her time anywhere in England after this summer.

He gave a laugh. 'I do like how you think, Miss Duval. Life's too short to choose, isn't it? Why not have it all? That's exactly right. I knew I liked you from the start.' Then he sobered, dangerously so for him. Everything was a laugh and a lark to Leo Eberley, even love. But she'd seen the glimpse of steel beneath, and she knew to beware. 'Splitting time might be in my future. My brother has an estate in Hampshire he's been eager for me to take on.' He gave a boyish grin. 'My brother means to make me responsible through land ownership, which I know nothing about. I suppose it's never too late to learn. Crops aren't for me, but horses are, and the estate is in the northeast, not far from one of the Earl of Hartvale's properties. I am hoping if I do go through with it that Hartvale will help me get started.' He smiled again, entirely winsome. He *was* trying. 'Of course, a man doesn't want to manage a property alone. A man needs a wife for such an undertaking. I think Lady Jane would like Hampshire very much, and perhaps you would, too?'

Her stomach lurched. She'd not expected such a respectable offer from Lord Leo. When she'd thought of bringing him up to scratch, it had been as a man who was footloose, a man with no attachments and pockets to let. How would he respond to her conditions now? She'd not meant to hurt him, but her plan seemed uniquely designed to do just that. 'Possibly.' She smiled prettily. He wouldn't expect more than that from her right now. He'd been somewhat ambiguous, too, perhaps feeling his way and taking stock before seriously offering. 'I think a lot of young women would be amenable to such an offer.'

His smiled widened. 'They might. But the real question is *who* is amenable to *me*? And that, my dear girl, is you.' He laughed and patted her hand. 'Have I succeeded in shocking you—the unshockable American—at last with my boldness? I know I should talk to Mr Cameron first, but I just couldn't without knowing where you stood.'

She laughed with him to cover her own sinking heart. Damn her plan. Damn her needs. Damn the deal she'd made with her father. She'd not meant to hurt anyone. She'd meant only to protect herself. 'I had been warned about the speed at which things occur during the Season.' By his own brother no less, right before Hale had kissed her beneath the plane trees.

'You needn't worry. I can take the rest of the business up with Mr Cameron.' He offered a reassuring smile and switched the topic. 'Now, tell me about your lunch basket. I will want to bid on it.'

Hale wanted to bid on Zephy's basket with a primal need to possess, to claim, to mark her as his, even as he knew how absolutely futile that desire was. He could not claim her, and because he could not, he had no business marking her, calling attention to her through his actions. The Tattersalls incident, the ride in the park, and for a certain few who'd seen it, the lapse at the cricket game had all conspired to call the wrong kind of attention to the two of them in no small part due to the comments of Miss Emerson. His enlisting of Tunney and Greenwood had come too late to be as effective as he hoped in focusing attention away from them. As a result, there'd been some inappropriate contretemps in the betting book at White's that he'd had to personally quash before it got out of hand.

Even here at the house party, Miss Emerson seemed intent on making trouble, remarking on the walk down to the lake loud enough for many to hear, 'I wonder which brother will win Miss Duval's basket?' He'd known then he could hazard neither a bid nor the smallest of glances Zephy's direction. It was making the day impossible, and he was failing at it.

How could he not look at her? How could he not be aware of where she was at every moment? Laughter followed her, joy and energy followed her, and of course the crowd followed her. Everyone wanted to be in Zephyrine Duval's orbit. Including himself. Hale strolled alone down by the lake-shore, keeping his distance but fully aware that Zephy and Leo were on the wide expanse of green where several others were flying kites and taking advantage of the breeze. Leo was lounging on the grass, reclining on his elbows and calling instructions while Zephy gamely manoeuvred the kite, the blue ribbons of her straw boater fluttering, the breeze pressing the fabric of her dress against the shape of her lithe body.

His own body stirred at the reminders the image conjured. Mere hours ago, he'd been intimately in her orbit. He'd not been able to sleep afterwards. His usually carefully managed emotions had run amok. He'd felt elated, almost euphoric as a direct outcome of what had happened in the kitchen. Pleasure like that was an aphrodisiac all its own, and it was as addicting as opium. He wanted more of it, soon and as often as possible. Therein lay the rub, to quote the Bard. He could not put himself or her through that glorious pleasure again. There was no purpose to it, nowhere it could lead. But it didn't seem to matter. He'd stayed awake the rest of the night. He'd watched the clock, wondering if she'd put the bread in the oven, wondering if he'd be able to smell it baking. Wanting to eat it, but that would require bidding on her basket. It would require undermining Leo very publicly. Miss Emerson would have plenty of grist for her petty gossip mill then. And it wasn't fair to Lady Julia, who still had not written to him, who still expected an offer from him perhaps when everyone returned to town and the Season hit its own frenzied climax.

He'd behaved as a man last night but not as a gentleman, and now he had to live with the repercussions. What he ought to do was put some distance between himself and the party. His own family seat, Glenmere, was not far from here on the other side of Woodingdean. He should ride over tomorrow and check in with the steward, take a look at the fields. Perhaps spend the night, or the rest of the week before heading back to town and Parliament. Epsom would be the first week of June, then the Southford wedding, and after that he could head to Cowes for racing. He would be too busy to think about Zephy Duval.

Her laughter caught his ear, and he used it as an excuse to look in her direction. God, she was beautiful, so natural, so alive with that expressive face of hers. Leo looked besotted. His poor brother. At some point, Leo had convinced himself he was in love with her, money notwithstanding. Leo had walked down with her and devoted himself exclusively to her this afternoon. And of course, there'd been no mistaking Leo's gesture with the coat at the cricket match. He'd been warning Hale off, staking his claim. If his brother was only after the fortune, it might go better for their brotherly relationship. It might give Leo the latitude to forgive him for last night's interlude. If it were only about the money, Leo would be happy to agree to her outlandish marriage requirements, perhaps sail off to San Francisco with her on a lark just to spite him. But Hale feared there might be more to it than that. Leo might be developing real feelings for her, might think himself in love—at least love as Leo understood it. Even if feelings were engaged, Hale could not let such an arrangement go through. A scandal of that enormity would taint the dukedom. One way or another, Hale had to dissuade Leo from that proposal and hope it didn't ruin his relationship with his brother beyond repair. Neither of them would thank him for the interference. Leo would sulk, and Zephy would have only a month to find someone else to take her deal.

There was a whistle from the large pavilion set up for the luncheon, and guests made their way towards the tent from their various activities, excitement ratcheting at the prospect of the basket auction. At the pavilion, Southford made a little speech about the school he and his fiancée were sponsoring, and all the young ladies lined up behind their baskets, encouraged by Southford to share the contents of their picnic.

'Miss Duval,' Southford said and moved down the line, 'have we saved the best for last? Tell us what has inspired your basket.'

Zephy gave a smile, and for a moment Hale thought he imagined her gaze lingered on him. She would be that bold. 'I wanted to share something of myself so that you all might get to know me, the real me, a little better,' she began, every man in the crowd already hanging on each word. Hale wanted to wipe those smiles off their faces, wanted to yell that she was his. She held up a cloth-wrapped circle. 'This is a wrapping cloth from my family's bakery in San Francisco. Inside is a fresh loaf of sourdough that I baked this morning from starter that I brought with me all the way from California. If you breathe deeply enough, you can still smell it.' Hale could have sworn he heard Tunney and Greenwood sigh.

'If you bid on my basket, we'll slice the bread and pile it high with ham bought from the village butcher and Lord Southford's prized cheese straight from his home farm. There is also cold lemonade, an American dessert and chocolate from my mother and father's store. My mother is the daughter of a chocolatier, so chocolate is part of my heritage as much as bread is,' she explained with a laugh.

'That sounds delightful. All the baskets are delicious, ladies. My mouth is already watering.' Southford moved back to the front of the line to Miss Emerson's pink-ribboned basket. 'Shall we start the auction?' Bidding ensued in good-natured competitions, some baskets more hotly contested than others, but all baskets bringing in a few pounds for the school. Major Tunney won two baskets, which was met with a great deal of humour and comment about the size of his appetite and bordered on the ribald until Southford reined the joking in as Tunney offered an arm to each of the Misses Calverts and their baskets.

The only problem with the auction process was that by the end it became obvious who imagined themselves to be in contention for the remaining baskets. Greenwood was clearly eyeing Leo and wondering how much of his allowance he had left and how much Leo would be willing to spend. A few others were eyeing Greenwood and likely wondering how impressed Miss Duval would be with the prospect of a title Greenwood wouldn't inherit for a decade or more. Other folks were covertly watching Hale watching Leo, as though wondering if he meant to compete at all.

'We'll open the bidding at one pound,' Southford began. 'This is our last basket, so bid well unless you intend on going hungry,' he said to general laughter.

'Of course, for a small donation, those without baskets are welcome to the buffet,' Southford chuckled.

'Two pounds,' Greenwood said, jumping up the bid.

'Two pounds, four shillings,' came another bid.

'Three pounds.' Leo raised his hand and now the battle was joined, Zephy offering a lively encouraging smile to each bidder as the price for her sourdough went up and up.

'Ten pounds,' Greenwood said to the quiet gasp of the crowd. Only Miss Emerson's basket had gone for more than seven pounds.

Zephy's gaze flashed in Hale's direction. He'd not meant to bid, had meant to make a donation and eat from the buffet instead of creating the impression that he favoured any of the misses when everyone knew he was all but engaged to Lady Julia. But Zephy was in need of rescue. Why didn't Leo say something? 'Fifteen pounds,' he said firmly, loudly, earning a sharp stare from Southford.

'Thank you, Your Grace. The school will be able to purchase lunches for students for a year with that,' Southford offered graciously.

'Twenty pounds.' Leo's answer was edged with fierceness, and Hale felt the force of his brother's stare even as he heard Miss Emerson's breath hitch in excitement. 'By Jove, let's make it thirty.' His brother grinned with his customary bravado. 'Can't have any of the little ones going hungry.' Hale was sure he'd have to cover that bid. Leo didn't have thirty pounds on him. It was probably no more than he deserved, though.

'Well done, Lord Eberley. The children thank you.' Southford applauded, and Hale quietly ceded the field. Something twisted in his gut. He could not stand there, smiling and clapping with the others as his brother was crowned man of the hour and claimed lunch with Zephy Duval.

Hale stepped out of the pavilion in time to see a footman heading straight for the tent. The speed at which the man approached, as if he'd run from the house, sent a tremor of foreboding through Hale. The man wasn't running to the pavilion, he was running to *him*.

'Your Grace...' The footman paused, trying to catch his breath. 'Your presence is required back at the house. Your mother...'

Sheer, naked, undisguisable fear rocketed through Hale. 'Is she well? Is my mother all right?' She'd seemed fine this morning at breakfast, although she'd remained behind, preferring to catch up on correspondence and do some reading in the garden. Had she been hiding an illness from him?

'She is well, Your Grace. I did not mean to alarm you.' The footman had caught his breath. 'There's been a message that requires your immediate attention. Her Grace asked for you to come at once.'

Relief flooded Hale to the point of nearly feeling weak. It was probably estate business, a broken plough or a collapsed stone wall, something that was impeding planting. But that was far better than an ill parent. His father's death had put a certain fear in him. He was not ready to be…alone.

## Chapter Thirteen

His mother sat alone, awaiting him in a sitting room, her expression stern. She nodded towards the note lying on the table. 'We have a problem, my son.' That sounded like more than a broken plough, and the note had come to her, not him. So it was worse than he thought.

She passed him the note, summarising its contents as he scanned the news with growing disquiet. 'Lady Julia's father would like to announce the betrothal. He's asking permission to put the news in *The Times*.' It wasn't hard to see why. The marquess wanted everyone to see it when they returned to town from their house parties. Julia's father was forcing his hand. It was a bold move, and it required a bold response.

'It is an audacious play, given that it is the bridegroom's duty to place the notice.'

His mother shook her head. 'We should have known. *That* branch of the Parkhurst family has always been wild, and their title is new. Still, I suppose it is easily handled as long as you intend to marry her?' That was the real problem, Hale thought, not that the marquess wanted to make the announcement, and somehow his mother knew it.

'Ah, it is as I thought,' his mother mused with soft eyes. 'Lady Julia has not claimed your affections. Perhaps there is another who has?'

Was there? Zephy had his interest, his curiosity, his passion most certainly. But his *affections*? *Was* he falling in love with Zephy Duval? Or had Zephy simply shown him all that he'd be giving up in a union with Lady Julia? Zephy had awakened wants in him he'd not thought he had, and now he wasn't sure he could commit to a marriage without them. It was incorrect logic, though, to think this was a choice between Lady Julia and Zephy. Zephy could not be for him. He could want the things Zephy had awakened in him, but he could not meet them with her; he could not have her. He'd have to meet those needs with someone else. Zephy had her own plans, which made the wanting all the worse. He was once more reminded that for all he had, he could give nothing she needed.

'Perhaps the marquess can be delayed.' Hale offered his mother a smile. It was not an answer to her question, but it was all he had to give at present. 'I think I'll take a walk in the garden for now, and tomorrow

I will leave for Glenmere. It's a shame to be so close and to not look in on the estate.'

He laid the note on the table and departed for the solitude of the gardens. He was not ready to rejoin the high-spirited company of the house party. The marquess's enquiry was acting on him as a tocsin, and he needed to think about what came next. Could he go through with the marriage? If he didn't, there would be a scandal as well as a breach of his responsibility to the family—the ducal succession would not be secured for yet another year, which was no mere consideration. His father's death had thrown that aspect of his duty into sharp relief. *Do not marry in haste*, his father had counselled in his final days. But also he had counselled not to tarry. *Marry by your thirty-fifth birthday*, his father had admonished, so that there was time for children and time for raising them, preparing them. Hale had taken his father's papery hand, looked into his tired eyes and promised he would.

At the time, a decade had seemed like forever. Surely, he'd find a suitable wife well before then. And he'd found Lady Julia, who was eminently suitable and who raised no fire in him. Still, a promise was a promise. His father would approve of Lady Julia: pretty, gently bred, athletic. She would know her duty; she'd been raised to understand estate life.

Hale stopped beside the roses in all their red, pink and roseate beauty, echoes of the last time he'd walked in a rose garden rising unbidden and somewhat unwanted in his mind. What would his father think of Zephyrine Duval? Would he find anything suitable about her? Did it even matter? Was there even an argument to make that would compel her to stay and take up a place beside him as his duchess? Was that what he wanted? For her to stay? There would be scandal in that as well. Everyone knew he was no supporter of these American heiresses. He'd look like a hypocrite. Everyone knew, too, that his brother had paid obvious court to her. There would be unkind rumours about two brothers courting the same woman. A few nights ago he'd used the term *complication* to describe his situation with Zephy. Now, he needed a stronger word. This wasn't merely complicated, it was convoluted and full of consequences that just kept spiralling.

What was a duke to do? If there was any place he could find those answers, it would be at Glenmere, the home he'd grown up in, his touchstone when the world weighed heavily. He was only sorry it would appear too suspicious to go today—it would look too much like licking his wounds from the basket-bidding, and that was the last impression he wanted to cultivate. Dukes didn't lick wounds or skulk away like whipped curs. Dukes were immovable granite, rock-solid pillars of society, not given to whims of fancy or emotion. Such men didn't have the luxury of leading with their hearts when two hundred and seventy years of tradition were on the line.

Zephy had the luxury of the kitchen to herself in the early hours of the spring morning. She closed her eyes and breathed in the silence more so than the scents, although they were there, too. The luxury wouldn't last. Southford's staff would be up about soon, preparing breakfast trays and hot chocolate. But her starter needed to be fed. It wouldn't take long, and after yesterday's picnic, the simple task of doing something associated with home would be a welcome reminder of why she was here. Then afterwards she'd take Lady Jane out for some exercise.

Zephy tied an apron over her riding habit and poured out a little of the starter, as was the bakery's practice back home. She added flour and water, stirring until the old was mixed with the new—a rather apt metaphor for her time in England. She'd come on this trip to better understand her path and to make some choices so that she didn't have to make others. The journey had been far more revealing than she'd expected, and not everything had been useful. Some of it had been complicated, and it was changing her: what she thought, how she felt, what she wanted.

She carefully poured the starter back into its jar. It would need to sit for a day before she could bake with it. She wasn't the only one changing here in England.

The starter was changing, too. She'd noticed it in the taste of the bread yesterday and made a note of it for her next letter home. Her father would be interested in how the environmental variables were affecting the dough.

'Are you baking again?' Hale's low tones drew her attention to the door. He was dressed for riding and looking entirely too dashing for dawn hours.

'No. I was feeding my starter.' She untied the apron and set it aside. 'It won't be ready for baking until tomorrow.'

He strode towards the worktable with a laugh. 'Feeding it? You make it sound as if it's a child.'

'In some ways it is. Raising sourdough can be like childrearing. It's temperamental, must be kept to a schedule, given structure if it's going to thrive.' She was glad for the table between them. The last time they'd been in the kitchen alone had been explosive. She was still sorting the aftermath of that out. He'd tried to ignore her yesterday and then thrown all caution aside when he'd bid exorbitantly on her basket against his own brother before stalking out of the pavilion, only to disappear for the rest of the day. She didn't know what to make of any of it or if she should even try to make sense of it.

'What are you doing down here so early?' She nodded at the saddlebags slung over his shoulder.

'Looking for food for the road. I am going over to

Glenmere today to check in with my steward while I'm in the area.'

Zephy knew a pretext when she heard one. 'You mean you're hiding.' She braced her hands on the work table and leaned forward, dropping her voice in case a servant coming in early heard them. 'What has happened, Hale? Something has, I'm sure of it. This is not you. You disappeared yesterday at lunch, and now you're sneaking out before breakfast.' She held his amber gaze, daring him to look away first, daring him to tell her. Or was it herself she was daring? What did she expect to hear? That he was running from her and the feelings that had been exposed two nights ago in the kitchen? That he was jealous of his brother?

'You once trusted me with a confidence. I will reciprocate if you promise not to tell a soul.' His voice was gravelly and low. 'Lady Julia's father wants to announce the engagement in *The Times*. It is a strategy to force my hand. He believes I have tarried too long.'

'I am sorry.' Zephy tried to ignore the irrational feeling in the pit in her stomach engendered by the reminder of Lady Julia—a phantom girl on the periphery of Zephy's world. Since the garden party, she'd not seen Lady Julia and Hale together. It was hard to remember the girl had some kind of amorphous claim on him. Not that it should matter, Zephy reminded herself. She would lose him, and it was ridiculous to mourn that. He wasn't what she needed, at least not for the long term.

'I'm not sorry,' Hale assured her.

'Right, I forgot. Apologies are only for regrets.' She gave a short, dry laugh, mostly for herself. Perhaps he didn't mind the marquess's intrusion. Perhaps he was simply playing the gentleman and informing her that his circumstances were changing. 'Are congratulations in order, then?' She was having difficulty reading him. Was he pleased about the development? Was his oddness earlier attributed to telling her, given what had passed between them in this very kitchen? Or was it something else?

He held her gaze, his eyes intent. 'I'm not sure I will allow the marquess to make the announcement. But his request has drawn into sharp relief for me the knowledge that it is time to decide what I want. I can't drag out the decision forever. It must be made, and it must be made now. It's really why I am going to Glenmere today. It's the place where I do my best thinking.'

She had to look away from those whiskey eyes. A girl could get drunk on his gaze, and right now there was so much to see in those eyes—feelings he would not give words to, the regret he denied, the frustration at having the decision put to him. It would be too easy to be lured into those depths and drown, to lose all sense of what anchored her. He was engaged in an internal battle even if he wouldn't admit it, and his struggle tugged at her. Every fibre of her being wanted to go to him, to offer comfort. But she knew where that led now.

Instead, Zephy busied herself, moving around the table. 'There's ham in the larder, and I have an extra loaf from yesterday that I set aside.' She felt his hand gently close about her arm, his words rough gravel and tinged with want.

'Come with me. To Glenmere. I want to show you my home. You're already dressed for it, and it's a beautiful day for riding. Leave a note for the Camerons, and we can be gone before anyone is up.' In other words, before anyone could catch them and make them stop.

That alone was an indicator of the risk behind his request. What would Lord Leo think if he found out? What would Lulu think if she knew? And yet, in the end, what they thought didn't matter. The request was simple: to stay or go. And her answer was simple, too. 'Yes.' She wanted to go, and so she did. Hale needed her, or he wouldn't have asked. She handed him the starter jar. 'Put this with the food and give me a moment to leave a note.'

'The dough?' He gave her teasing, sceptical smile.

'Habit. I never leave home without it.' If Glenmere was the place where he did his best thinking, perhaps it would hold true for her as well. She also had decisions to make.

The promise of the morning held true. The blue sky, the green fields burgeoning with May flowers, all served as testament that this had been the right choice. Apollo and Lady Jane were in fine form and ready for exercise on the open road or cross-country as the terrain allowed. As were they. She and Hale were happy to ride, the conversation limited to Hale pointing out some sights as they passed. They took advantage of open fields for gallops and low stone fences or logs for the occasional jump, and the miles flew.

'We'll make Glenmere in time for a late breakfast,' Hale joked as they turned down the tree-lined drive leading to Glenmere.

'*Late* breakfast? Most of London isn't even up yet.' Zephy laughed. It was likely no more than half past eight. The house party wasn't even awake yet. No one would have seen her note.

'Half past eight *is* late in the country.'

Zephy tilted her head upwards, taking in the leafy green canopy overhead. 'This drive is lovely. It must be cool in the summer.'

'They're European ash. They are indeed cool against the heat, but you should see them in the autumn. They turn all the colours of a flame, gold, orange, red. It's spectacular.' He spoke about his land the way she talked about her bread, Zephy realised:

with intimate depth and detail. He *knew* his land, inch by every inch—the leaves on the trees, the crops in the field, the stone in the quarries.

Zephy gave an appraising nod that was not entirely for the trees but for the man beside her as well. Such knowledge that they two possessed! Knowledge that went bone-deep, that was called up without thinking. Knowledge that was not acquired quickly but over years of learning until it was as natural to them as breathing. His roots went deep here, as deep as those of the European ash. He would not be easily uprooted. Neither would she. She belonged in San Francisco.

She looked up once more at the trees, shielding her eyes from the sun filtering through the leaves. Sorrow nudged. She'd be long gone by autumn. She wouldn't be here to see the leaves change. For the first time, sadness accompanied that thought. 'My family has a home in Napa Valley, outside of San Francisco. We say it's our summer home, but I like fall there better than any of the seasons. The hillsides turn golden. There's nothing more beautiful than riding out on horseback to see the foliage and picnicking beneath the leaves.' Although even that fond thought of home brought another wave of unlooked-for sadness.

That autumn horse ride would be without Lady Jane, whom she was fast coming to love. When she rode the hills this fall, memories would ride with her.

She would think of Lady Jane and Glenmere with its resplendent ash trees and the man she'd left behind.

'You're unhappy. I fear I have inadvertently been the cause of it.' Hale made a concerned frown. 'Was it something I said?'

She gave a small shake of her head. 'No, it was something I realised. For the first time since coming to England, the thought of leaving here is lacking its usual joy. Home doesn't beckon as I thought it would.' It was the best way she knew how to explain it. When had that happened? How had that happened? Or more importantly, *why* had it happened? She'd been prepared to like England, of course. She'd wanted to come, had dreamed of London for years. But she'd not expected to want to stay. She suspected that had less to do with liking England and more to do with the man who rode beside her—a most unsuitable man given her position.

'Then, don't go back.' His low tones gave the words a hushed gravitas as they fell amid the quiet clopping of the horses' hooves.

'Don't go back? You speak nothing short of treason,' Zephy joked, trying to tease away the seriousness she heard in his words. What did he think staying would solve? 'I have to go back sometime. I promised my father I would be home by July. My word is my bond.' Home with a husband in some shape or form, no less. 'Besides, the bakery needs me. And

I've learned how much I need the bakery. To stay is to give up that part of my life.' It was more than that. It was a need to protect herself. To leave the bakery would be to lose a part of herself, her independence. She would be subsumed into a different life entirely, and by extension, she would become a different person, perhaps a lesser person.

Hale said nothing but gave her a long, considering stare, his gaze soft. 'You should be able to see the house now.' He directed her gaze to the end of the ash alley, and her breath caught. This home was so different than the cluttered Elizabethan style of Wheaton. The neoclassical lines of Glenmere were clean and symmetrical. Some might call the architecture plain, but she found it calming. 'It suits you. It's like you.' She cocked her head and smiled at Hale. 'It's honest. It makes no secret of what it is.' Imposing, yes. There was no doubting the magnitude of the home or the consequence of the man who lived here. But it was also straightforward, like Hale.

In the carriage circle before the steps leading up to the wide oak doors, they dismounted and handed the horses off. The doors opened on cue, the butler welcoming them as if they'd been expected. 'I sent word yesterday so that my arrival wouldn't be a surprise,' Hale murmured in answer to the question in her eyes. She did not miss the thoughtfulness behind the gesture. Not everyone would consider the servants and the effect a spontaneous arrival would have on them.

Inside, the house matched the promise of its exterior. After introductions, Hale had politely dismissed the butler, insisting on doing the tour himself, saying, 'We want time to stretch our legs before sitting down to a late breakfast on the terrace.' The tour was only of the public rooms on the first floor, but Hale's pride in his home and region was evident just as it had been beneath the ash trees. The blue sandstone exterior had been quarried in Sussex, and the floor was made of Sussex marble. The artwork on the walls depicted scenes from the Battle of Hastings and the Peasants' Revolt. The former she knew had taken place on Sussex soil, but the latter she was unfamiliar with.

'The Peasants' Revolt? That seems an odd choice for a nobleman's home.' She studied the painting with a squint. 'Was there one here?' Her knowledge of English geography and history was not deeply specific. Perhaps Lady Julia's would be?

'This one was in Essex, but the people here participated, too. My father always said it was a reminder to tend towards humility.' He answered with a smile that she thought might have been more in memory of his father than the lesson. 'Are you ready to eat? We can see more of the house later.'

The bricked terrace was the ideal setting for an al fresco meal. A table set with china bordered in a colourful wildflower pattern paired with matching cups for tea and chocolate overlooked an immaculately groomed garden that featured striking animal topiaries. 'It's like a zoo.' Zephy gave a delighted laugh as Hale held a chair for her.

'You can study them more closely after we eat.' He gave an easy smile, looking more relaxed than she'd seen him in days or perhaps ever. He belonged here; he fit here in a way that was so completely organic it required no explanation. 'I am glad you decided to come. I have other estates, but this one is my home.' He reached for her hand, something warm and comfortable unfurling within her at his touch, something as arguably as potent in its own way as the heated, physical intimacy they'd shared.

Zephy curled her fingers around his in return. 'It is an honour to have you share it with me. I think seeing a person's home is like seeing a piece of themselves.'

His gaze held hers, his voice a low, intimate rumble imbued with meaning that washed over her like a slow, soaking wave. 'Then, you truly understand why I wanted you to come.'

To see him, to know him in a way that transcended words or any experience London could provide. To see him in his element. It was the height of honesty and vulnerability on his part. That he had done it purposely for her was a stunning and powerful realisation that left her only able to breathe a single word in the quiet morning. 'Yes.'

She was in no hurry to have him let go of her hand, to move his gaze away. There was nothing else. It was hard to believe that somewhere, far away at Wheaton, the Camerons would just now be waking up and reading her note. That fact seemed to belong to another life, another world.

## Chapter Fourteen

'The topiaries are part of the world of my childhood,' Hale explained with a laugh as he toured her through the garden. 'The trees are like our very own menagerie here. You're not wrong about that.' They stopped beside a giraffe with a long, elegant neck, and Zephy noted Hale absently gave the foliage a pet as if it were real, as if it weren't the first time he'd done such a thing. 'My father put them in for me when I was three. He said it was for my education. A three-year-old couldn't go on safari, but the safari could come to him. I was never too young to learn.' He gave a light laugh. 'I didn't think of it as learning. I thought it was great fun to come out here with my nurse and run about. I made up my own safari games. As I grew, I had atlases with great maps of the world, of Africa, and always there were books about animals and trees along with history and Latin.' He gave her a wink. 'Animals and trees made the Latin bearable, enjoyable even, once I realised how their worlds intertwined. Then, eventually, I had a brother to share all of that with.'

This conversation was intoxicatingly personal, and she was drinking deeply of all of it. There was so much here to like, to fall into: the warm smile that lit his face, the fond and repeated mentions of his father since they'd arrived, and the realisation that he'd just shared with her more personal information in a single conversation than he'd volunteered in any of their previous conversations. The underlying truths were plainly laid out: He was devoted to family and committed to his duty. His people could count on him. And a larger truth loomed large and unavoidable: *He* was like *her*. The duke and the Sourdough Heiress shared fundamental beliefs that governed their lives, their choices. Six weeks ago, she would not have guessed it possible, and it shook her.

'Your father sounds like an astute parent, recognising that the education of a child takes place beyond the schoolroom.' As her *grand-père* had been. Another unlooked-for similarity. She smiled, remembering *Grand-père*. What would he think of her, here in England? Of her plan to keep the bakery in the family? What would he think of this man beside her who could in no way be part of that plan?

'You miss your *grand-père*,' Hale divined.

'I do. We're a French family. We do everything together. Each one of us is an extension of the other. So to lose someone is like losing a part of yourself. He was a great man.'

She looked up at him, at the sunlight over his shoulder. 'My father tells the story of the night my *grand-père* decided he would go to America. He came home with two tickets for a ship that was sailing. It was just he and my father. My grandmother had passed away by then. He said to my father, "Pack your things, only what you can carry. We leave in the morning. It's all been arranged". And that was that. My father never thought to contest it. What was there to contest? He wasn't going to let his father go halfway around the world without him. We do everything together. We've built a life in San Francisco, together.' There was so much she wanted him to understand in that story: who she was, the way in which her family was important to her, why she *had* to go back, even if it wasn't her personal choice, even if it meant leaving Lady Jane, Lulu, *him*. Maybe she shouldn't count him. She was leaving him anyway. She had to marry, and so did he. Their duties required it.

They started walking again, and he reached for her hand. This had become a natural gesture, a comfortable gesture. Their hands knew their way to each other now with ease. 'I think this might be the first real conversation we've ever had.' Hale slid her a glance and a smile.

'We've had several conversations. There was the night at the ball. You were quite eager to talk with me that evening, as I recall.' She gave him a sly smile to go with the teasing. 'At the Rivercross garden party, you were also eager to lecture me.' She meant it as humour, but she remembered too late that Rivercross would be a reminder of Lady Julia, and she wished she hadn't mentioned it. 'Then, there was the yacht ride home.'

'Those conversations all ended poorly. I'm not sure they count.' He smiled. 'They were more argument than discourse.'

She laughed. '*Discourse?* Is that what you call this? Such a stiff term for walking and talking.' And being entirely oneself.

'Whatever this is, I like it.' He brought her hand to his lips and kissed it, a rare spontaneous, demonstrative gesture from him. But the day seemed made for such things, or perhaps it was that Glenmere was made for such things.

'I like *you* here.' She probably ought not have said the words out loud. It would only add another level of entanglement to a knot they couldn't unravel. 'I see why you wanted to come, to think.' Not just because the home was beautiful and peaceful but because *he* was peaceful here, too. They reached the edge of the gardens where the curated landscaping met the rugged verge which extended out to a tree-line. 'It must be difficult to be away from here.' It was no wonder there was such an edge to him in town. How he must miss this place.

'I do miss it. But it's the price and duty of being a duke. I must sit my seat and see to the business of England in return for the privilege of governing this small portion of it.' He glanced down at her feet. 'Are your riding boots comfortable? Can you walk a bit farther? I want to show you something.'

She could walk to Wales if it meant being with him like this. They stepped out into the verge and made their way to the tree-line and the forest beyond, trodding a well-worn path until they stopped at the base of a wide tree.

'*Quercus robur*. English oak.' Hale leaned against the trunk. 'My tree-house is up at the top, or at least what is left of it. There's nothing more than a platform these days. But you can see for miles in reward for the climb.'

Zephy eyed the hand-holds leading up the trunk. She could probably do it, although she'd prefer to do so in trousers. 'Are we going to climb it?' She was starting to suspect today was not for climbing. It was for falling, and she was falling hard. They did not need to ascend the platform for her to be touched by the glimpse of the little boy within the man who wanted to share his treasure with her, and it was positively irresistible.

He shook his head. 'I wouldn't risk it.' It was quiet in the forest, and they spoke in hushed tones.

'If you had no intention of climbing, then what are we doing here?' The forest suddenly seemed intimate, dangerous. It was madness to be here with him. Good madness, though. A madness that might be managed. After all, if an heiress fell for a duke in the forest and no one knew, did she really fall?

They were standing close, and she could feel the heat of him, fire stirring between them, a fire that had been slowly unbanked all morning. Perhaps the whole morning had been leading towards this. Perhaps it wasn't the forest that was dangerous but the man in the forest. After all, this was the same man who made her not want to leave England. He was the variable in her changing heart. This was his fault: his willingness to argue with her when all the other gentlemen were so eager to please her; his love of family and his stubbornness which mirrored her own made him admirable even as it made him difficult. He challenged her because he understood her. He made her feel things, *want* things she'd not considered before. Then he'd given them to her in proof that she *did* indeed need them, and in the giving, he reminded her that her plans did not allow for them.

His eyes were steady on her, her body heating from his gaze, his mouth hovering just inches from hers. 'Do you want to go back?'

'I think we've come too far to go back now,' she whispered, swallowing hard, her tongue running tentatively over her lips, her own gaze gauging his want, his hunger. Then she twined her arms about his neck and drew his body against hers, his mouth against hers.

*She* was kissing him, and his body was rousing quite thoroughly to the overture. Not just the uniqueness of the overture—when had a woman ever *initiated* such intimacy with him?—but the sheer magnitude of the want behind it for both of them. It was as if the morning had been leading to this since he'd seen her in the kitchen and the spontaneous words *Come with me* had slipped from his lips. He'd not planned to ask her or even to encounter her before he'd left for Glenmere, but the words were right. She was meant to be here with him.

Her tongue tangled with his, slow and confident, tasting of breakfast's chocolate, and a little moan of enjoyment escaped her. He caught her sigh in his mouth, let it echo throughout his body. Her hand slipped to his trousers, and he felt her fingers trace him, hold him through the fabric, and his body strained against her, his hips trapping her between the tree trunk and himself.

'Seems like there's another oak in the forest.' She laughed up at him, her sea-mist eyes alight with the thrill of discovery and exploration and her own naked want.

'Careful,' he cautioned. 'You'll have us beyond reason. It would be the work of a moment to have your skirts up, taking you against the tree trunk.'

'Really?' She kissed him hard on the mouth then, her teeth sinking, fiercely, deliciously, into his lower lip, her breath coming in laboured gasps. 'That sounds quite fulfilling, actually.'

Good God, yes, it did. She'd get no argument from him. But he could not let that happen. They would both regret that within minutes of it occurring once the haze of passion cleared. He fumbled with the fastenings of his breeches thinking to distract, to redirect them both. 'Take me in your hand.' They could have this at least.

She stroked the length of him, there in the forest, beneath the tree he'd spent his childhood climbing, pretending he was king of all he surveyed. He felt like that king now, with her hand on him, the powerful thrum of life coursing through him, summoned to his hard core by her touch. Had he ever felt so alive? So aware of himself as a living, breathing man than when he was with her? Racing? Galloping? Waltzing? She was an aphrodisiac all her own. God help him, he was hard, so very hard. All he wanted was to bury himself inside her and slake his need the way water slakes a fire. His body was gathering itself for release. Someone was making sounds, guttural, unconstrained cries, groans, part begging, part exultation. They were *his* sounds, Hale realised, coming from his own throat, his own soul. Thank goodness that when a duke came in a forest, there was no one to hear.

At last, he could hold back the pleasure no longer. His body spent in the column of her hand as a final roar ripped from him, leaving him gasping. He drew her close, wrapping his arms about her tightly as she murmured a single word, 'Magnificent.'

They stood that way for a long while, their bodies pressed together, their breaths eventually coming in long, slow draughts as his body lingered in its pleasure, loath to leave the forest, but the morning was passing, and he had fields to see and a steward to meet with. Those plans had already been laid.

'Will you be all right on your own?' he asked quietly as they walked back to the garden, hands linked. Their bodies, it seemed, were reluctant to not be joined in some way, no matter how small. 'The house is yours. You can make free use of it.'

'I only need the kitchen.' She smiled. 'I'll look in on my starter.'

'There are books in the library. Mrs Hepburn, the housekeeper, can finish the tour with you,' he offered. 'I don't like the idea of leaving you alone.'

'I'll wait and finish the tour with you. Come find

me when you're finished with your work. We'll take the rest of the tour and then—'

He silenced her with a swift kiss. He didn't want to hear the next words *and then we'll ride back to Wheaton.* They'd be there in time to change for supper, to rejoin the world they'd left behind for a day. 'I'll hurry.'

'Take your time.' She stepped back, letting go of his hand at the edge of the garden, but he held her with his eyes, drinking her in—the walnut hair that had come loose in the forest, the sea-mist eyes full of laughter and life, the smile that was for him alone. In that moment, he was struck with a sense of clarity: that she belonged here. With him. That they belonged here at Glenmere together, building a life. This was what the days would be like: early morning rides, walks in the forest, passion given free rein for passion's sake not procreation's, the promise that there would be enough time, that he was enough, not because he was the duke but because he was a man. Her man.

He found her a few hours later, not in the kitchen as he'd suspected but on the back terrace, in an apron— proof she had at least been in the kitchen at some point—staring worriedly at the sky. So he'd not imagined the roll of distant thunder he'd heard in the fields and attempted to dismiss. The weather had changed drastically from the blue skies of the morning. Grey clouds had rolled in, the wind had whipped up, and now rain was imminent.

Relief shone on her face when she turned and saw him coming through the house. 'You're back! I was worried you'd be caught in the worst of it.' She twined her arms about his neck in quick hug that felt all too right—this moment, this sense of homecoming in this place, to her, to her concern.

'I've survived rainstorms before.' He laughed and watched her eyes darken, remembering the cricket match. He'd not been wrong that day: There had been something potent between them, something sparked by a simple gaze—and by his wet shirt. He'd give credit where it was due. 'I think there's a bigger concern, though. We can't ride back to Wheaton. The clouds will break at any moment, and with thunder in the air lightning is sure to follow. There's the coach, of course, but I wouldn't want to risk the carriage horses. If they were to spook it could be disastrous.' He grimaced. He wouldn't risk the carriage horses, but he would risk her reputation and his. The logic seemed off somehow, and yet safety demanded this decision. They could not travel, and they had a perfectly good home, fully staffed, in which to weather the storm until they could travel.

Her arms were back around his neck again, that saucy smile of hers playing on her seductive mouth. 'Are you asking me to spend the night, Hale?'

Oh, wicked woman. He would give in to her teasing but not yet. They did need to take these circumstances seriously. 'I suppose I am. There is no choice. We'll have to make our situation very clear to Southford and to the Camerons for the sake of your reputation. And mine.'

'Yours?' She laughed. 'You're a duke. You will recover if there's any talk. But there won't be. No one could expect us to travel in this weather. It is only common sense to stay put.' To an American who didn't live by nearly so many rules as the ton, Hale thought, but he wisely kept the comment to himself. Airing it wouldn't change their circumstances. Thunder clapped, a loud cymbal reminding them they were here for the duration.

## Chapter Fifteen

There were certainly worse places to wait out a thunderstorm, a spring rainstorm, a lightning storm, of which the latest occurrence was a strong mix of all three. Hale had been right not to try and travel. One might have pushed for leaving with the argument that the rain would abate, that it was only late afternoon and there would be daylight to navigate by until supper time. But those would have been losing arguments. Mother Nature seemed intent on this storm lasting through the night. The thunder and lightning had moved on, but the torrents of rain were still drenching the windows of Glenmere long after sunset.

They were dry inside, although Zephy was keenly aware of the invisible crackle that sizzled between them with all the intensity of a lightning strike as they finished the tour of the house. As beautiful as the house was, Zephy wasn't sure she'd heard a word Hale had said. Her body was sharply attuned to his, to the heat of him as they strolled side by side, the feel of his muscled arm beneath her hand, the scent of him, all bergamot and citrus, the scent of vitality and comfort.

She'd experienced that vitality in the woods today. He'd been hard and hot in her hand, ferocious in his passion, and she had revelled in it, in watching him come undone because of her. She'd felt powerful, glorious in those moments. She'd not guessed it was possible to feel so much pleasure while giving pleasure to another. Zephy slid a glance at Hale's profile, watching the play of evening shadows and light over the planes of his face. He was a handsome man. She'd always thought so, although it was becoming more of a mystery as to how she'd once believed he was a prudish traditionalist. He was far too faceted to be a dried old stick. He was quite the opposite in fact. He was fascinating.

'This is the gallery. I've saved it for last.' Hale ushered her through a curtained archway and into a long, expansive corridor with windows banking the far side, draped in elegant portières of forest green velvet and copious amounts of gold fringe. 'The Sunderland ancestry hangs in here.' He gestured to the wall opposite the windows. 'The house was begun by the first duke in the late 1600s, but his son finished it. He had grand ideas about using the gallery as a place for his wife and daughters to walk in the winters and for his sons to practice their fencing.' They stopped at the far end in front of a stern-faced man bewigged in long dark curls. 'He had twelve children, so perhaps an exercise gallery was a good idea.' Hale laughed.

'He looks like you,' Zephy commented with a sly grin.

'I'm not that serious,' Hale argued, offended.

'You are, but that's not what I meant. I was referring to the dark hair and the nose.'

'It's not his real hair,' Hale countered, still feigning insult over her observation.

'No, but it *is* his real nose. The Sunderland nose, perhaps? You have it too. Long, regal, narrow, strong. It's definitely a duke's nose.'

'You are very observant. I didn't think you were paying that much attention,' Hale teased back, but she wondered if there was something more beneath the cajolery. She was indeed paying attention when it came to him. She noticed every detail, every nuance. Too much for her own good, probably. Lady Jane wasn't the only one she was going to miss when she went back to San Francisco, with another man in theory and in name, nonetheless. Her plan was getting worse all the time.

That plan was all she had—a point that had been driven home to her as she'd worked in the kitchen waiting for Hale to return. She was powerfully attracted to him as a man, but she could not be his duchess. A place like this would subsume her as would a life like Hale's. She'd become part of him. The baker's daughter would disappear into the consuming expectations of being a duchess. She would lose herself. But she was borrowing trouble. That version of her future wasn't going to happen. Hale was going to wed Lady Julia. There was protection and permission in that knowledge. She'd come to Glenmere because this was all there was ever going to be between her and Hale. There was no risk of a future, and there was bittersweet solace in that. In that regard, she was safe. She could return to Wheaton and her plans, and he could return to his.

They walked the length of the gallery, alternating between the view of the rain against the windows and the generational portraits on the wall. 'I'm impressed.' Zephy smiled when they reached the end. 'I think you're the handsomest duke of them all. Your ancestors must be very pleased at how you turned out,' she teased. 'I must revise my earlier opinion, though. You look like your father.'

'My mother would be glad to hear it,' he laughed. 'Her side of the family is blond. Leo takes after her. How about you? Do you take after your father or your mother?'

'In looks it's hard to tell. They're both dark-haired. But people say I have my mother's eyes and my father's temperament. Which is probably why we butt heads like goats. We're too alike, too stubborn.' She gave an awkward laugh, uncomfortable with the admission. 'I don't think I ever told anyone that before. I love my father. I don't want to seem disloyal. It's just that sometimes we disagree on the path forward.'

'I don't think you're disloyal.' Hale offered a reassuring smile. 'I disagreed with my father, too. Someday my son will disagree with me. I think it's an occupational hazard of parenting.' What a father he would be, too. It was easy to imagine him with a child on his shoulders strolling the topiaries or with a young boy beside him rebuilding the tree-house. But it was hard to acknowledge that child would not be her child. It would be the product of a union he made with someone else because he was the worst possible choice for her. That was a difficult argument to believe in the moment, though, as she watched him bend down and retrieve something on the other side of the square viewing ottoman.

'I had Mrs Hepburn prepare an indoor picnic for us.' He held up a wide-bottomed open basket. 'There's even a quilt for authenticity.' In the far-off distance, a remnant of thunder rolled in sonorous ambience.

Zephy's stomach took that moment to gurgle its presence. She laughed and pressed a hand to her midsection. 'I skipped lunch while you were out.' The late breakfast on the terrace seemed ages ago.

They spread the quilt on the floor in front of the

last portraits, and Hale brought a lamp near while she unpacked the basket. 'I'm glad we didn't eat the bread this morning.' She held up the sourdough loaf they'd brought from Wheaton. 'How much food did Mrs Hepburn think we'd eat?' The basket was burgeoning with cold chicken, scotch eggs, raw carrots cut into long, slim sticks, cheese, currant cakes, and a bottle of—wait, was that really Champagne? 'Champagne on a picnic?' She held the bottle up. It was still cold. His staff had impeccable timing.

'Of course. It's a ducal picnic, after all.' Hale took off his coat and set it aside, rolling up his sleeves. 'You don't mind the dishabille, do you?' he asked, his hands stalling on one cuff as if he'd thought better of his choice.

'Not at all. We're indoors. Be comfortable.' She'd nearly pointed out that there was no one to see but decided against it. They didn't need any reminders of that, ridiculous as it was. Dear heavens, it was nearly the twentieth century. Surely Society had more to worry about than a man and a woman being alone together. Society's sensibilities must have evolved beyond such strictures. And yet, look what *had* happened when they were alone in the kitchen, in the woods...

Hale stretched himself out along the length of the old quilt, the swoop of his dark hair falling in his face. He looked boyish and charming. 'I can almost imagine you in the countryside with trees at your back instead of portraits.' Zephy reached to slice the bread. 'But you'll have to get up and pop the Champagne cork.'

'Wait.' Hale's hand closed over hers. 'Don't cut the bread. I want to see it. What's on the top?' He squinted in the dim light, and she held it up for him.

'It's a fleur-de-lis. It's our score. It's how you know the bread is from our bakery. Bakers score the top of the loaf before they bake it. Pierre Fontaine is our scorer. There's an art to it. You have to cut the mark deep enough so that it doesn't bake out. Pierre can make beautiful bread art with his scoring.'

'But you did this. This is lovely, almost too lovely to cut.'

'We must or we'll starve. I can bake you another loaf.' She laughed and set to work, slicing the bread and building each of them a sandwich while he poured the cold Champagne.

'To indoor picnics,' Hale toasted when all was ready.

'To spring storms,' she replied softly, catching his gaze over the rim of her glass as she sipped while the lightning between them crackled and recklessness rumbled.

For the sake of her sanity, Zephy let her gaze drift past Hale's shoulder to the portrait on the wall of the father who'd shaped the man who sat beside her. 'May

I ask, how did he die?' she asked gently. She did not think it had been natural causes. Hale was still young, and he'd been duke for a while already. His father could not have been much older than he was in the portrait when he'd passed.

'Consumption. Suffocating is a terrible way to die.' His brow knit as she watched him think. 'But I was so grateful for every day he lingered. We had time to do what needed to be done and to say what needed to be said.' Hale's voice was quiet, thoughtful. 'Those days cost him. He held on for me, for his family, for his people. Towards the end, he fought every day for every breath.' There was a catch in his voice, and Zephy reached out a hand.

'We were with him when he passed, gathered around his bed, all of his affairs in order. His death was much as he lived in that regard—orderly, organised.'

'Thank you for sharing that.' She squeezed his hand. 'My father was ill this past year with a lung ailment. Pneumonia. Recovery was long. It pained me to see such a strong man unable to climb the stairs of his home, unable to go to the bakery. He is fine now, but it was an abrupt and difficult reminder of mortality. My father will not live forever. The future must be contemplated.' She paused. Perhaps she should not have shared. 'I know it's not the same as your father's situation, and I don't mean to minimise what happened to him, but I do understand some of the agony of the lessons such an experience teaches us.'

'I appreciate that.' He offered a soft smile. 'I think we are shaped by someone's death as much as we are by their life. How my father lived was meant to be a model for me, a standard for me to aspire to. But so was his death. Even if I wish he'd been a different kind of father who was more present in our lives, he was still a *good* father and an extraordinary duke. He never faltered, never failed.' He blew out a breath, his gaze troubled.

'You are a good duke, too,' Zephy offered. And in time, he would be a good father, a *better* father than his own.

Hale shook his head and threaded his fingers through hers. 'I am already failing him. I made him a promise right before he died.' At his words, it seemed that a hush fell on the gallery, that perhaps the ancestors were straining from their frames to hear. 'It was our last conversation. He'd sent for me earlier than was our usual habit for a daily meeting. He was sitting up in bed, pale to the point of greyness, his breathing so laboured that it was hard for him to speak more than one word at a time, and the interval between each was long.' He paused. 'I'm sorry. The details are morbid and perhaps unnecessary.'

'It's all right. They are part of your memories, too,' Zephy soothed quietly.

'He told me not to marry in haste but not to tarry in the decision either. He wanted me married by my thirty-fifth birthday. I promised him I would be. I was twenty-four. There was plenty of time. For me, at least. He asked me to send for my mother and Leo. He was gone a half hour later. But ten years later, I have not fulfilled my pledge.'

'But you will,' Zephy urged, undone by the hopelessness in his eyes. Hale was a man of confidence. He was not meant for desperation and defeat. 'Lady Julia…' She hated to say those words.

'What if I don't *want* to marry her?' he interrupted sharply. 'Beyond common courtesy, I feel nothing for her.' His words implied what his eyes did not bother to hide. They were ablaze with the desperate truth—he did feel something for someone else, for *her*. 'You've brought me to life. You've shown me what passion feels like, how it feeds the soul. Having tasted ambrosia, a man cannot go back to porridge. Not happily, at least. Don't deny that you feel the same.'

She swallowed hard. This was bad. Very bad. 'You cannot give up Lady Julia.' Not for her. She could never make him happy no matter how much she wished she could. All she could do was ruin him, wreck him inside and out, just as he could do the same to her.

His eyes were aflame, and she was burning with their heat. She was running out of arguments. 'Giving

Lady Julia up assumes I wanted her in the first place. I only ever *needed* her. The two are not the same.'

'You still need her. That hasn't changed,' she reminded him gently. This night would end. She would return to San Francisco. He would still need a bride.

'But I want you.' Time slowed at his words. Argument withered. Passion bloomed. The truth stood naked and uncloaked between them. She wanted him, too. Perhaps they could have their heart's desire for a night. Perhaps that would be enough. Perhaps he already understood that the wanting could go nowhere beyond this room. He was not talking about a wedding, only want. She could give him that.

The world faded. No more portraits and velvet portières, ancestors or anecdotes. Their world was a single lamp, their life raft a picnic blanket, and in that moment it was easy to believe they were more than enough for each other. Hale took her glass and set it aside with his, the action deliberate, the quiet deafening even as the moment thundered with intent. He reached for her, their bodies coming together in an embrace, a joining of mouths and bodies that was softer, gentler than their previous encounters but no less intense for its tenderness. This was not a fierce act of competition but a compassionate act of cooperation, two souls searching, seeking and finding one another. This time there would be completion. The day demanded nothing less. Whatever came after was irrelevant. The time for half measures was past.

Zephy reached for his shirt, her fingers drawing loose his neckcloth and pulling it from him before moving on to work free the buttons of his shirt. She tugged the shirttails from the waistband of his trousers and pushed the garment from his shoulders.

'Zeph,' his voice was a growl, her name voiced in warning.

She let her eyes hold his, her hands resting on his waistband. 'Do not tell me to stop. We have come too far for that.' Her mind was made up. She didn't want to hear his arguments. Zephy moved into him, her mouth sealing his, her hand covering the evidence of his need with its palm.

'Then, we'd best even the playing field a bit,' he murmured against her lips, his hands undressing her, fingers warm and competent at the buttons of her blouse, his gestures mirroring her earlier ones until she could feel the heat of his hand through the thin linen of her chemise. His hand slid beneath her chemise, covering her breast with its warmth, his thumb rubbing the tip of her nipple, sending a jolt of raw heat through her. She gave moan of surprise, of delight at the sensation.

'Like that, do you?' His mouth was at her throat, working its way down her body, the lingering exploration of one another quickly becoming something hotter, less languorous, more fierce. Her own palms ran over his bare chest, revelling in the contrasting textures of him, the smooth planes and rough muscles that gave him his masculinity.

'You'd better get those trousers off,' she murmured, breathless as her need outpaced her patience. She was hungry for him, wrapping her arms about him, drawing him down to the quilt with her as he pushed at his trousers. He was hungry, too. She could see it in the darkening of his eyes as he came over her, his arms taking his weight even as his hips meshed with hers, their bodies meeting.

It would be soon now, this satisfying of need and fire that drove them, that made her writhe with the heat of its flame. She pushed her hips against him, urging him to embrace the madness, and he answered, his phallus testing the readiness at her entrance, ensuring her body's want matched her mind's, working himself inside inch by slow, delicious inch. She arched her neck and let loose a groan. She felt so wickedly, decadently alive, his careful sheathing making her acutely aware of him and of herself, stretching, accommodating a man intimately for the first time, wanting with an intensity that obliterated her patience and fired her blood with an intimate heat.

She was not alone. He was burning, too. She could feel it in the heat of his body, in the tightness of his muscles. There was an edge to his breathing, a roughness to the last inch of his sheathing. A harsh groan worked its way up the corded length of his throat as he reached his destination. 'Wrap your legs around me,' came the guttural instruction, and she responded, tightening her legs about his lean hips, holding him close, keeping him within her. Then he began to move—and oh, this was wondrous territory, an unexplored terrain of sensations. She was torn between wanting to linger and savour the newness of it and wanting to seize the sense of completion that lay beyond the next thrust, and the next.

It did not take long for savouring to lose the battle. Hale was driving them forward, stroke by stroke to the inevitable outcome. She held on. She gripped his hips with her legs, she dug her hands into the muscled breadth of his shoulders. He was her anchor, her compass in this new world of pleasure. He gave a final thrust and she broke, shattering like glass, shards of her soul scattering, so immense, so overwhelming was the release. He broke a moment later, his body shuddering as he tore himself from her and spilled beside her. She had a vague idea of what that effort had cost him and what it had cost her. She had felt the warm seed of him against her hand in the forest. It was not meant to be spent carelessly. It was meant for life. Just not for the life she required of him.

He was breathing hard as he lay down beside her, and she moved towards him, fitting herself to his side, to his comfort, his strength. There was security in the shelter of his body. His arm went about her, holding her close, and they lay in silent harmony, recovering together as if they could not bear to be parted even when pleasure had been spent. Outside, rain pounded the windows. She didn't want to move. Not ever.

## Chapter Sixteen

He had to move. The knowledge that he must, however, provided him with no motivation to do it. Hale was too content, too replete, too satisfied to want to change anything about these waking moments. Never mind that sun streamed through the gallery windows. Never mind that the spring storm had passed while they'd slept the night away at their makeshift picnic site on an old quilt. Never mind that some of their clothes lay adrift like flotsam on that quilt or that their remaining garments were wrinkled and askew. There was no hiding what had taken place in this space last night—something wonderful, something extraordinary and powerful, something that had and would continue to change their lives in some fashion yet to be determined...and not all of it for the better.

Hale looked down at Zephy asleep in his arms, her dark hair loose and streaming over his chest. He waited for the remorse to hit him. There were several reasons he ought to feel regret, to in fact be swamped with it. She had plans he could not be part of. He had a life she did not fit. Yet he'd made love to her knowing how impossible a future was, knowing that despite her boldness and her openness to passion that she was untouched. He touched her anyway, taken that which could not be returned or given again.

He'd been raised to be a gentleman, and on those grounds alone he should be riddled with regret, but the regret didn't come. He wasn't sorry this had happened, even knowing there would be hell to pay for it. He would have to live with the memory of last night for the rest of his life. Another secret he'd have to carry alone. Still, he would try to do the right thing. Duty and desire demanded it. In some ways, he was glad for those traditions. They had taken the burden of choice from him. There was only one choice now.

Zephy stirred, sea-mist eyes opening to his gaze, a smile curving on her mouth as the night came back to her. 'Who knew English hardwoods could be so comfortable?' She gave a throaty laugh. 'I slept surprisingly well. Did you?' She was teasing him with her smile, her eyes already laughing.

'*You* are a morning person.' He uttered the revelation with a sense of incredulity and amazement, as if he'd discovered a new land.

'Bakers usually are.' She shifted on her side and propped her head in her hand, the curtain of her hair falling over one shoulder, long and loose and entirely provocative. 'We start our work before the city is up so that when the people need to eat the bread is ready.' She slid a hand between them, and he felt her warm fingers close over his roused shaft. 'The question is, are *you* a morning person?'

He gave a knowing chuckle. 'Morning, afternoon, night, there is no clock where you are concerned.' To prove it, he rolled her beneath him, delighted in her inelegant yelp and astonished laugh. He was even more delighted in her readiness to engage in lovemaking with such casual abandonment. He entered her with a playful swiftness that matched her own willingness, and then they were both holding one another, she laughing up to his face, and he laughing down at her in sheer joy of the joining.

Pleasure came fast, engulfing them both, and when it passed, he collapsed beside her, an exultant sigh purling up his throat. When had he ever felt like this? So happy? So *giddy*? That was usually a term he reserved for silly girls. Not so now. He was nearly dizzy with the emotions coursing through him. He indulged the feeling as long as he dared, but it didn't change the fact that they still had to move.

Hale exchanged a look with Zephy, who answered with a soft, knowing smile. Without words, they rose, gathered their things, repaired their appearances and tidied the space. Cleaning up was like reliving the night in reverse, each used item holding a memory. They folded the quilt, packed the empty bottle and the remnants of food back into the basket, and tucked it beside the viewing ottoman for a footman to discreetly retrieve later. He looked up from his chores to find her gaze on him, and he wondered if she was thinking the same or whether her thoughts were already running ahead to what must come next.

He reached for her hand. 'Mrs Hepburn has a room prepared for you,' he said quietly. 'You can use it to freshen up. I will go to my own chambers and meet you on the terrace for breakfast in a half hour.' He was stalling now, he realised, putting off the two inevitable events that would shape their morning. They had to talk about last night, and they had to return to Wheaton. They needed a plan; at the very least, they needed an understanding between them before they had to meet with others. They could argue with themselves that last night, that this morning, had been moments out of time, but that wasn't true. Those moments didn't exist in a vacuum, nor did they exist just between the two of them. Those moments would affect people around them—people they cared for—and those moments would affect hopes and dreams each of them held individually. It was a conversation Hale was dreading and also one he was wishing to get over with as soon as possible.

Thirty minutes later, Zephy was waiting for him

on the terrace—a surprise, as he'd thought he'd be the first one down. Her back was to him, her gaze looking out over the gardens. He couldn't see her, but there was a pensive quality to the rigidity of her posture. Perhaps she also sensed this breakfast would be different than the one they'd enjoyed yesterday. That gave him pause. Had they only been here one day? It seemed a lifetime ago that they'd ridden away from Wheaton. So much had happened in the span of twenty-four hours; so much had changed. He had changed.

'I see Mrs Hepburn has baked her sweet rolls.' He strolled towards her, keeping his tone casual. It would get serious soon enough, and he'd hold on to these last moments of easy bliss for as long as he could. 'They're probably no match for your sourdough, but we're fond of them,' he joked, holding a chair for her. 'Did you find everything you needed in your room?'

'Yes, thank you.' She helped herself to a roll. 'I love the morning after a hard rain. The world seems cleaner. The storm has washed away all that is bad, and we may start afresh. We get some fierce storms in San Francisco, too, off the water.' She smiled, and that little word *we* skewered as sure as a spear. He was jealous of that *we*. He wanted it to be for them, not for a family thousands of miles away that he'd never met. He took the word and made it his own—a small act of rebellion against that envy perhaps.

'*We* should talk, Zephy,' he began only to be silenced by the swift dart of her gaze.

'About last night?' Her tone was sharp. This was the Zephy he'd first met on the dance floor and in the rose garden.

'Yes, about last night.' He bristled. 'Do not treat it so cavalierly as if it were a casual encounter, as if it meant nothing.'

Her sea-mist eyes narrowed. 'But it doesn't have to mean everything, Hale. You are acting as if last night changes anything. It changes nothing.'

'It changes *everything*, Zephy.' He dropped his voice to a low growl. 'How can you say it changes nothing when you felt what I felt last night and this morning. I saw it in your face, and I felt it in your body as assuredly as I felt it in mine. *That* was not ordinary.'

Her expression softened. 'I did not mean to imply that I felt nothing, only that there may not be room for feelings in the decisions you and I need to make as individuals. You made it clear last night there was a difference between what we wanted and what we needed. We do not need each other, Hale.'

'I think that depends what the need is based on.' He was prevaricating. He knew what she meant. Their plans could not be fulfilled through each other. 'I find that I need you quite a bit more than I thought. Will you marry me, Zephy?' It was what he wanted, he realised. 'I want you here at Glenmere, building a life with me, raising our children, watching them run among the topiaries, playing games in the gallery, riding the forest paths on their ponies, baking bread in the kitchen beside you, flour smudging their cheeks.' Zephy would not be a traditional duchess, but she'd be his. Whatever she lacked in Society's eyes, his consequence would be enough for the both of them. He would make sure of it. He would protect her.

What arrogance! To think that a mere few hours last night would outweigh *her* hopes, *her* family, the very reasons she was here to begin with. Damn him and his proposal! She wanted to yell at him, wanted to scream how ludicrous his suggestion was and how impossible. That had not changed. But this was not the time for a hot temper and an even hotter head. Emotions were simmering for them both after a night of what could only be classified as extreme passion and a morning of sweet, explosive pleasure. And because of that, Hale was talking marriage. Every titled Englishman's end game, it seemed. It was what he knew. Tradition. She could not be part of that.

'Perhaps.' She answered his heated question coolly, taking a slow sip from her teacup, willing her nerves to stay steady. Marriage to Hale wasn't an unpalatable option, just an impossible one. She had to help him see that, even though it would be a painful exercise for them both. She could not be gentle about this, or he would persist. The pain would be his fault. He was the one putting them both in this position.

She set her teacup down and cocked her head. 'If I say yes, will you come to San Francisco with me?' she asked evenly, although she knew the answer.

He answered her cocked head with a stern expression of his own. 'Zeph, you know I cannot be that far from home for extended amounts of time. There are the estates and Parliament. It's a year-round job, really.'

She nodded in understanding. He wasn't wrong. His position was demanding. 'But I can? I can forsake my home, my responsibilities? Is that it?' she queried. 'Because that's what you mean when you say you want to build a life together. You want to build your life with me alongside. You want children to run through the topiaries of your childhood, to fish in the rivers of your land, ride through your forests. What about my family? I want my children to know my parents, to know the bakery the way I know it, to learn to make bread as soon as their hands can work the dough. Are my wants no less demanding? Who will do the bakery books? Who will meet with our suppliers and our retailers? Who will open up new markets for our bread? Oversee partnerships to extend our market lines? Who will care for my parents and my legacy? My father cannot shoulder that burden alone.'

'Neither can my land stewards, to say nothing of my seat in Parliament, which no one else can fill. Surely your father could hire someone, Zeph. It's not that you're not valuable to your bakery, to your family, but—'

'It's not inherited? Is that what you mean?' she snapped. Good heavens, the man could be conceited at times. And stubborn. 'It's just skills that someone else could learn and then practice?' she filled in for him, her temper escalating. 'Knowing the steps, Hale, doesn't automatically make someone a good dancer or else we'd all dance as well as you. It takes more than just doing the functions to make that bakery succeed. And it's a family business. It can't be that if I am not there, if we're hiring outsiders. We may not be a dukedom with our ancestry hanging on a wall, but our business has its generations, too. My great-great-*grand-père* started the bakery in Picardy.' She paused to control her tone. Her voice was rising, a sign she was giving way to her emotions. 'My father took it over from his father, and I will take it over from him. This is *our* way, our legacy, as much as Glenmere is yours.'

'Only if you marry. I can give you that, at least.' His reminder was a punch to the stomach, a feeling she'd known all too well recently. If he wasn't playing fair or nicely, she wouldn't either.

'Fine. I'll marry you and go back to San Francisco alone.' She knew full well he wouldn't tolerate that, *couldn't* tolerate that. The sweet roll turned to something hard and heavy in her stomach. She didn't want that either. How could she leave Hale? In its convoluted way, it was another reason not to marry him. Before, in her imagined plan, the marriage had been to a fellow towards whom she felt indifferent. Leaving that gentleman had never been something she'd viewed as a difficulty. Leaving Hale, though, a man with whom she'd shared bodies and pleasure, conversation and argument, a man she cared for, would definitely be much harder. For them both. She'd be leaving him behind to ridicule and shame, a man abandoned by his wife, a succession not secured, a promise to his father broken. He didn't need her money. He needed a wife and an heir. She could not give him those things. She would in fact steal his freedom to achieve those things with someone else.

'Zephy,' he began to launch his rebuttal, 'you know how impossible that is. You would need to stay here. I am not an obscure second son who has the luxury of a temporary marriage and a bit of scandal in exchange for your settlements. The kind of scandal you propose would taint a dukedom.' He sighed. 'Perhaps I have been too delicate in my arguments. Perhaps I should be more practical. Look around you. This would be our home, your home. With me. With our children. Don't you want that? You belong here. With me. Can you look at me at say you don't feel the rightness of that? That you didn't feel that connection, too, yesterday?'

'You ask too much.' She wouldn't deny what he said, but that didn't make it any more attainable. 'It's not the picture you paint that I object to. It's the price of it. I would lose myself here. My life, my sense of self would be gone entirely. I would become an extension of you, nothing more,' she said quietly, solemnly.

'There are other prices that are just as high or higher.' Hale was pushing hard now, and she braced for the onslaught, for the argument he'd so discreetly avoided, perhaps in the hopes he wouldn't have to use it? 'What about the price to yourself? Going home means a marriage to a man you loathe. You would prefer that to a marriage to me?'

She wanted to wipe that satisfied gleam from his eye. He knew he'd hit bull's-eye with that reminder. She fired back. 'I do not want a marriage with Mathieu Aubert, but that does not mean I can have a marriage with you. I will continue to seek the middle ground. A second son here who will be able to bear the temporary burden of scandal, as you put it.'

He gave a rueful smile. 'I admire your tenacity, even when you're beaten. I think that option might be off the table for you now.' He sobered, and his sobering made her more wary than his arguments. There was a deadly earnestness now that he exuded. 'I don't pretend to know how it is in America, Zeph, but you're in *my* country now, and you are living by England's rules while you are here. When a gentleman such as myself takes a woman's virginity, it is understood that marriage is a foregone conclusion.'

'That is archaic. It's not the Middle Ages, Hale. I do not expect—' She was rambling as the implications of his words became clear.

'It's not about what you expect, Zeph. It's what others expect that matters.' He covered her hand with his where it lay on the table. 'Rest assured, I would have offered regardless. But also be aware that whether you agree or not, others will expect it after last night.'

'No one knows.' But even as she said it, Zephy knew it was an argument that would not stand.

'Everyone who matters knows. My mother knows. The Camerons know. That alone would be enough. Our families will expect it. It was enough that we spent the night here alone even if nothing had happened between us. But it's not just them. We were gone overnight. Our absence will be noted by the entire house party. Letters are written daily back to friends in town. I see the post go out. The troublesome Miss Emerson is a prolific letter writer, and she has already made difficulties for us on more than one occasion.' He had the grace to look abashed. 'I should not have bid on your basket. It raised suspicions that I hoped had died.'

'What suspicions?' Zephy's own panic was starting to rise.

'You weren't to know. A lady *shouldn't* know. There was a page in the betting book at White's about you and me and Leo.' He closed his eyes, his brow knitting, his discomfort palpable. She squeezed his hand. Despite their disagreement, she did not want his pain. 'It was about who you'd choose. It happened after Tattersalls.' And Miss Emerson's tasteless remark. Oh, how she'd like a few words with that impertinent snob. 'You do see, now, Zeph, that there is no middle ground anymore. It's me, or whatever fate awaits you in San Francisco. I do hope you pick me. I would save you from the latter. You deserve better. We can work it all out, if we just take it one step at a time and if we believe in us.'

'That's easy for you to believe. You have no risk. I am entirely on your ground.' She swallowed hard. She did see. It had taken only one indiscretion and her plan had come to naught. Tears formed. She was cognizant of his hand squeezing hers as her options slipped away.

'Let me ask you again. Will you marry me, Zephy?'

She blinked her eyes dry. No man wanted his proposal received in tears. Hale deserved that, at least.

'I need time to think, and I believe it would be good to not rush into any hasty decisions. We should wait and see how all of this plays out. Your noble sacrifice may not be required.'

He nodded sombrely. 'I can give you time, but make no mistake, Zephy. I do not consider this a sacrifice.'

'Not today, maybe. But you will,' she whispered. 'We both need time to think more clearly.'

He rose and offered his arm. 'Shall we go, then, and face down the scandalmongers at Wheaton?'

She laughed. 'Perhaps there won't be any. Perhaps people will be more understanding of our circumstances and the weather.'

He arched a brow. 'I wouldn't take those odds. You'd best accept that I will be right about this.'

## Chapter Seventeen

Hale was unerringly and irritatingly right about his prediction regarding what lay in wait for them at Wheaton. There was indeed scandal, and it wasted no time. The moment they dismounted, there was a summons to attend Southford and the Camerons in the rose drawing room.

Zephy exchanged a look with Hale. *So it begins* his eyes said to hers as they made their way to the house. His hand at her back was warm and strong. She took encouragement from that.

'All they can do is rant and break themselves against the rock of our togetherness,' he murmured into her ear. 'Let us begin as we mean to go on. Together.' But they weren't together, not really. Their togetherness was an illusion as was the idea that they meant to go on like this. She couldn't allow that to happen for both their sakes and for the sake of those affected—Leo, Hale's mother, her family, even Lady

Julia and the Camerons. What should have been a decision made between two consenting adults had become a group affair.

The rose sitting room was full. The Camerons, Southford and his mother, Lord Leo and Lady Sunderland all sat arrayed in a half arc of chairs, a tribunal of sorts. Southford greeted them with stiff formality from the fireplace mantel. 'I am glad to see you both looking well. When you didn't return I feared there'd been some mischief on the road, a stuck carriage wheel or a thrown shoe.' He smiled, but it was not warm. She'd not seen Southford like this.

Hale's smile was easy. 'To avoid such calamities, we opted to stay at Glenmere. The estate is fully staffed even in my absence, and my housekeeper was more than able to provide for an impromptu guest.' Hale's reply skillfully reminded everyone present that there had been chaperones and that all measures to make her visit decent had been taken. She appreciated his effort to protect her reputation. If his argument was persuasive there'd be no scandal, no need for him to press his proposal even though his argument fronted a lie. This simple lie, if believed, would solve everything. Well, *almost* everything.

'Nonetheless,' Southford began, his unease more evident now that Hale had taken the righteous moral ground from him. He was an earl, Hale was a duke, and the duke had implied all decent protocol had been upheld. If Southford wanted to respond he'd have to question Hale's word and honour. The question in the room was no longer what had happened at Glenmere but who Southford was to challenge Hale's word, given that Hale had a pristine reputation and was arguably in pursuit of another lady. For a moment, Zephy thought Hale's gambit might succeed.

'You do understand, Your Grace, that as the host of this house party, every young lady here is under my protection.'

'And this particular young lady is also under mine,' Mr Cameron put in gruffly, crossing his arms over his not-insubstantial-chest, remnants of his sporting days. 'I have pledged to her father to keep her safe.' Mr Cameron didn't care about dukes and earls.

Hale acknowledged him with a nod. 'I understand, sir,' he began calmly, only to be interrupted by a low, fierce voice at door.

'Well, *I* don't understand. You have behaved awfully, Sunderland,' a voice boomed from the doorway, and the tall imposing figure of the Marquess of Barrow strode forward, fire flashing from his dark eyes, the accusations no one in the room had dared to speak rolling easily off his tongue. 'You, sir, rode off alone with another woman when you knew there were expectations with my daughter.' Zephy found the marquess to be incredibly imposing, but Hale did not flinch.

'Nothing has been formally settled, as you well know, despite your efforts to the contrary. The matter of those expectations should be discussed in private, as should the attempt *you* made to force my hand.' Hale deftly turned the tables and the man's own tactics back on him.

'My daughter is prepared to honour those expectations in marriage,' the marquess ground out. 'But you would jilt her at the very last! When the Season is halfway spent! Her time wasted on you! You will have made a scandal of her.'

Hale met the marquess's gaze with a hard stare, meeting the man evenly even though Barrow was his senior in age by twenty-five years. 'We do not suit. I am helping us both avoid a lifetime of unhappiness. On those grounds, I am not prepared to marry her. She is an accomplished young woman. She will have no trouble finding someone who suits her better. If you wish to do this before witnesses, so be it. Let everyone in this room bear witness. I will not be offering marriage to Lady Julia. My attentions are engaged elsewhere.'

The marquess's eyes flashed once more, and Zephy felt the thunderous force of his gaze—and his blame—fall on her. 'Is she the *elsewhere*? This trumped-up baker's daughter from San Francisco?' he spat. 'I will tell everyone what you've done, Sunderland. There will be scandal. I know how you abhor that.' He smirked, and Zephy felt her toes curl into the soles of her shoes. Scandal was the last thing she wanted for Hale.

'Not if you're smart. Any scandal over this touches your daughter. It is in both our interests to quietly bury the subject and, if asked, to reply that it was a mutual agreement that we no longer suited.'

'You're slumming, Sunderland.' The marquess scoffed with a frown at having his threat so easily deflated. He had nothing but hard words left to strike with. 'You, with all your vaunted talk of resenting the American heiresses. I didn't count you as a hypocrite, but perhaps she has newly discovered *charms* after a night away.' His insinuation was clear. The room gave a collective gasp as Barrow let another unspoken truth spring to life with his words.

Zephy opened her mouth to respond, but Hale took a half step in front of her, blocking her from the marquess. 'I will thank you to watch your mouth regarding the woman I intend to marry.'

No! Zephy's knees threatened to buckle. What had Hale done? He'd promised her time... This was only supposed to be for looks until the storm passed. Instead the storm had burst overhead, and she was drowning in it, her control over the situation swept away. She was torn between wanting to flee the room and feeling the need not to abandon Hale in this moment, torn between wanting to present the united front she'd promised him and wanting to call him out on breaking his word.

The room was deadly silent. The Duchess of Sunderland spoke calmly, her tones reminiscent of her son's. 'I think congratulations are in order. Perhaps a footman might fetch some Champagne.' She smiled serenely at Lord Barrow. 'If you will excuse us, this is a private, family celebration. My son will want to leave immediately for London and a special licence if there's to be a wedding next week at Glenmere.' She looked about to the group, her gaze landing on Southford. 'Everyone from the house party is invited,' she said in a gesture of magnanimity.

No amount of Champagne could erase the horror that raced through Zephy. With a single sentence, Hale had broken his promise to her. *That* might have been remedied with discussion behind closed doors and a healthy amount of forgiveness if she were willing. But not this. With the simple action of ordering Champagne, his mother had sealed her fate and given it a timeline. It seemed Hale was going to allow it. Of course he was. It gave him what he'd advocated for this morning, what he wanted. Never mind that there were others present who weren't happy at the arrangements. Lord Leo's eyes flashed with anger, his hands fisted at his sides. Lulu was shaking, perhaps shocked on her behalf—or something worse? Had she lost her friend for good?

Hale's words had resolved the issue of the marquess, but it had also created others. She wanted desperately to believe this was all a scene, play-acting for the marquess. Perhaps there was nothing that could not yet be undone if she could get Hale alone. 'Might we speak?' she asked him quietly once the toast had been made. But before they could leave the room, Lulu broke through the pretence of celebration.

'Will none of you put a stop to this madness?' Lulu broke the silence with a tear-clogged voice, and for a brief moment Zephy thought her friend might come to her aid, but even the safe harbour of the Camerons was closing against her. The enormity of that swamped her. She was truly alone now, in a strange world, with no one but Hale to rely on, and he'd not stopped this. Panic clawed. *All they can do is rant and break themselves on the rock of our togetherness.* All they could do was be upset. But at the present, it seemed like that was quite a lot.

'There is no madness, there is nothing to stop,' Hale said evenly, and Zephy's own panic grew. He did not mean to deny his intentions and to assure everyone it was all play-acting now that the marquess was gone.

Lulu's gaze narrowed. 'She doesn't love you. She plans on leaving you. Do you know that? She just wants your name, and she'll go back to San Francisco and work in her bakery. She won't give you a real marriage.' She spat the words at Hale. Hale didn't flinch, but Zephy felt as if she'd been stabbed, a blade to the back. Her friend had betrayed her plan in a room full of people, although it wouldn't have the desired effect on Hale. He already knew, had known all along. *And it hadn't stopped him.* That was the sort of man she was dealing with.

'I am aware. We have details to work out.' Hale used the moment to clear the room. 'Which is why I want to speak with you immediately, Mr Cameron, about marriage settlements. Southford, if we could use your office? Mother, Leo, I would like to speak with you after that. If you would wait here?' He was masterful in this crisis just as he had been at Tattersalls. Zephy would give him that, but she could not forget for a moment what this marriage would cost her if it went through.

Lulu stormed past her with a hard stare. 'Lulu, wait.' She reached for her friend's arm, but Lulu was gone. 'I'll go talk to her,' Zephy said to no one in particular before gathering her courage and taking the opportunity to leave the room. Hale had his own dragons to slay at present, and so did she—two tasks which they must accomplish alone. Hale might need her forgiveness, but she needed Lulu's. The shoe was quite suddenly on the other foot, and it pinched.

## Chapter Eighteen

Upstairs, Zephy knocked on Lulu's door and entered on tiptoes. Lulu had thrown herself on the bed, her head buried in a pillow, sobbing. 'Lulu, what's really wrong?' Zephy sat tentatively on the edge of the bed.

Lulu looked up, rage in her eyes. 'Did you expect me to be happy for you? Happy that you came here to be my bridesmaid, but now you're getting married before me? Happy that you'll be marrying a duke? A duke you don't even want! You'll be the toast of the Season, and I'll just be another advantageous marriage. You stole my moment from me. When I walk down the aisle, everyone will be comparing me to you, and I will come up short.'

'You know that's not what I intended,' Zephy said trying to console her. She'd not realised how much the pageantry of a wedding had meant to Lulu.

'I'm not sure I know what you intend anymore, or what you ever intended. You said you wanted a desperate second son, you said you were going to go back to San Francisco. But for all I know, you meant none of it. Maybe you were just leading Lord Leo on to grab his brother's notice. And it worked. You have Sunderland, the duke who doesn't need your money, the most eligible man of the Season, and you don't even want him, don't even appreciate him. You despise him. Unless that was a lie, too.'

'I didn't like Hale at first, but I do now,' Zephy confessed. More than liked him. 'He has depth. He is responsible and kind and passionate.' She paused. She was starting to act as if the wedding were real. She couldn't do that. It wasn't going to happen.

Lulu gave a horrified stare. 'So something did happen at Glenmere! You went to bed with him,' she accused. 'No wonder he has proposed. You trapped him into it.'

'No, Lulu, it wasn't like that,' Zephy rushed to explain. Lulu made it sound sordid and conniving. 'I hadn't planned to go to Glenmere. I didn't even know he was going, and I wouldn't have known if I hadn't been in the kitchen with the sourdough starter when he came looking for food for the journey.'

Lulu gave her a critical stare. 'You've always been good at spotting an opportunity.' Lulu's gaze turned mean. 'But perhaps you've overplayed your hand this time. He'll never let you leave.'

'He has given me his word. We will work something out.' She wasn't sure that word meant very much, though. He'd also promised her time. He'd broken that promise within hours of making it.

Lulu gave a cruel laugh. 'He'll be less keen to work something out when he has you and your settlements under his control and there is no motivation for him to grant your wishes. Don't be naive, Zephy.'

'If he doesn't help with the solution, I'll just leave on my own. He can do very little about that when I'm three thousand miles away and not dependent on his money. He'll have no leverage if it comes to that.' There were other things she could do if the marriage took place. There was consolation in that. She couldn't threaten him with a public divorce, though American women could do that. She had the funds for it, but perhaps not the heart. She didn't want to fight with Hale. She didn't want to be aggressive with him, to attack him in order to get what she needed. She liked to believe Hale felt the same way: that the best way forward for them was to amicably talk through their problems, as they'd done so far.

'He'll have leverage if there's any chance you're pregnant,' Lulu said smugly.

'We were careful.' Somewhat. They'd not been careful this morning.

'This time. There will be other times. Sometimes passion doesn't wait for sheaths, sometimes sheaths fail, sometimes a man can't withdraw fast enough,'

Lulu enumerated rather bluntly. 'That child will be reason enough to drag you back to him. Sex is his weapon. It's every man's weapon, that spear between his legs.' Lulu sneered. 'Just as gossip is a woman's.'

She did not like this iteration of Lulu. 'This is not you, Lulu. You're overwrought with the stress of the wedding and the Season.' Zephy reached for Lulu's hand. 'Should you break it off with Southford? Are you not sure of him? Certainly, your father could handle the details for you.'

Lulu's eyes filled with desperation. 'I cannot cry off now. We have been engaged since the holidays. I am trying to warn you, Zephy. These noblemen are laws unto themselves. My father can protect my money in my settlements and provide for future children, but my father cannot fully control Southford. Just as you won't be able to control Sunderland.'

'What has he done, Lulu?' Zephy's concern was immediately fixed on her friend. She was understanding Lulu's outburst better now.

'He has a mistress he's madly in love with,' Lulu whispered. 'He promised to give her up, but he's only become more discreet. He has no intention of fully giving her up. They've been together for years. She has a house off Jermyn Street.' Lulu blushed. 'I suspected it was still ongoing when we returned to the city. I followed him one day.'

'Oh, Lulu.' Zephy's heart went out to her friend. 'You must tell your father and cry off.'

Lulu shook her head. 'I can't.' She held Zephy's gaze steadily. 'I thought I could make Southford love me the way I love him.' She paused. 'Zephy, I'm pregnant. We anticipated our vows back in March while my parents were in New York.'

It was early days yet, then. She couldn't be more than two months along. 'You're sure? Does Southford know?' This was shocking news indeed. Southford was always so doting, seemed so genuine when they were together.

'Yes, he knows. He's thrilled.' There was a bite to Lulu's words. 'Genuinely thrilled. I can hardly complain about a mistress now, and he could have an heir by Christmas. He gets everything he wants, and I can do nothing.' But stand by and watch her heart break, her trust shatter. It gave new meaning to Lulu's concerns about Southford returning to his usual pursuits after the wedding. Zephy had not understood that until now. Nor had she fully understood how much it meant when Lulu had said Southford was her only ally. Hadn't Hale said almost the exact same thing to her today? But surely she and Hale were different than Lulu and Southford.

'Lulu, I am so sorry.'

Lulu nodded. 'I just want you to know what you're

walking into. I learned too late, but it's not too late for you.'

'I can't go home and marry Mathieu Aubert,' she reminded Lulu.

'No, he's the far worse choice.' Lulu squeezed her hand. 'But protect yourself within your marriage so that you have options, and we'll hope that Sunderland makes good.' Lulu worried her lip. 'I am sorry about earlier. I said mean things. Wedding stress or not, I should not have said them.'

'But they were true. You felt them, and I am sorry you thought I was upstaging you. But I am even more sorry that I've been so wrapped up in my own concerns that I didn't notice what was happening around you, that I didn't understand how important the wedding is. I would offer to wait, but I don't think the scandal will allow it.'

Lulu nodded. 'I understand. All is forgiven.'

'I will not forgive you for this.' Leo turned from the fireplace, his features pale and drawn, his green eyes blazing when Hale stepped into the room. Hale gave a terse nod. He shut the door behind him and waited for the storm that was his brother to break. At last. Perhaps this storm was inevitable. It had been brewing for years despite Hale's efforts to defuse it.

'You knew I intended to propose this week.' Leo pushed an agitated hand through his blond waves. 'I am such a fool! I told you everything on the ride here from the train. I wanted your approval, as the duke, as *my* brother. And you...' he sputtered with deep-seated betrayal '...*you* put up a resistance worthy of Kenilworth Castle, and I, ridiculously, kept trying to break myself against your walls, to win you over while all along you wanted her for yourself.' Despair warred with fraternal fury in Leo's eyes, and Hale felt his own heart break. He'd been reckless this morning with his announcement. Words made reality. More than that, he'd been reckless with Zephy's trust and his brother's always-fragile feelings, two things he cared deeply about. These were two people he would not wilfully or needlessly hurt. But he had, in order to save face. He drew a steadying breath and counselled himself to patience. Leo was not done yet.

'I asked you directly on that ride if you had intentions towards her.' Leo ground out the last accusation. 'I should have believed my eyes. I knew what I saw that day at the cricket grounds.'

He could argue against none of that, but he could speak the truth now that the storm had blown itself out. 'Leo, she chose me—'

'Because you took her to your bed and made love to her. She had to choose you. For the first time in your entire, perfect life, you broke the rules.' Leo gave a harsh laugh. 'The irony of it is that, for the first time in my imperfect life, I didn't. And look what it got me.' He made an impotent fist. 'I needed her, Hale. When I was with her, I felt important, like I could do something, *be* something, like I could go to the Hampshire estate and make something of it with her beside me.' He rubbed at the bridge of his nose, a tic jumping in his cheek. 'We could have had a life, Hale.'

They could have. Hale would admit to that. 'You may feel you needed her, but you don't love her, and she was never going to go to Hampshire with you, not to stay,' Hale offered sternly. Leo kept forgetting that piece. 'The life you want with her is not the life she can give you.'

Leo's eyes simmered like hot coals. 'But she'll stay for you? Is that it?'

'No, that's *not* it.' Hale moved to take a seat for the first time since Leo had begun speaking. 'I don't know that she'll stay for me. But I knew her plan all along. It was one of the reasons I was so adamant that you not propose. I wanted to tell you, but it was not my news to impart. She and I have to work it out. Her family is important to her.'

Leo slouched wearily into the remaining chair. 'So you've both betrayed me, then. She was going to use me and pay me off for my name, and you were simply going to bed—'

'You don't need to finish that thought. You've already made your point there,' Hale cut in sharply. 'I am saving you from a mistake.'

'Like you're saving Lady Julia? You're quite the saviour, today,' Leo groused, but the heat had ebbed from his anger as understanding began to dawn: He was not his brother's victim so much as a victim of circumstance.

Hale leaned forward. 'Leo, you are my brother. I will always love you, and I will always want the best for you. You don't need Zephy to be successful in Hampshire. You are enough on your own, if you want to go. I would like you to stand up with me at my wedding and, God willing, I want you to stand with me as I hold my first child and in all the times to follow. I am sorrier than you can know that things have evolved as they have. It was not my intention. Can we get past this?' He held Leo's gaze, his own eyes pleading silently. He did not want to have to choose between Zephy and Leo.

Leo gave a slow nod. 'I can, with time. I will be there next week for the wedding, I will put on a good face. Then, I will go back to London for the duration of the Season, take the *Aquatica* to Cowes for racing in August, and take some time after that. This has been…a lot.'

Hale offered his hand, and Leo shook it, letting Hale rise and draw him into a brotherly embrace. 'Good man,' Hale murmured at his brother's ear. 'You'll be all right.' And for the first time, Hale believed it. Leo had grown up at last, even if it had been painful. When he released his brother, he turned to his mother who was discreetly wiping away tears. 'It seems we have a wedding to plan and a short time to do it. Are you up for it?' He smiled, and his mother smiled back. She would enjoy the challenge. Most of the weight had been lifted from his shoulders. He had settled with Cameron, reconciled with Leo. That just left Zephy, perhaps the most difficult discussion of all, for last. In many ways, her absolution meant the most.

'Can you forgive me?' Hale had found Zephy in a quiet little-used sitting room upstairs. She'd changed out of her riding habit into a light blue muslin and re-fashioned her hair into a soft bun that lay at the base of her neck. She looked misleadingly serene. He knew better. She would be seething over what had happened in the rose room.

He took the chair across from her and waited. He'd done enough talking—to Mr Cameron, to the marquess, to Southford, to Leo, to his mother. Talk had accomplished much, but he sensed in this case listening might accomplish more. If he waited too long, though, he'd miss the last train to London. He counselled himself to patience. There'd be other trains tomorrow if it came to it.

At last Zephy turned her gaze towards him, her calm tones damning. 'Three hours, Hale. That was all it took for you to break your promise.'

'The marquess was an unlooked-for wrinkle.'

'So you took away my option of time to consider your proposal. You took more than time away from me. You took my choice. You railed at the marquess for trying to force your hand, and then you did the same to me.'

He supposed he deserved that. 'In part, you are not wrong. But I think the situations are different. Your choice was inevitable. Whether you want to admit it or not, your choice has already been made.' He braced for her response. Regardless of how true it was, she wouldn't appreciate hearing it.

Her chin went up in a defiant tilt. 'So your pledge to offer me time was merely an act of pandering to my wishes, to create the illusion of caring about what I want.'

He was not going to say yes to that. He matched her quiet tones. 'Hopefully, you know me better than to assume I would patronise you. I am trying to protect you.' Her stubbornness was not her greatest asset at present. She needed to see beyond it.

She gave a little nod. 'And I am trying to protect *you*, although you are too obstinate to see it.'

He was the obstinate one? A smile twitched at his lips at a most inappropriate time. 'How do you reason that?'

'I will ruin you, Hale. I can't be a duchess. I must think about my family. The marquess was right. I'll always be a baker's daughter. I don't want to be anything else. The marquess and others like him will make you pay for *slumming*.' She used Barrow's word, and Hale found himself bristling.

'Before you start protesting, it's more than the social scandal. I will ruin *you*, and you will ruin me, who we are at our cores. I don't want you to compromise the man you are any more than I want to compromise who I am. We are too unalike to fit together. You are, in fact, the very worst choice of a husband I can make.'

'So you've mentioned.' He gave a sigh. 'I disagree. We have powerful things in common, Zephy. A love of family, a commitment to duty. We might not be from similar social backgrounds, but we share values and beliefs that run deeper than that. We don't have all the answers right now, but we will find them.'

Zephy rose and went to the window, looking out over the grounds. He barely heard her words. 'I'm scared, Hale.'

It was quite an admission from his brave Zephy. He went to her and wrapped his arms about her. 'What scares you?'

'Going home and facing Mathieu Aubert. Staying here and giving up my old life. Hurting you. Losing myself. There's no way out for me.'

'Sometimes the best way out is through,' he murmured, breathing in the scent of her. 'Do you want to know a secret? I'm scared, too.'

'Like at Tattersalls?' She gave a soft laugh, and he felt a little of the tension leave her. 'But you leapt anyway.'

'It's all right to be afraid, but it's not all right to let the fear win, to let it paralyse you. I learned that while climbing up to my tree-house one summer. I was so high up that I was too frightened to climb back down and too frightened to keep going up. I was absolutely too far from the ground for anyone to reach me. I had to take care of myself. Eventually, I kept climbing. The view at the top was worth it, and I learned I could do it. The next climb was easier. Be scared, Zephy, but keep climbing. I am there to reach for you.'

'It's not easy, though. This is not what I sought. I don't want to hurt you, but I fear I already have. How did it go with your mother and Leo?'

'Well enough. Leo and I have made peace. Mother will take you to Glenmere tomorrow and make the wedding preparations. You can rely on her. She is to help you settle in. I'll stop by the Camerons' townhouse while I'm in London and bring the rest of your things back with me. All has been easily arranged.'

'Will you do something else for me in London? Will you call on Lady Julia and make sure she is all right? This will be a blow to her.' Zephy's consideration for another touched him.

'I will.' He offered a reassuring smile. 'You are kind to think of her amid all of this. She is young and lovely and well-dowered. She will be resilient, I am sure of it. Everything will be well, you'll see. I promise, Zephy. Do you believe me?'

'I do. I must,' she whispered, the words a balm to his soul after the tumult of the day.

He knew how much it cost her to put her faith in him again and that she felt she had no choice. 'I will be worthy of your trust.' Already a plan was forming, gleaned from everything she'd ever told him about her family. He would put the initial steps in motion in London and once he was certain, he would tell her, he would show her that her fears would come to naught. He pressed a swift kiss to her cheek and made his farewell. If he left now, he'd be just in time to make the train and put their future in motion.

## Chapter Nineteen

It was time. For her wedding. Zephy was all nerves and nausea, alternating between wooziness and worry. She stood before the mirror in her new chamber at Glenmere—the duchess's chamber, complete with adjoining door to the duke's chamber—a reminder of all that went with marriage: a joining of lives and bodies. 'The dress looks well, yes?' she asked Lulu, and not for the first time.

She'd chosen a pale blue gown she'd not yet worn, one of the dresses she'd brought from San Francisco. There'd been no time for a new dress, and although Hale's mother had offered some older wedding gowns from past Sunderland duchesses, Zephy had wanted something of her own. This one had been among the things Hale had retrieved from the Cameron townhouse.

Lulu stepped up behind her and placed comforting hands at her shoulders. '"Something old, something new, something borrowed, something blue". This applies to two of those things. It's new and blue, so it's perfect. *You* are perfect in it. Blue is your best colour.'

'But blue is a bit unorthodox. Everyone is expecting a white dress. Your wedding dress is white,' Zephy worried. 'I don't want to start off on the wrong foot by reminding everyone that I'm different, an outsider. There's enough that's unorthodox about this wedding as it is.' That it was happening under a cloud of scandal, that up until two weeks ago Society had thought the perfect, handsome Hale Eberley, Duke of Sunderland, would wed the equally perfect and beautiful Lady Julia Parkhurst, daughter of a marquess; that the bride was an American upstart, a baker's daughter from the wilds of the West. Add to that the duke's previous penchant for eschewing American money and that his own brother had been perceived as a contender for that money and the scandal doubled. She and Hale weren't just marrying under a cloud. They were marrying under a veritable rainstorm, which was an apt metaphor given the circumstances that had required the marriage to begin with.

'Are you sure you don't want to eat something before church?' Lulu urged. 'You hardly ate anything at supper last night. We could start with toast. It works wonders, I've been living off it.' She laughed. 'I've been passing morning sickness off as wedding jitters. I only have to keep the charade up for two more weeks.' She smiled mischievously. 'That reminds me. I have something for you.' She pulled out a plain wrapped package. 'They're sponges for contraception,' Lulu whispered, tucking them into the top drawer of the dressing table. 'That way you can decide what's right for you.'

'I am sorry I won't be there for your wedding. You were counting on me.' Zephy felt miserable about that. Lulu had been good to her despite recent developments.

'You and Hale are supposed to be on your honeymoon. It will be far too soon for you to put in a public appearance.' Lulu squeezed her hand. 'Besides, I'd like everyone to be looking at me and Southford for just a few minutes. If you came, everyone would be looking at you and Hale.' They laughed together, and Zephy felt her nerves settle.

'You will have a beautiful day, Lulu.' Zephy smiled in the mirror at her friend. 'Can you believe this? Two American girls from a mediocre boarding school are marrying English noblemen. That's quite a jump up in Society's eyes. I am sure Mrs Trainor, the headmistress, will be aghast. We weren't exactly her favourites. Too spirited.'

'Aghast *or* over the moon. Think what this will do for her enrollment.' Lulu laughed and reached for the veil, a pretty, filmy length of fabric attached to a wreath of fresh flowers hand-picked that morning.

'Flower-wreath veils are all the rage. You'll be traditional in that, at least. If you're not going to eat, then we should go.' Zephy bent her head, letting Lulu settle it and fix it in place with a few hairpins. 'There, that should hold it.' Lulu stepped back satisfied. 'You're ready now. You look like May itself—youthful, happy.'

She did look happy, although that surprised her. The past week had been fraught with plans and worry. Was she doing the right thing with this marriage? Could she trust Hale? Everything was new. She was surrounded by new people, by new places. Even Glenmere had seemed different without Hale beside her. But she'd been firm, grasping the situation immediately. She wasn't a guest here any longer but a resident. The staff were watching her, waiting to see if she would be her own mistress or simply be swallowed up in the large shadow of Hale's mother.

Her business experiences at the bakery had stood her in good stead, and she'd found a path to walk that both established the beginning of her tenure here and honoured the dowager duchess. Hale had been pleased when he'd returned. And she'd been pleased, too. More than pleased. *Relieved*. Perhaps she might not lose herself just yet. She took a final look at the chamber. A maid would come to tidy it and lay out a nightgown in anticipation of the night to come. 'The next time I am in this room, I won't be Zephy Duval anymore,' she whispered to Lulu. 'I'll be Her Grace, the Duchess of Sunderland. Wife of Hale Eberley.' She would forever be linked with a man, interdependent on his identity. The old fear sent a tremor through her.

'Don't be a goose, Zeph. You will always be Zephy Duval. You can't help it.' Lulu gave her a gentle squeeze. Zephy hoped Lulu was right. Underneath the names and titles, she would always be herself—a baker from San Francisco. But legally, Zephy Duval would be erased by this marriage. No encouragement from Lulu could change that. She just hoped the baker's daughter wasn't buried too deeply.

'Here's your bouquet. The flowers will hide your hands if they shake.' Lulu pushed the collection of blue forget-me-nots twined with cream roses into her hands. Hale had put the bouquet together himself and had it delivered this morning—staunchly sticking to the old tradition of not seeing the bride before the wedding. The bouquet had come with an explanation: *Forget-me-nots symbolising respect, love and a promise of fidelity; cream roses for thoughtfulness and charm.* There was a postscript at the bottom: *Also, the forget-me-nots are known as scorpion grass, and that seems fitting to me as well, considering your temper, if you don't mind me saying so. Yours, Hale.* The note had made her misty-eyed, and Lulu's gaze had gone soft. Zephy's hands closed around the bouquet now, taking strength from it. *Love* might be putting it too fine. Their association was too new for that perhaps, but not for passion, and the nod towards fidelity and his promise meant more than either of those.

She smiled and felt her nerves settle once more. This was her wedding day. The sun was out, and a good man waited for her at church. She was going to live in the moment of it. She could worry about whatever came next later. For today, it would be enough to have Hale beside her.

The procession to the little chapel on the Glenmere property began with the first step she took out of her bedroom. The staff had lined the hallway and the foyer downstairs to send her off, each of them bowing or curtsying as she passed. She gave each of them a piece of that smile, thanking them for the welcome they'd given her. She understood they saw this day differently than she did. To them, she was marrying their duke, becoming part of their world. They didn't see the turmoil beneath, the problems left to resolve, and today she didn't want to think about those.

At the front steps, Mr and Mrs Cameron waited to join her on the walk to church. The chapel wasn't far, and Zephy had insisted she walk instead of taking a carriage. They'd take a carriage home. The village had turned out for the walk, some children adding wildflowers to her bouquet. She wondered if they'd turned out on their own or whether Hale had had something to do with it, to ensure she felt welcomed, that she belonged. The crowd left her at the church door. They would remain outside until after the ceremony. Inside, the Camerons left her in the small narthex that separated the chapel from the entrance and took their seats at the front on the bride's side, across from the dowager duchess.

A violin began to play from somewhere inside the chapel, the strains of Pachelbel's 'Canon in D,' a cue for Lulu to make her entrance. They exchanged one last smile and Lulu was gone, looking lovely and dignified in a gown of sage silk, her own signature colour, a bouquet of cream roses in her hand. Alone at last, Zephy thought, watching her friend. She'd not been alone, not really, for the entire week. She took the opportunity to draw a few deep, settling breaths and to make a quiet survey of the chapel. It was small and built of stone. There were perhaps only ten rows of pews inside, but they were filled with local notables: the squire's family, the vicar's family, a baron's family who lived nearby, and a few of Hale's close friends who'd come from London, as well as a few house party guests who'd stayed on at Southford's. Fortunately, Miss Emerson was not among them.

Hale's mother had outdone herself, planning a wedding that gave no impression it was a rushed affair. Spring garlands draped the pews on the aisle, sporting pink, blue and yellow blossoms, each garland tied with an elegant cream bow. At the front, the altar was draped in a pristine white cloth, flanked by two large floor urns burgeoning with cream roses and draped in swathes of blue satin. Between the music and the flowers, the effect in the little chapel was stunning. For her. All of these little details were for her. She looked down at her bouquet, remembering what it stood for, and her eyes teared up. Again. She couldn't cry just yet.

Lulu reached the front, and Hale stepped forward into her line of sight, Leo beside him. She'd seen Hale last night, but looking at him now, she felt as if it had been ages. He was resplendent in a morning coat of dark blue with grey trousers, a silver waistcoat embroidered in blue flowers and linen so white it practically shone. His black hair was brushed to a sheen, his usual swoop in perfect place. But it was his confidence she noticed the most. His shoulders were straight, his posture unerringly erect, his gaze direct. He was not looking at the gathering or at the decorations, she realised, but at her. Zephy stepped forward and began the walk down the aisle in measured perfection, the guests rising as she passed, but she barely noticed them. She was intent on the man who waited for her. He lifted her veil and smiled into her eyes. Somewhere in the congregation, a woman sighed. Zephy smiled. 'Thank you for the flowers,' she whispered.

'You look stunning.' He took her hand as Lulu took

her bouquet, and Zephy and Hale turned together towards the vicar. Zephy was glad she'd taken a moment to appreciate the decorations and the details when she'd had the chance. She certainly wasn't able to concentrate on them now. All of her attention was riveted on Hale, on each expression that flickered across his face, on his gaze, on the silver buttons of his waistcoat. Each detail absorbed her. This man was to be her husband, their lives irrevocably joined—a thought that she both thrilled to and feared.

Hale slipped a plain gold band on her finger. Were they at that part already? The service had sped by. 'I thought this would make baking easier,' he said in quiet tones, a soft spark in his amber eyes. She smiled her appreciation. There was no time for more words, but his gesture was not lost on her. It was hard to keep gems clean, to pick miniscule pieces of dough out of their settings. His thoughtfulness bordered on astounding. Amid the chaos of the week, he'd paid attention.

'Time for the kiss, my favourite part,' Hale murmured, and they exchanged a private smile before his lips pressed to hers, a sealing, a promise. She'd have liked nothing more than to race away with him right then and celebrate in other, more intimate ways. But there was pageantry to honour and people to meet before that—hours of it, in fact. Outside, an open-air carriage festooned in matching garlands pulled by an immaculately groomed grey horse waited to take them back to Glenmere, along with the eager villagers. There were pennies to toss, and there was a joyous parade that followed the carriage to the house. 'Today is about villagers, the merchants and the tenant farmers as much as it is about us. Maybe more. It's a communal celebration,' Hale explained, melting her with his smile. 'Our marriage is a promise that life will go on here at Glenmere as it has for nearly three hundred years. There might be a new century coming, but the life they know remains intact.'

'Thanks to you.' Zephy smiled.

'Thanks to *us*,' Hale corrected, leaning over to claim a kiss while those nearest the carriage cheered. 'You are a part of this now.'

At the house, tents and tables had been set up on the front lawn. There was a dance floor laid out and music. There were games organised for the children and prizes, too. Mementos were gaily wrapped and placed on the tables. Everyone would go home with a bronze medallion imprinted with the ducal crest and the date of the wedding. 'It's a handsome token.' Zephy turned one over in her hand as they stole a moment alone.

'There's something etched inside your ring as well. May I?' Hale slipped the ring off her finger and held it up for her to see. *'H and Z, May twenty-fifth, 1890. Forever.'* He slid it back on.

'I like it very much, Hale. It was thoughtful.' She gave a sigh. 'I like this, being with you, just you. I wish we could slip away.'

'Not yet,' Hale teased. 'We must do our duty and dance.'

She laughed. 'May I dance with you more than twice today? Now that we're wed?' It seemed surreal to say that, surreal to experience the feelings that came with it.

'You may.' Hale smiled. She liked this iteration of him, a man at peace, comfortable in his surroundings, who gave away no sense of regret that today was his wedding day or that he'd married the least likely of women. A little spark warmed her. Perhaps it was because he had no regret. Perhaps it wasn't an act and he was truly happy. As long as he kept his word, perhaps there was hope for them both inside this marriage. It was a good note to start on.

He was married. To an American heiress. To a woman who laughed out loud as they went through the steps of a country dance with their set. The realisation carried its own level of unbelievability with it, as did the flood of feelings that coursed through him.

Hale swung Zephy around and passed her on to the next partner with a good-natured wink. He'd not expected to feel this way—like he was dancing on air, floating on sunshine anytime she looked at him, anytime he caught sight of her in a room. And heaven help him, anytime he touched her or she touched him, which she did quite often. He loved that. Good English girls didn't initiate touch with dukes. And Zephy touched all of him: his hand, his arm, his cock... He loved her boldness. She'd touched him with her eyes today when she'd come down the aisle, so proud and brave. He'd not wanted to look away, had not wanted to miss a moment of their wedding.

One would never guess, looking at her now, dancing with their guests, laughing with them, how hard today was for her, or how hard the week had likely been, surrounded by so much new, aware of how alone she was. Every consideration had been made to ensure she felt this was her wedding, but the fact was her parents weren't here. Her friends, outside of Lulu, weren't here. She wasn't marrying in her home church. Her father had not been here to give her away. And yet, she'd faced the day with joy, and the kiss she'd given him in the chapel had been warm, open, encouraging. He did not fool himself that a marriage solved everything. It did not. But perhaps it did portend hope. Hope that they wanted to work on a life together. And it would be work. They were from two different worlds. But perhaps it would not be insurmountable if they were honest with one another.

They danced until they were breathless, greeted people until their hands hurt and their faces ached from smiling. They ate until they were full, drank Champagne until their world was slightly, delightfully blurred at the edges, until Hale could not recall ever being happier or wanting anything different, until the lights in the pavilions came on as dusk fell and new platters of food were brought. The guests were welcome to stay and celebrate. But he'd done his duty and now it was time, at last, to do a different duty, one he'd been looking forward to since he'd picked forget-me-nots for his bride in the dew-drenched dawn right after sunup. Zephy gave him a secret look over the rim of her Champagne glass, her eyes asking the same question. He gave her a little nod and took her hand, leading her discreetly from the party, edging them slowly into the verge beyond the gaslight and then into the house undetected. At the stairs, he swung her up into his arms.

'Are you going to carry me to bed?' Zephy laughed up at him.

'Yes, tradition holds it's to protect a man's bride from evil spirits.'

'Oh,' Zephy replied with mock coolness. 'I thought it was because the bride was reluctant to leave her father's home.'

Hale paused on a step. '*Are* you reluctant, Zeph? I know events have been chaotic and unexpected to say the least and that today…' *was not the wedding she'd likely imagined.*

She silenced him with a hard kiss. 'Perfect. Today was *perfect*. And no, I am not reluctant in the least. I think you'll find that out very soon if you'd keep moving.' She slid him a sly smile.

'It was perfect.' He continued to climb, juggling her in his arms. 'Perhaps both explanations for the tradition are true.'

'Perhaps they are,' she agreed, and he thought it wouldn't be the last time they'd make peace in this way. Acknowledging that they could both be correct was a step in the right direction, a step towards an amicable future.

## Chapter Twenty

Hale pushed open the door to his bride's chambers and stepped inside to a candlelit, rose-petalled bower complete with more Champagne. 'We'll be too drunk to do anything if we drink any more,' Zephy laughed when she saw the bottle.

'We'll save it for later.' Hale set her down and shut the door behind them. 'All I want to do right now is look at my bride one last time in her beautiful wedding gown before I help her out of it.' He did not bother to hide the desire-tinged husk to his voice. It was just the two of them now, at last, and he wanted her. He'd wanted her all week from the moment he'd ridden away from Wheaton to seek the special licence.

'Hmmm.' She stepped close to him and wrapped her arms about his neck, hips pressed to his. 'We are in accord, then, because that's all I want, too. I am looking forward to seeing you naked.' It was a bold reminder that there were still firsts to be had between them.

'I see you've given this some thought,' Hale teased, but he didn't mind. He'd had a taste of that boldness and was well-warned. He liked that his wife knew what she wanted, and that she wanted it from him. That boded well for their marriage in the bedroom, at least. He stepped away from her, the fire at his back. He stripped out of his coat and tugged off his shoes. 'I hope you're a quick study because next time you'll be the one undressing me.'

'That depends on how good of a tutor you are.' She sat on the edge of the bed, mischief flashing in her sea-mist eyes, the skirt of her blue gown flowing about her, her dark hair loose over one shoulder. Looking at her was like looking at spring itself come to life. Hard desire speared him as he discarded his waistcoat and pulled his shirttails from the waistband of his trousers before pulling his shirt over his head. He hadn't the patience or dexterity for buttons at present. He heard her breath catch in appreciation and saw her gaze go still, riveted on him. He held that gaze with his own as he divested himself of his trousers and kicked them away so that he stood before her, a fully naked offering.

*With my body I thee worship.* The words intoned slowly in Zephy's head as she looked upon him and comprehended the import of what he had done in this very literal offering of himself. It was a physical pledge to match the one he'd made this morning in words. His body was made for worship, every inch of him from the tips of those fingers that had caressed her to the ruddy, hard length of the phallus that rose between his thighs—all of it was made for the giving and receiving of pleasure, her pleasure. Her blood already hummed with the knowledge of it.

She rose from the bed and came to him. 'May I?' She pressed a palm to his heart, felt the life and the strength beating beneath her touch. 'You are beautiful,' she whispered. 'I did not expect it to be so much. I did not expect a man to be a work of art.' She traced the lines of his torso with an inquisitive fingertip, feeling the ridges and planes where muscle met sinew. 'You must be a sculptor's dream.'

'I am only glad I am *your* dream.' Hale gave a slow smile, the desire in his gaze heating her own. 'Shall I help you with your gown?' His words were steady even in the midst of burning. She envied him his control even when desire was riding him hard.

'Yes.' Her own voice was a breathless wisp. She was impatient with her own desire now, impatient to have him in bed, to claim again the pleasure she'd experienced in the gallery.

He turned her about and whispered at her ear as if he'd read her mind or perhaps he'd just read her body. 'We have all night, Zeph. We have as long as we want, as long as we need. There is no risk of anyone intruding.'

Her gown slid from her body, and her corset followed, his hands proving more than up to the task. She turned to face him, making short work of her remaining undergarments, but she could not read the expression on his face. Perhaps he'd wanted a show from her, some tantalising foreplay of rolling down a silk stocking, but she hadn't the willpower for it. She wanted only to be naked with him, skin to skin with him in the big bed that stood at the centre of her room. When he said nothing, she met his gaze evenly, bravely. 'Have I disappointed?'

'No. Whyever would you think that?' His Adam's apple worked in his throat, swallowing as if his mouth were dry.

'It's just that some people look better with their clothes on. Perhaps…' Zephy ran her hands over her ribcage.

'You are definitely not one of them.' Hale closed the distance between them, dispelling any notion of disappointment as he drew her against him, and she felt the full warmth of him, the strength of him for the first time without any impediment. Warm skin to warm skin, and she was flush with the joy of it. 'If I hesitated,' he murmured at her throat, 'it was because I was overwhelmed. I wanted only to look my fill, to celebrate my great luck having a bride, a *wife*, who pleases me so thoroughly.'

She twined her arms about him and lifted a leg to rest at his hip. He hefted her then, allowing her to wrap her legs about him with a throaty laugh. 'I thought you'd never ask.'

In answer he bore her back to the bed, coming down over her. Why did she like looking up at him from this position so much? She didn't know, only that she did like it, quite a lot: those amber eyes with their slow-burning flame, those arms locked to hold his weight, that body running the length of hers and then some, the heat of his phallus at her entrance. It was a multisensory experience to be sure, and she revelled in it, in him, despite knowing this was an imperfect union. He came into her with the confidence of a man who knew he'd be well-received, who knew this was where he belonged, and she pushed the reminder away. Not tonight. Tonight it was perfect. There would be time to deal with the imperfections later. For now, there was only to be pleasure. But that created two problems.

The problem with *now* was that one moment was followed by another moment and another until *now* stretched into what once had been the future and the present was all that mattered, all that existed. The other problem was with pleasure. Pleasure was addicting. Once tasted, never relinquished. Desire became a craving that ruled the day from sunrise to sunset and into the night: delicious, delirious, demanding. And yet, Zephy had no will to break from its chains. Quite the opposite. She wanted more of it.

They woke in the mornings to slow, friendly lovemaking, rode out on their horses before breakfasting on the terrace, sneaking off to make love before going their separate ways on estate business—he to the office and his ledgers, she to the kitchen to feed her sourdough and meet with Mrs Hepburn over menus and meals or to the village with the dowager duchess for visits. There was luncheon in the topiary garden or a picnic in the forest beneath the tree-house tree, which led to the need for a nap and lovemaking before or after the nap—or both. It was a favourite treat of hers to wake up in the early summer afternoon to blue skies filtering through the green boughs, her head resting on Hale's chest, his arm about her. She loved waking up first, to watch him sleep. There was supper and cards with Hale's mother, who promptly left at ten each evening for the dower house. They might share a late-night sherry in the library after her departure, but most evenings they went straight up to bed the moment the door shut behind her. Not because they couldn't wait to be rid of her company but because they couldn't wait to get back to their own.

This was a good life, an unexpected life. As long as she didn't think beyond the now, Zephy didn't need to worry about it ending, and so she didn't. Late May slipped into June. They read about the world beyond them in the newspapers as they lazed on blankets in the wild strawberry fields, their fingers stained from berry-picking, their stomachs full from tasting. The Derby at Epsom came and went, Basingstoke's favoured colt going nose to nose from start to finish with Sainfoin who was ultimately declared the winner. The newspapers covered Lulu's town wedding to Southford extensively, calling it the wedding of the Season, and printed pictures of the bride. There was the annual Buckingham Palace garden party. There'd been shocking news in the Society pages that Lady Julia Parkhurst had eloped with long-time friend of the family Oliver Tymount, the second son of Viscount Harrington, and was honeymooning happily at his estate in Yorkshire. Zephy was happy for her. It seemed that Hale had indeed done her a favour.

As June ebbed, people in the world beyond Glenmere were looking forward to Ascot and the regatta in Cowes. Lulu sent a quick note to say she and Southford would be honeymooning in the South of France until autumn. Leo sent word he was headed to Cowes early.

'It's not that early, I suppose.' Hale propped himself up on one arm as he sprawled on the picnic blanket spread in the shade of the tree-house tree. 'The regatta is in August, and that's just a week or so away.'

'August. Where has the summer gone?' Zephy laughed and looked up into the sky.

'Do you want to go to Cowes?' Hale asked in slow, careful tones as if he were feeling his way into a conversation he didn't want to have.

'No.' Zephy shook her head. 'Do you, though? Because if you did...' Perhaps he was being reticent because he wanted to go. Sometime, perhaps soon, they'd have to leave the cocoon of Glenmere, but not yet. Not now. *But when?* a little voice in her mind whispered. *When is* now *over?*

Hale lay back on the picnic blanket, hands tucked behind his head, face turned to the sky. 'I don't want to go. If it were up to me, I'd never leave Glenmere again. Everything I want is here.' He turned his face towards her with a warm smile and reached for her hand. 'So, that's decided. We won't go to Cowes. If we're lucky, we won't have to go anywhere until next spring,' he chuckled.

They wouldn't be that lucky, Zephy thought, snuggling up against him. She wished they hadn't brought up Cowes, wished Leo hadn't written. The spell they'd so carefully woven was starting to break. Perhaps it was a sign of just how fragile the fantasy had been or a reminder that a fantasy was all it had *ever* been. All dreamers wake up. She'd promised her parents she'd return by July, and July was nearly past. How were they faring without her? How much longer could she keep putting aside the issues she and Hale needed to work on in order to make this marriage viable for the long term? Honeymoons did come to a close and hers was running out of time.

His time was running out. Hale could feel it in their lovemaking, see it in Zephy's eyes. There was desperation mixed with the desire. Honeymoons didn't last forever, but promises were binding. He'd given his word that she needn't give up her family in exchange for his. The marriage had done its job. It had squelched scandal, restored decency to his dukedom and ostensibly secured the succession in the eyes of outsiders.

The marriage had in fact done more than its job. It had made him feel things he'd been unprepared to feel, had not expected to feel. He'd always thought his marriage would be one of mutual respect, not passion. But this was both, and it was highly satisfying. More than satisfying. It was addicting and elating, and two months later, he could not get enough. But now that elation was joined by fear—fear that he might lose all of that because he might lose her. He wished they'd never talked of Cowes a week ago. His brother's letter had been the little crack that had let the world seep in. Now, Hale had to confront it and live up to the promises he'd made Zephy.

Hale pushed the ledgers aside and sank his hands into his hair. Sometimes ignorance was indeed bliss. He did not have that luxury. He'd known Zephy's plan from the start. One could even say he'd given her the idea for it. She'd always meant to go home. She'd never meant to fall into passion any more than he had. Was that passion enough? And perhaps, in ostrich-head-in-the-sand-fashion, he'd hoped it would be. For a while it had been. The honeymoon had lasted far longer than he would have guessed. But that made it all the harder to contemplate change. He wasn't ready for it to end. He didn't want things to change.

He'd hoped the plan he'd set in motion in London three months ago would have borne fruit by now. But there'd been no word. Yet. That was no excuse. Things had to change. For them both. There was the succession to consider. They couldn't keep practicing safety measures indefinitely. But there could be no thought of a child until the situation with her family was settled, and that could only be settled one way. She had to stay in England. There could be no more talk of her going home, not only because of the scandal but because he simply didn't think he could bear it. She had become integral to him in such a short time.

There was a knock on the door, and a footman entered. 'The post has arrived. I thought you and Her Grace would want to see it at once.'

Hale sorted through it. He'd been hoping for word from France, but there was none. Most of it was for him regarding estate business from his other properties. That was one more thing that would require changing the routine. He couldn't stay at Glenmere interminably. In the fall, he'd have to make a tour of his other estates. Amidst the letters and reports was a thick envelope addressed to Zephy from San Francisco. He'd telegrammed her parents news of the marriage two months ago, and they'd sent back their congratulations, but this was the first letter to arrive since their wedding and since they would have realised she wasn't coming home.

'Where is Her Grace?' he asked, rising from his desk. Zephy would want to see the letter immediately.

'In the kitchen, Your Grace. I believe she is baking bread today.' The staff had gotten quickly used to the sight of her in her apron kneading dough. Hale personally found the sight of his wife baking bread quite erotic, perhaps because it was associated with other memories, other intimacies.

He stood in the kitchen doorway for a long moment, watching her with the dough. She broke off a piece and held it up, sniffing, then putting a bit on her tongue to taste, her brow furrowing before she bent to scribble some notes. He waited until she looked up and saw him. 'Is everything all right? You look concerned.' He smiled and strode towards the worktable. They had the kitchen to themselves for the moment. It was market day for Cook, and the assistants were taking their half day.

'The dough is changing.' She wiped her hands on her apron as she explained. 'The dough I brought to England was influenced by the climate of San Francisco. Many bakers feel the fog and the weather affect the yeast in the dough. I suppose it's like the argument that it's the quality of the grass that impacts the success of Irish sport horses. It's the same theory. The starter is changing. It's taking on the effects of the new climate.'

'It's adapting. Evolving. Like us,' Hale said, wanting to find an allegory of hope in that.

'It's losing its unique properties,' Zephy countered sharply. With a sinking heart, he definitely saw the unfortunate allegory in *that*. 'It's not San Francisco sourdough anymore,' she said. If his fear was losing her, *her* fear was losing herself.

'It will still taste delicious,' Hale cajoled, not liking where the allegory might be headed. Perhaps it was time to redirect the conversation. 'I have a letter from home for you.' Although, he was less pleased to give it to her now than he had been a few minutes ago. He'd hoped the letter would be filled with further congratulations and excitement about their marriage and that excitement would buoy Zephy's own. She set great store in pleasing her parents. If they were pleased with her marriage, perhaps it would encourage her to stay, to give up the desire to go home. Now, he worried a letter from home would also remind her of all that was waiting for her, pulling her away from him.

Zephy's face lit up as she took the letter. 'Shall I leave you to read it?' Hale asked, wanting her answer to be no; wanting her to say they'd go out to the terrace with a pitcher of lemonade and she'd read it aloud. It was nearly the time of day they took tea or lemonade when it was hot. They could share the news together.

'Yes, I think I'll take the letter out into the garden.' She paused, perhaps sensing he'd sought a different answer. 'Unless you'd rather I wait to read it? Was there something you wanted to discuss?'

'No, not at all.' Hale smiled to cover his disappointment. Her family was still her family; it had not yet morphed to being *their* family. Perhaps it was too soon to hope for so much. 'Go, enjoy your letter, and I'll see you at supper. I need to talk with the gamekeeper anyway. I'll ride over and do that.'

She smiled. 'You don't mind, truly?'

'What I mind is missing out on our afternoon *tea* together.' He smiled back with a teasing grin.

'I'll miss that, too. But I'll make it up to you tonight. I promise.' Zephy set aside her apron and kissed him as she passed, off to read her letter and news from home that Hale hoped wouldn't kill the remaining vestiges of their hard-won happiness.

## Chapter Twenty-One

Mathieu Aubert had been killed in a gunfight in the wharf district. Zephy stared in disbelief at the words, the letter slipping from her hand and fluttering to her lap while she digested the import of the news. She was glad she was sitting down on a bench in a quiet bower, glad she was alone because she couldn't control her reaction or how that reaction might be viewed by another.

There was, of course, the initial dissonance of the news in general. She'd not been expecting the letter to open with such a morbid announcement. It seemed to violate the conventions of letter writing. She'd been expecting a felicitous enquiry about her marriage. Perhaps an opening like Ma chère fille, *I hope this letter finds you well and enjoying your honeymoon in England.* Instead it started with *There has been devastating news to our community. Mathieu Aubert was killed in a gunfight on the wharf.* There were details, too, now that the initial news had been imparted.

Zephy picked up the letter and re-read those details, this time more slowly. There'd been a married woman of questionable repute, the wife of a gambler, involved. Both men had been playing cards and drinking. Alcohol, women and gambling. All three of Mathieu's vices had done him in simultaneously. It was an all-too-fitting end.

When had her mother written this? She studied the date at the top of the letter. The tenth of July. Seven weeks after her wedding. Too late to make a difference. Otherwise, her mother would have sent a telegram and not waited for the news to cross a continent and an ocean. Zephy had been picking strawberries and making love on picnic blankets for weeks by then and quite enjoying it, thoughts of San Francisco far from her mind. Which was not to her credit. Was that why her mother had begun the letter so audaciously? To remind her of her real life? Her purpose? Her promise? And to remind her that she had strayed from all three? That Mathieu Aubert was not the only one who had vices?

That was the second level of shock—the shock of implication and consequence that lay beneath her mother's news. If she'd waited, if she hadn't rushed into anything, she could have gone home in July without needing a husband at all, the agreement with her father null and void. Everything could have gone back to normal. Until the next time her father had a marriage candidate in mind. The next time, she wouldn't have an escape to England available. Or perhaps there wouldn't be a next time—that was the other piece of news in the letter, buried at the end almost as a postscript: Her father was tired, he could not run the bakery on his own for long.

The implied message dangled like a tempting carrot. Perhaps her father was desperate for her return, desperate enough that he wouldn't require her to marry. Maybe he'd even have realised he loved harmony within his family, harmony with her, more than strife clashing over archaic ideas of what a woman could and could not be.

That was all conjecture about a future that no longer existed. It had been erased the day she'd said *I do* to the duke, to Hale. The only thing that mattered was that the path towards home was cleared. All she had to do was take it. In theory, it was simple enough. She could purchase a ticket, sail from Southampton and be home in two weeks, the adventure behind her. Her marriage and husband behind her, just as she'd planned.

Zephy crumpled the letter in her hand. Was that what she wanted? To leave Hale? To leave this marriage behind and go back to her old life? The very fact that she hesitated over the answer, that she thought in terms of her *old life*, told her all she needed to know, all she feared. Those words suggested it was something she'd cast off and set aside the way the sourdough was casting off its old elements while it worked hard to adapt, to take on the elements of its new world.

It was a damnable position to be put in, having to choose between family tradition and her heart. That too, was a damnable realisation—to know that her heart was indeed engaged when it came to Hale. That was not part of any plan. Four months ago, she hadn't even known his name. All she'd known was that he was the man she was least interested in marrying. Now she knew his body as intimately as she knew her own, and she was coming to know his mind just as well.

Cold logic reared its head. If it was this hard to contemplate leaving him after just a couple months of marriage, it would only get harder after six months, a year. If she didn't leave now, then when? The old arguments lined up alongside the logic. When there were children at stake? When she had deep ties with the community? When the scandal to him would be worse? To linger would be the height of selfishness. Unless…unless there was middle ground? There had been once before. Perhaps there would be again.

Zephy floated the middle ground at supper that night. She'd dressed thoughtfully in her gown of sea-mist blue and had her maid take care with her hair, piling it high in an elegant heap of curls secured with mother-of-pearl pins that matched the pearls at her neck. She wanted to look her best when she made her argument. Timing and setting were everything when it came to persuasion. She'd even gotten Mrs Hepburn and the staff in on it, having them set the table out of doors in the garden and light the lanterns so that they dined amid a fairyland.

'What did I do to deserve all this?' Hale exclaimed with a smile as he came down the garden walk. 'I should have known something was afoot when my valet insisted on a close shave and extra toilet water.'

'It's our two-month anniversary. I thought we should celebrate.' She kissed his cheek and breathed in the citrusy bergamot scent of him. He held her chair and she sat.

'I know this dress.' He took his seat across from her, his eyes twinkling, two amber stars. 'It's the one you wore the first night I met you.' A footman approached with two glasses of Champagne on a tray.

'What's this?' she asked in surprise.

He gave a lift of his shoulder in a show of nonchalance. 'I wanted to be prepared in case we were celebrating something. It's probably not as chilled as it ought to be. After all, I didn't have the afternoon to plan.' He gave her a teasing grin. He was in a good humour, much better than he'd been when they'd parted in the kitchen. Would that help or hurt her cause tonight? He was happy, and she didn't want to ruin that for him.

He took both glasses and handed one to her. 'Shall we toast our anniversary now, and we can toast whatever other news the evening brings later? Here's to two glorious months of marriage, and to a lifetime of happiness.' Now she was truly starting to worry that her plan for a romantic setting was going to undermine her. He suspected there was something afoot, some grand news she wanted to not only impart but celebrate.

'To happiness.' She clinked her glass against his with a smile. Her toast was a wish, a hope, a prayer. She didn't want to lose this, to lose him. But he would have to meet her halfway if they stood a chance. A footman served the first course, a clear gravy soup full of fresh summer vegetables and slices of homemade sourdough bread. He was barely able to conceal a smile as he withdrew. Even the servants suspected something was going on. She'd not meant to convey such a message with her request.

'How was your meeting with the gamekeeper?' She took a sip of the soup.

'It went well. We discussed fish levels in the rivers and water depths. It's important to watch in the summer when the creeks get drier.' His eyes twinkled as if he were humouring her. 'How was your letter from home? Are you going to tell me your parents are coming for a visit?'

It was the perfect opening, although she'd not thought to bring up the subject so soon. She'd hoped to wait until after the fish. But one learned in business to seize opportunities when they arose. 'No. Why would you think that?'

For a moment, his gaze became guarded as if he'd been surprised in a less-than-pleasant way. He gave a shake of his head. 'I assumed they'd be eager to see their daughter, to see her new home, to meet their new son-in-law and family, perhaps be here for the December holidays and any other events that might be happening later in the year.' He gave her an encouraging look, his gaze expectant. Then it dawned on her, and for a horrifying moment she saw the evening through his eyes—through ducal eyes—and her heart sank. He would be so disappointed.

She lowered her voice and reached for his hand with a meaningful look. 'Hale, I'm not pregnant.' They'd taken precautions, they'd *agreed* to wait, and yet Hale's features could not conceal their disappointment. 'Why would you think otherwise?'

'Of course.' He tried to dismiss the disappointment. 'It was unrealistic of me. I suppose I just hoped that perhaps something had slipped past our careful considerations. It's not unheard of.'

'You hoped? We agreed it would be important to

wait. How could you hope for such a thing?' His comment had been quite revealing of inner thoughts he'd not yet shared with her, perhaps had never meant to share. That concerned her. He'd told her one thing and had hoped for another. It wasn't hard to see why. A child would tie her here.

'Zeph, please don't be angry. I meant nothing by it. I had a letter from Southford in the post. He shared the news that he's to be a father later this year. They are expecting already after only a month.' There was a wistfulness in his eyes that did things to her heart, making it soft and malleable. Her mind rushed in to fill the cracks with reality.

'It's not what you think with Southford and Lulu. She was pregnant before they married. She thought it would persuade Southford to give up his mistress.'

'I'm sorry to hear it.' Some of the wistfulness left Hale's gaze. 'Perhaps it might change things yet. A child, especially a son, can bring a man to heel, and Southford values family. This child could be the making of them. It could be what they need to get over this hurdle.'

Zephy nodded noncommittally. Is that what he truly thought they needed, too? A child to bind them together? Lulu was right. If that were to happen, Hale would hold all the power. She'd have money to leave, money to spend on courts for a divorce. But she would never get that far if there was a child. It was already nigh on impossible to think of leaving Hale. To leave him *and* a child of theirs was improbable. She had to strike now, and if he would not agree to the middle ground, she would have to leave while she still could.

'My parents aren't coming for a visit, but I thought we might go to them. It could be a second honeymoon. You could see my home, and you could meet *your* in-laws.'

Meet *his* in-laws? The underlying message bowled him over more than the request itself. Zephy wanted to go home. Wanted to leave Glenmere. Hale played with the stem of his Champagne glass. 'A few days ago you didn't want to go to Cowes, didn't want to go anywhere. But the truth is, you don't want to go anywhere in England. You want to go home.' Saying the words out loud hurt more than he'd anticipated. Zephy going home meant leaving him, and he was far too cognizant of her original intentions when it had come to her marriage plans. She'd never meant to stay. He'd foolishly believed he could change her mind.

'I'm not leaving you, Hale. I'm asking you to come with me. I've seen your life, lived your life these past months. It is not unreasonable for me to want to show you mine,' she pleaded with him gently.

'We *can* go. But not now with the harvest to think about in the autumn and the estates to tour. We'd hardly get to California and we'd have to turn back.

Maybe we could go next spring? In March before Parliament really gets up a full head of steam. We could spend the month and be back by Easter.' It wouldn't be ideal. Time away was at a premium except in the winter when his estate and parliamentary duties eased. But winter travel of that magnitude was a difficult issue for a man with no heir of his own. Maybe by spring, travel would be a moot issue if Zephy was expecting.

Guilt pricked at him. He'd promised her they'd work through this issue, and here he was delaying a trip and hoping for things she did not want. He was being selfish. He drew a deep breath, aware that she had let go of his hand. He needed to see this from her perspective, and from her perspective he was botching the evening. She'd set it up in order to make her request. He'd gotten caught up in the servants' misreading of the reason for her arrangements. Southford's news hadn't helped. He'd been thinking about babies and envying Southford ever since.

He reached for her hand, wanting the connection of touch with her. He laced his fingers through hers, the candlelight catching the gold band of her wedding ring. 'Zeph, why the urgency for a trip home? Are your parents well? Is everything all right?' Perhaps there was an unspoken reason behind the request.

'They are well. My mother wrote to say that Mathieu Aubert has died. He was killed in a gunfight on the wharf.'

'And now you are free, or you would be free if it weren't for me.' Hale held her gaze with steady eyes while his insides roiled, anger clashed with sorrow, with loss, with grief for what might have been but would never be. He saw the implication immediately. If only she had waited a few more weeks, she might have had all she wanted without having to pay the cost.

'That's not what I said.'

'It's what you think. Too bad you hadn't gone home earlier. You could have married him and been widowed by now. Which is what you'd hoped for anyway. I'm afraid I won't be so obliging.' Anger was winning out, its heat cauterising the open wound in his heart, searing it into numbness, sealing the hurt inside before it could spill out.

Zephy's eyes flashed lightning bolts. 'How dare you insinuate such a morbid thing. I do not wish you were dead. I asked you to come with me.'

'To what end? So that once we were there, you could simply announce you'd not be returning with me? The ground would be all yours. Short of throwing you over my shoulder and carrying you off, I'd have to accept your wishes.'

'The ground would be all mine? Like the ground is all yours here?' She raised her voice. 'You promised me we'd be partners. But so far, it's been all you. We live in your house. We live your life. This is not all about geography, Hale. This is what I was afraid would happen. This is the subsummation I feared. I am being overtaken by your life while my father is struggling and alone. I should be with him. He needs me. *I* need me.'

'You seemed to be enjoying it just fine right up until today,' Hale ground out.

'Because I thought we were going to find a compromise, a solution. You promised me we would. Now all you can talk about is babies despite our agreement. A baby will trap me here, and you know it. Lulu warned me that was how aristocratic men solved everything. A pregnancy overrides all of a woman's preferences. You know I could never leave a child behind, and I know you'd never allow me to take the child with me.'

'Damn right.' The topiaries surrounding them loomed like dark, threatening shadows. He wasn't imagining them as a childhood playground now as much as he was imagining them as monsters closing in to rip the last of his happiness from him. Damn Mathieu Aubert for dying! It was the height of unfairness that a dead man who he'd never met had the power to upend his life so thoroughly.

'You've made your position abundantly clear. You leave me no choice. I should have known this would never work.' Zephy rose in evident anger, her motions quick and jerky in testament to her level of upset. In her haste, her hip bumped the table. The Champagne bottle tottered from the impact and fell, shattering on the garden pavers, its liquid seeping away into the cracks. Like his marriage.

'Zephy, wait.' He rose, wanting to stop her, wanting to take her in his arms. If he could touch her, hold her, if she would touch him, then perhaps they could find their way back, they could remember all the potential between them.

'I *have* been waiting.' She threw down her napkin and stalked away out of reach. 'How long did you think you could keep me waiting? Keep me thinking you would come through on your end? Goodnight, Your Grace.'

He felt like a cad even as his own anger with her burned hot inside him. He'd done this to her. To them. Every fibre of his being wanted to run after her and make her listen if that was what it took. But what would that solve? Anger only fuelled anger. He had no new arguments to make. Perhaps the best option would be to give her space, to let them both sleep on the situation. Tomorrow, there might be word at last regarding his plan to meet Zephy halfway. There should have been word a few days ago. Yes, he assured himself. Things would look better in the morning. They could hardly look worse. He glanced back at the ruined table and gestured for a footman. 'We're finished here.'

## Chapter Twenty-Two

She was finished here. It wasn't the way she wanted it to be, but it was how it had to be. It had always been how it had to be. Zephy threw some clothes into a travelling bag. She'd have her trunk sent on later. She'd been fooling herself these past two months that it could be different because believing that was the easiest path, the most enjoyable path. It was the path that let her have all that she wanted.

*All that she wanted.* She knew what that was now. It had not always been clear. She wanted her family and the bakery, of course. But she'd wanted other things, too, like the chance to travel, to discover who she might be beyond the bakery, what she might want. This journey had been a chance to do that and more.

Her hands stilled, gripping a garment. She wanted Hale. She wanted to be his wife not just in name. She did not want to live apart from him. She *wanted* to live here at Glenmere. She loved this place *because* of him. She wanted his happiness. But she wanted the bakery and her family's happiness, too.

Zephy's gaze drifted to the connecting door between their rooms—a door that had seldom been shut since their wedding day. It was shut now. She could change that. She could cross the room and open that door. She could find the words to mend the quarrel. But what would that solve? The dilemma, which had travelled with her from San Francisco, still remained. Travel had not resolved it. Marriage had not resolved it.

All her plans had come to naught in that regard while the question remained: How was she going to live her life? Who was she going to live her life for? The candidates for that answer were actually many: For her family? For the bakery? For herself? For Hale? For the Sunderland dukedom? If she chose herself, would that choice guarantee her happiness? What would that happiness look like? Could it even exist if it came at the expense of others' happiness? She shot another look—a lingering, longing one—at the closed door. She wanted to open it, to see if Hale had come upstairs, to take back her harsh words, to lay this burden out between them. She wanted to tell him she'd choose them if she knew how. But she didn't. She didn't know how without hurting people she cared for.

Tears smarted in her eyes. That was the answer,

then. She didn't know how to choose him. So she couldn't. She had to go back to San Francisco, back to her family, back to a life she understood, and hope that Hale would understand. She'd been open with him about her plans from the start. Family was important to him as well. He would see reason. Eventually.

She closed the clasp of the travelling bag as if she were closing a chapter of her life and looked out the window, making another decision at the sight of soft July rain dripping down the panes. She would go in the morning, then. With luck the rain would stop. She sat down on the bed and looked about the room. She whispered 'I am sorry' into the air. Now there was nothing to do but wait. In the morning she and Lady Jane would take a last ride to the train station. She should try to sleep. Soon, all of this would seem like a distant fairy tale. Soon, she'd be gone. No, the better way to think about it was that soon, she'd be home, back where she belonged.

She was gone. Hale stood in the centre of Zephy's chambers in abject shock, chilled to his very core by this physical proof of her absence—her very permanent absence. 'Show me the note again,' he demanded, holding out his hand. Her maid timidly handed over the paper with too few words on it. *Send my trunk with all haste to Southampton.*

She'd left. Him.

She'd not just been angry last night, she'd been honest. It should not surprise him. Zephy had always been honest, even when he'd not liked what she had to say. There was nothing for her here, and so she'd acted on that damn plan of hers. She'd not even left a note for him but for the maid. *Send my trunk.* She'd been too angry to wait until she could pack everything herself and take it with her. But that was Zephy, too. Honest, direct and spontaneous. Once her mind was made up, there was no dissuading her. She didn't merely take what she wanted, she seized it whether it was sex or business. She did nothing slowly or by halves. It was an admirable quality until it wasn't. Right now it definitely wasn't.

He sat on the edge of her bed, unsure if his legs would hold him much longer. He'd had time to say goodbye to his father, time to close all the loops. But Zephy had ripped herself from his life. There'd been no closure at all, no second chances, no safety net. He pushed a hand through his hair. That was a mistake. It called to mind all the times Zephy had run her fingers through his hair, anchoring her hands in its depths, or twining her arms about his neck, her fingertips playing with it.

Was this what it was going to be like? Remembering her at every turn, at every touch? He could lock up this room, but he couldn't lock away the rest of the house. How would he ever ride past the tree-house tree and not think of her? How would he ever walk in the topiary garden or sit at the terrace table? Dear heavens, the kitchen. He could never go there again without seeing her with her bread dough. That was the difference between the loss of his father and this. What he felt for Zephy went deep and cut deeper, like the score on top of a sourdough loaf. He hadn't loved his father, not the way he loved Zephy. Zephy had become his heart.

Did she know? Had he ever said the words? Ever told her? He'd made her a promise. He was trying to keep it, but she didn't see it that way. Her words had made that clear last night. His stomach clenched at the memory of those accusations—that he'd hoped for a child to trap her, to take away her choices. Is that what she thought of him? It was what she thought of aristocratic Englishmen. She'd made that opinion well-known to him on more than one occasion, and then Southford, the cad, had gone and made the stereotype true with his treatment of her best friend. But Hale had hoped he'd risen above that. Even more than that, he'd hoped he and Zephy had defied that classification together. Apparently not, if she was so willing to believe the worst of him so quickly.

His conscience was quick to prick. *She thinks you haven't honoured your promise. You did not tell her of your plans. How was she to know, when you didn't share? She knows nothing of the deed in your desk.*

*She knows nothing of the letter you sent to her cousins in Picardy.* Would that have been enough to keep them from this impasse? If she did know, would that be enough now? Was he really going to let her leave without knowing for sure?

A groom rushed in, winded from the dash between the house and the stable. 'Her Grace is asking for the coach. She has a valise with her. It seemed odd, as there was nothing on the schedule about a trip. I thought you should know.'

She was still here. It wasn't too late. Hope surged. If she was still here, he could tell her. Hale rose, his sense of purpose returning, his thoughts focusing. He needed to make a quick stop in his office to grab what he needed.

He was nearly out the door when a footman called after him. 'Your Grace, what about the guests?'

'Guests? What guests?' Hale turned, trying to hide his impatience. He wanted to get to Zephy before she decided not to wait for the coach and rode out in the rain on Lady Jane.

'Your Grace,' he sputtered, 'the couple who arrived at breakfast this morning. They have a letter from you.' Ah, the breakfast he'd missed because he'd slept late after struggling to fall asleep after the quarrel with Zephy.

Hale sighed and reached for patience with grasping fingers. 'Thank you, George. I'll see them. Where are they?'

'We put them in the breakfast room, Your Grace.'

Hale strode to the room, determined to dispatch with this latest ducal business with all haste, postpone it if need be. The couple rose when he entered. They were dressed in the sturdy garb of artisans, and the man whipped his cap off his head. *'Bonjour, monsieur.'* His voice was thick with the accent of northern France and its hard sounds. Hale felt his low spirits rise.

*'Bonjour,'* he replied. 'You must be Edmund Duval.' He came forward to shake the man's hand, the action catching the man by surprise and no small amount of discomfort that a great man would shake a baker's hand.

Edmund gave a nod. 'This is my wife, Cecile. We arrived by train early this morning and came straight here.'

'That's fine. I would have sent the carriage, had I known. I was expecting a letter in response to mine,' Hale explained.

Edmund gave another nod. 'I thought it best we save time and come in person because we are also expecting.' He beamed proudly. 'We want to be settled in San Francisco well before the baby arrives.'

It took Hale a moment to take in the news. This explained the delay in their response. 'Yes, of course.

You will take the offer, then? This is wonderful. My wife will be so pleased.' At least, Hale hoped so. This was the first piece of his plan. The second was contained on the paper in his pocket. 'I am sorry to be abrupt, but I need to go and meet my wife. Mrs Hepburn, my housekeeper, will have a chamber for you and anything you need. Please, make free of the house. We will talk when I return and you can meet your cousin, Zephyrine.'

Edmund cleared his throat. '*Merci*, you are too kind. May we use your kitchen? We have sourdough starter and it needs—'

'To be fed.' Hale gave a laugh. 'I know. I am married to a baker's daughter. Please, visit the kitchen. Her own starter is down there.' Unless she'd taken it with her, but since she was going home to all the starter she could want, Hale thought she might have left it. She didn't need it. Just like she thought she didn't need him. He was going to prove her wrong. He was going to show her he was a man of his word, a man she could trust. And he was going to show her there was a way through all of this for them.

The rain hadn't stopped. Zephy shook the droplets from her coat, already soaked from the walk to the stable from the house. Luck was not with her. The late-night drizzle had become a morning shower. She would be drenched by the time she reached the train station. She set down her valise and requested the coach, hoping to sound casual, hoping no one would think to question her and tell Hale. The last thing she needed was to see him before she left. He'd always been the last thing she needed, and yet she fell for him every time.

As she waited for the coach to be readied, she clung to last night's resolve. This was the right decision. She had tried, Hale had tried, and the one thing they needed to get right they simply couldn't. They couldn't compromise their families, so they were faced with compromising themselves instead. It was not tolerable. They would make each other unhappy.

That was the form the narrative in her head had taken over the long night of waiting. As the hours ticked by, her anger had been suborned by something less blameful. Last night, in the heat of the argument, she had wanted to blame Hale, to see him as the villain who'd been looking to cheat her, to lie to her. That kind of hot anger was hard to sustain, though. She needed something else in the light of day. And the blameless goodbye was born.

This was for the best; they'd both tried, but there were limits they couldn't overcome. It allowed room for her to remember their passion, to remember the idyllic days at Glenmere without seeing them as a plot to manipulate her. That wasn't Hale. He was not a manipulator. That's not where his power came from, and neither did hers. Her power came from straightforward honesty. She'd not lied to him about her plans and what she needed. Sometimes things just didn't work out. If they'd been different people…

No. If they had been different people she wouldn't have loved him. Would he come to realise that she *had* loved him? She'd not told him. She'd shown him, though, with her body every time they touched. With her willingness to take the leap of faith with him. She closed her eyes. Perhaps remembering wasn't the best course of action just now when it was still possible to go back inside the house, apologise and try one more time. Perhaps she ought to leave the remembering for when she was on the train or, even better, for when she was at sea and there was no more choice…

'Zephy.'

It was as if she could hear him. Not just in her head.

She could smell him, the faint scent of bergamot on the summer rain, as if he were here beside her. There was a brushing touch at her arm, and her eyes flew open in disbelief. 'Hale?' His name was a whispered question. He should not be here.

'You didn't think I'd let you leave without saying goodbye?' His amber eyes were solemn, flecked with hurt. He was wet. He'd left the house without anything more than his morning coat. She pushed the damp swoop of his dark hair out of his face.

'I thought we'd said enough last night,' she offered quietly.

He nodded slowly as the coach rolled up. 'But not everything.' He held out his hand. 'May we talk? There are things I should have told you sooner, and I think they will make a difference to you, to us. Please? Come back to the house with me and let us talk. There are things to show you, to tell you. If you don't like them or if they don't change your mind, the coach is ready and you can go.'

*He was prepared to let her go.* The offering was staggering. She was overwhelmed by it because she knew what it would do to him if she did leave. It was not a hurt she'd willingly chosen to inflict. He must be quite sure of himself, and her curiosity could not refuse. 'All right. I'll come in for a little while. But, Hale, I will not be delayed,' she warned.

She took his hand, but they did not speak until they were inside. 'Where are we going?' she asked as they walked past the sitting rooms and the estate office.

'To the kitchen. Good things happen for us in kitchens.' Hale smiled at her, and she was reminded of those times kitchens had indeed provided them memorable experiences. 'Your cousins are here from Picardy. They arrived this morning. I am surprised you missed them in the driveway.'

'I went out the back,' she stammered as if that mattered compared to his other news. 'My cousins? I've never met them.'

'It's about time you did.' He stopped in the narrow hall and faced her, his voice low. 'They are waiting for you, for us. I sent for them. I meant it as a wedding gift for you, but it took longer to locate them than I expected.'

Her mind was racing as she looked up into his amber gaze, so intent, so earnest. 'I don't understand.'

'You've been clear that the family needs you, or someone young to run the business, someone who understands it, who has vision, who is family. You've also been clear that you cannot abandon them, even at the expense of your own happiness. Am I correct?'

He held her gaze, his own eyes soft. 'I understand those obligations better than anyone. I'm a duke. My burdens are the same as yours: People depend on me, my family depends on me for their very survival. I know the privilege of carrying that responsibility and the costs of it. Perhaps like myself, you constantly ask yourself, where does my happiness fit in with those burdens? Or am I not entitled to any happiness because it is a burden to others if it conflicts with my duties. Am I right, Zephy?'

Dear heavens, he was going to make her cry, and she sensed he hadn't even come to the point. All she could do was nod. Her resistance was slipping away fast. She did not want to leave this man who understood her so completely. She could not throw the rare miracle of him away, and yet how could she keep it? That hadn't changed.

He withdrew something from his damp jacket pocket. 'I have something for you. It's a copy of a letter I sent from London when I went up for the special licence. Take a moment and read it, carefully.'

She took the paper and unfolded it, reading it once, then twice. She looked up, disbelief coursing through her. 'You wrote to my cousins? And now they're here?'

'The night of our picnic you told me there was still family in Picardy. I found them. Edmund and Cecile Duval. They work the family bakery with Edmund's parents and his brother. I wrote to the whole family with my plan and let them sort out what would be best for them.' For a moment, her confident husband looked boyishly shy here in the dim kitchen corridor. 'Saying it out loud, I hear how heavy-handed or arrogant it might have been to do that. It didn't seem that way at the time, though. I introduced myself, and I explained the situation to them, how our marriage was leaving the bakery shorthanded. I asked if they might be interested in sending someone to San Francisco, to your father.'

He cleared his throat. 'Edmund and Cecile arrived this morning. They are ready to go to San Francisco and make a life there. She's expecting, so they are eager. I think you'll like them.' His smile turned impish. 'I offered them the run of the house while I came to find you, and all they wanted was the kitchen because—'

'They had starter to feed.' Zephy laughed softly. The enormity of what Hale had done was washing over her in rather large waves that threatened to knock her off her feet.

'I didn't say anything because I was waiting to hear from them. I didn't want to get your hopes up,' Hale confessed. 'Then, when I didn't hear from them, I began to worry.'

'But they're here? At Glenmere?' Zephy was still trying to grasp that. Not one but two pair of Duval hands to run the bakery for her father. It would be more than enough.

'Yes.' Some of the hurt eased in his gaze. 'Are you angry? It was high-handed of me.' He gripped her hands tightly. 'I just wanted to show you I was a man of my word.'

'I'm not angry. I am overwhelmed.' She felt tears forming. He had been working all along on his end of the promise. 'I doubted you.' She bit her lip. 'That was arrogant of *me*.'

Hale let out a breath. 'My mother once told me that a man doesn't come to his marriage ready to be a husband, but he learns.'

'A wife, too.'

'Will you consider my promise kept? Will we be able to move forward together, Zephy?' His thumb ran over the gold band at her finger. 'You didn't leave this behind. Perhaps you still hope?' The thought swept her with a fierce intensity. She could have nearly everything she wanted—her own happiness and her family's because Hale had cared enough to make it possible. But one question remained. Could she stay here and not lose herself?

'I have something else for you,' Hale said softly. 'I should have made a gift of it to you the night we wed instead of waiting until I had your cousins sorted. In hindsight, I think it would have been proof that I meant to keep my word and that I heard your very real concerns about being my duchess.' He reached once more into his pocket, and her brow knit. What more could there be?

'Zeph, you are a baker. I would never want you to change that. I would not want you to feel that you had to give that up to be my wife or Sunderland's duchess. This is proof that you can be all of those things.'

She opened the paper and smiled, joy pouring through her. 'A bakery? You've bought me a bakery?'

'In the village. Not just a bakery, Zeph. A business that is all yours.' A smile suffused Hale's handsome face, and they were laughing together, foreheads touching in this private moment. 'I think the industry will be good for all of us. I discussed it with our current baker. He's getting older. His son wants to learn the business of sourdough, so there will be work enough for both of you, a kind of partnership. You can focus on bread, and the baker can focus on buns and cakes. And you can teach other girls.'

'I like that,' she said softly. 'Hale, thank you. This means...' She couldn't find the words.

'Everything?' he supplied.

She shook her head and raised her hand to stroke his cheek. 'No, it does not mean everything. You do. I didn't want to leave, I just didn't know how to stay without losing myself.'

He took her hand and kissed her palm. 'I didn't want to lose you either.'

She held his gaze, aware that people were waiting for them beyond the corridor. 'Hale, I want you to know that I am overwhelmed with the gift of the bakery and what you've done for my family. It does matter. It lifts a great burden from me. But I am staying with you because I love you. If I didn't love you, none of these gestures would have mattered.'

'You'll stay?' Hale's eyes burned with hope.

She nodded slowly. 'I'll stay because you gave me the choice to go.' Not even her father had given her that choice. But the man she loved had understood how much making that decision on her own had mattered to her. It was perhaps even more precious to her than the deed or that he'd reached out to her cousins.

Choice was everything. A person wasn't truly free without it.

His nose bussed hers as he gave a low laugh. 'And I love you or I wouldn't have made the gestures at all.'

'Ah, the things we do for love. I'd like to do them again, beneath the tree-house tree, in the topiary garden, in our bed, in our new bakery,' she whispered against his mouth.

'We will, but *after* we meet your cousins. They're waiting on us,' he admonished.

'*Us*. What a powerful word that is.' She wrapped her arms about his neck and held him close. 'I never thought I'd have an *us*, not like this.' She moved against him with her hips, watching his eyes darken. 'Like good sourdough, you're rising to the occasion, Hale,' she murmured.

He nipped at her neck with a chuckle. 'Like good sourdough, I expect to be fed.'

She laughed up at him. 'You're learning. Perhaps we'll make a baker of you after all.'

'Why not? If a duke and a baker's daughter can fall in love, anything is possible. We've proven it.'

# *Epilogue*

*San Francisco, New Year's Eve 1899/1900*

San Francisco Bay had proven to be the ideal place from which to watch the city's firework extravaganzas hosted by various private citizens. From the water, one could see all of the displays lighting the night sky. It was quieter out here too, far quieter than the streets, filled with riotous celebrations. Zephy stood at the rail, warm in the embrace of Hale's arms as their rented yacht bobbed on the waters. The bay was blessedly and unusually calm for the evening. Perhaps the water understood it was a momentous night as the calendar turned not just from one year to the next but from one century to the next.

Not far from them at the rail, their seven-year-old son, Alex—named for her father—and their four-year-old daughter, Edwina—named for Cousin Edmund—stood under the careful supervision of their grandparents, oohing in awe as red, white and blue fireworks burst in the midnight sky. She could hear her father telling Alex that these were colours of the American flag *and* the French flag.

Hale chuckled quietly at her ear. 'Your father never gives it a rest does he? Should I tell him the British Union Jack also uses those colours?'

Zephy laughed. 'I think we've made astounding progress this visit. Let's not ruin it.'

'It has been a good visit,' Hale said. 'I like San Francisco. It's a city with potential. I especially liked Napa Valley. It was as beautiful as you said it would be in the fall.' They'd spent considerable time at the château. For the children it was a lot like Glenmere. There'd been plenty of time spent outdoors hiking and riding. There'd been plenty of time, too, for the children to meet their cousins, Edmund's children. What a joy it had been to watch all of them play.

'It's been four months, and it's time to go home.' Zephy sighed. They would begin the journey back to England in a few days. She would be sad to say goodbye to her parents, but she was eager to get back. Hale's mother had graciously volunteered to watch over the estate in their absence, but there was much to do at her bakery and at the bread-baking school Zephy had opened. There were plans to make for the new year...

'It's good to hear you say that. *Home.*' Hale's arms tightened about her. 'I worried once we got here you wouldn't want to leave.'

'*Glenmere* is home. Wherever you and the children are is home, Hale.' It was all true. She didn't worry any longer about losing herself or being subsumed by Hale's life. They had a life of their own, one that they had built together by growing together.

The fireworks intensified, leading towards the grand finale. 'A new century,' Hale murmured. 'What an amazing time to be alive, to see it born, to be part of it.' He nodded towards their children. 'Will they remember this?'

'Alex might. Edwina is young yet. But I saved a copy of today's *Chronicle* with the date on it so they can look back and remember.' A rogue wave bumped the yacht with slightly more force than the others, and Zephy gripped the rail tight, her stomach lurching.

'Are you all right?' Hale was all instant concern.

'Quite fine.' Zephy turned to face him. 'There are a lot of reasons I am excited for this year and eager to be home, but the biggest one of all is that I want to get ready to welcome the next member to our family.' She loved watching his face change, loved watching the emotions of joy and pure happiness wash over him when he realised he was going to be a father again. He'd turned out to be a good one. He was made for fatherhood. Alex had gotten too big for shoulder rides through the topiaries, and Edwina would soon be too big as well, but now there'd be a new baby to trot through the gardens.

'A baby? When?' Hale breathed.
'June.'
'Or maybe late May? An anniversary baby?' Hale asked hopefully.

She laughed. 'Perhaps.' He grimaced. That was their word for *most likely not*. It always had been from the start, from that very first dance when they had not liked each other very much.

'Happy New Year, my darling.'

'Happy New Century, my love. Do you remember our first yacht ride together?'

She nodded. 'We argued the whole time.' More than continents had separated them then. They'd come a long way, not just in geography but in the maps that are charted on the heart.

\* \* \* \* \*

*If you enjoyed this story, make sure to read Bronwyn Scott's Wed Within a Year miniseries*

How to Court a Rake
How to Tempt an Earl
How to Seduce a Viscount

*And why not check out these other captivating reads by Bronwyn Scott*

Cinderella at the Duke's Ball
The Captain Who Saved Christmas

# MILLS & BOON®

## Coming next month

### RESCUED BY THE RAKISH LORD
#### Sarah Mallory

'It is a rather delicate matter. It concerns Lord Graddon's guest, the one with the roguish epithet Devil Blackbourne.' Lady Kenton declared. 'You will recall we all thought he had quit Graddon Hall.'

'But he has returned?' Selina replied cautiously.

Lady Kenton nodded.

'And now, I suppose, it is all over the town and all the poor mamas are once again anxious for their chicks. But is this all, ma'am?' Selina asked, still anxious. 'I cannot think it warrants you driving here especially to tell me.'

'You are quite correct, if it was only the rake's return I would have left it until we met, or you heard it from one of your other friends. As it is, Sir Alfred came home today with the most alarming report and as soon as I heard it, I came to warn you.'

Selina was now thoroughly alarmed. Was news of her masquerading as a serving maid all over Torrisford now? She waited anxiously while Lady Kenton tapped her fan against her palm, clearly struggling to find the right words to express herself.

'Oh, my dear Selina,' she exclaimed at last, 'The rogue has made you the subject of the most outrageous wager!'

*Continue reading*

**RESCUED BY THE RAKISH LORD**
Sarah Mallory

*Available next month*
millsandboon.co.uk

Copyright © 2026 Sarah Mallory

# COMING SOON!

We really hope you enjoyed reading this book. If you're looking for more romance be sure to head to the shops when new books are available on

## Thursday 23rd April

To see which titles are coming soon, please visit
**millsandboon.co.uk/nextmonth**

---

MILLS & BOON

# TWO BRAND NEW BOOKS FROM
# Love Always

Be prepared to be swept away to incredible worldwide destinations along with our strong, relatable heroines and intensely desirable heroes.

## OUT NOW

Four Love Always stories published every month, find them all at:

**millsandboon.co.uk**

# FOUR BRAND NEW BOOKS FROM
# MILLS & BOON MODERN

Indulge in desire, drama, and breathtaking romance – where passion knows no bounds!

## OUT NOW

Eight Modern stories published every month, find them all at:

**millsandboon.co.uk**

# OUT NOW!

Available at
millsandboon.co.uk

## MILLS & BOON

# LET'S TALK
## *Romance*

For exclusive extracts, competitions and special offers, find us online:

- **f** MillsandBoon
- **X** @MillsandBoon
- **○** @MillsandBoonUK
- **♪** @MillsandBoonUK

Get in touch on 01413 063 232

For all the latest titles coming soon, visit
millsandboon.co.uk/nextmonth